RECLAMATION

Praise for
ERUPTION

"Quintana's debut is a standard fast-paced techno-thriller, its momentum set more by intrigue than action as her characters question each other's motives and loyalties."

–Publisher's Weekly

"An impressive debut novel, "Eruption" clearly documents author Adrienne Quintana as an especially gifted writer with an enviable knack for deftly crafting surprise twists and unexpected turns in a compelling suspense thriller that never lets up from first page to last."

–Midwest Book Review

"Quintana's writing creates a great balance of tension to keep readers engaged. The potentially tricky subject of time travel is nicely handled and doesn't present questions of the semantics of the process. It reads smoothly and adds to the story beautifully."

–Deseret News

"Adrienne Quintana delivers with a plot that erupts with action and keeps you guessing."

–C.J. Hill
Author of Erasing Time

ADRIENNE QUINTANA

RECLAMATION

PHOENIX, ARIZONA

ISBN 13: 978-0692776162
ISBN 10: 0692776168

  Published by Pink Umbrella Books
     Quintana, Adrienne, 1976- author.
  Reclamation / Adrienne Quintana.
     pages cm
When Jace Vega wakes up three years after the eruption of Mt. Hood, she races to recover her memories about the Point of Origin before Omnibus destroys what's left of the world she knows.
ISBN 978-0692776162 (perfect : alk. paper)

Cover design by Adrienne Quintana
Cover design © 2016 by Adrienne Quintana
Edited by Marnae Horejs

For Carly—whose courage inspired me to finish this.

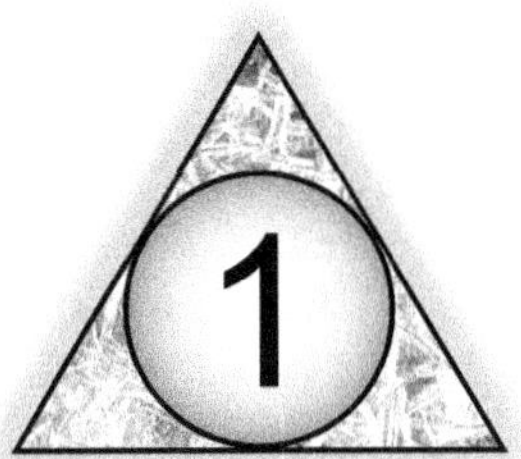

Beeping. Unrelenting, steady beeping. Water running. Footsteps. Breath hissing. Inhale, exhale, inhale.

"I think she's back," a female voice whispered.

"You're overreacting. They said it's not unusual to pass out, especially with an emergency C-section," a deep voice replied. Familiar.

I tried to lift my eyelids, but they were heavy.

"She asked about her father and Corey like she had no idea why they shouldn't be here," the woman whispered. "We're going to have to contact him."

The rate of the beeps increased, matching the pounding of my heart.

"She's waking up." Damien's voice. I was afraid to open my eyes.

A hand touched my forehead. "Jace. Can you hear me?" The voice of the woman with the scar. Claire. Damien's mother. She was supposed to be dead.

I pinched my eyelids even tighter together before slowly opening them. The light in the room overwhelmed me.

Claire and Damien's faces hovered over my head, blurry splotches of color. I blinked a few times until they began to come into focus.

"How are you feeling?" Claire's smile was filled with compassion. Pushing my hair gently away from my face, her fingers caught on a tangle.

"How did I get here? Where am I?" My voice was muffled by the oxygen mask that covered my face. I couldn't breathe. I struggled to lift my arms from under the heavy blankets, but they were tucked in tight. Pinned down. Paralyzed.

"Try to stay calm, Jace." Claire carefully lifted the mask away. I gasped. "This must be terrifying for you." She stroked my hair again. My fully focused eyes locked in on the jagged purple scar on the left side of her face. Damien thought she had died in the World Trade Center, but Victor knew she was still alive—he said he knew where she was.

"Where am I?" I asked again.

Damien touched my shoulder softly. "Jewish General, remember?"

"In Montreal," Claire added.

"Where are my father and Corey?"

"I told you before your surgery. Do you remember that, Jace?" Claire asked.

I did remember, but I didn't want to think about what had just happened to me. Tears welled up in my eyes. A baby. Damien had been the only one in the delivery room. The full gravity of my situation hit, and I couldn't stop the tears from falling. One devastating thought filled my mind: *My choices don't matter. They never mattered. The future on the tablet is set in stone.*

"You told me they're in Washington," I managed. "Are we married?" I asked Damien, still struggling to keep my thoughts coherent. "Did I…marry you?"

Damien's eyes widened. "You don't remember anything? Tell me the last thing you remember before the C-section. Do you remember coming to the hospital to be induced?"

His voice was desperate. He was begging me to remember. I shook my head. "I don't remember being pregnant. The last thing I remember is a volcanic eruption on Mount Hood. You were shot. Your father left us there to die." Damien took a step back. "A helicopter came in at the last second and rescued us. I was strapped to a gurney, tethered to the helicopter. I lost consciousness, then I woke up here."

Damien closed his eyes and rubbed them hard. "Unbelievable. He was right."

"Who was right?" I heard my heart rate kick up on the monitor again.

"Corey," Claire said. "He said that Victor had programmed his machine to send your memories back in time, and you told him to change the numbers just before a timer ticked down to zero. He was in such a panic that he did what you told him to do."

43 15 13 02. 43 03 07 11. The numbers Corey had given me in the flash of memory from that white room. I closed my eyes and pictured myself strapped to the gurney in Victor's laboratory. The flashes of memory from kindergarten had been coming so quickly just before the volcano erupted. I hadn't had time to make sense of everything completely. But I knew that somehow my memories had been sent back, that I had shown my father and Claire pictures that I had drawn from the future. I had told them about the World Trade Center. Then I had asked my father to help me forget.

I opened my eyes and scrambled, trying to push myself up in bed. "What happened to me after the eruption?"

"The helicopter brought you to the safe house in Edmonton. You'd had a stroke." Claire reached for my hand, pulling it from under the blanket. "You almost died. You were in a coma for over a month."

"And when you finally woke up, you couldn't remember anything," Damien said.

"Amnesia?"

"Beyond retrograde amnesia. You couldn't even speak or walk. You had to relearn everything." Claire squeezed my hand. "Corey was convinced that your memories had been sent forward instead of back when he changed the numbers. He said that you would be coming back, but he didn't know when."

Damien rolled his eyes. "Or if you'd be wearing a red coat and coming from the east."

Claire shot him a chilling look. "Damien was skeptical. But your father and I have been waiting for you."

"How long?" My heart began to pound again as I tried to do the math in my head. A month in a coma, then no memories at all. And a baby takes nine months. "How long has it been since the eruption?"

"Just over three years," Claire answered.

The words rang in my ears. Claire and Damien became a blur as my eyes darted around the bleak white room. They honed in on a large, flat-paneled digital screen mounted to the wall opposite my bed. Six emoji faces that graduated from an exaggerated smile on one end to a frown and streaming tears on the other were displayed in bold colors, inviting me to rate my pain. Next to it a message was displayed in both French and English.

April 6, 2018: Your nurse is Sophie. Please press the red call button for assistance.

Three years of my life—completely gone. I couldn't take my eyes off the yellow emoji with the streaming tears.

A soft knock sounded at the door. Without waiting for a reply, a nurse noiselessly pushed in a clear bassinet. I caught a glimpse of the baby's tiny fingers, reaching above the white blanket she was bundled in. The baby that would grow into the little blonde girl from the tablet. *She was real.* On the end of the bassinet nearest the nurse, a small digital screen displayed an animated heart symbol and a thermometer. 133 beats per minute. 37 degrees Celsius. I pulled my hand away from Claire.

"She's had her bath and her tests. We just need a name now for the birth record." Seeming to sense the tension in the room, the pretty nurse glanced warily at me, then from Damien to Claire.

"Can I hold her?" Damien asked, stepping toward her eagerly.

"But of course." The nurse smiled and waited for Damien to come to her. He ran his fingers through his sandy blonde hair while the nurse reached into the bassinet. She lifted the baby and smoothly transferred her into Damien's arms. He tensed his shoulders, shifting the capped bundle of blankets until it rested comfortably in the crook of his elbow. The shift pushed his grey t-shirt sleeve up above the middle of his bicep, revealing the bottom of a trident tattoo. Did he have that before?

He drank in the baby's features for a moment before sidestepping toward the bed. I had never seen deeper dimples on his face, and they stood out more against a day's growth of stubble than when he was clean shaven.

"You wanted to see her before we decided on a name."

I wanted to see her? If I didn't remember it, could it have been me?

Nurse Sophie was mesmerized by the sight of Damien holding the baby, but the spell was broken when he spoke to me. She turned a patronizing smile toward me. Holding a stylus in one hand with a tablet tucked in the crook of her other arm, she was ready to record the baby's name. "After I get this, I can show Madame how to administer her own pain medicine."

Could they all really be expecting me to choose a name for this baby? The tears I was holding back felt hot now. They were choking me. I couldn't say anything, and the silence felt painfully long.

Claire cleared her throat. "Can we give them a few minutes alone with the baby before they decide on a name?"

"Of course," the nurse said. The smile never left her face, but her eyes drifted up to the ceiling before she put the tablet back on the bassinet.

Claire gathered up her purse from the chair next to the bed. "I think I'll go down to the café. Can I get you anything?" she asked Damien.

He shook his head, his eyes never leaving the baby's face. "Thank you."

"I'll be back soon." The nurse sighed, following Claire to the door.

I was left with Damien standing at my bedside, holding the baby. Alone with my family. *No, not my family.* Somehow, when my memories were gone, another version of me had chosen the life on the tablet. She had chosen Damien.

But she had complete amnesia. That meant the other Jace didn't remember kissing Corey in Central Park or our intimate conversation in Victor's laboratory. She didn't remember the flash of Corey standing over me in that white room, when he'd told me he loved me. *That's never going to change.*

Damien looked away from the baby, catching my eyes just as the thought passed through my mind.

"I guess she must have had…" I looked away, clearing my throat "I never thought about…her name when we saw her on the tablet."

"The tablet?" he said. "It's funny to hear you mention it."

I shifted uncomfortably. "Why's that?"

"Whenever Corey brought up the tablet, you would completely shut down."

Corey. Why did he leave? What had happened to his promise that he would never do anything to give Damien an unfair advantage? I took a deep breath in through my nose and released it through my mouth.

"How long was it before I could walk and talk again after the stroke?" I asked. "Claire said we were in Edmonton at a safe house. Was Corey still with us?"

"The doctors couldn't even promise you'd recover fully, but you proved them wrong. We spent every waking hour working. Your speech was normal within three months."

"Was Corey still there?" I repeated. "Was he…at the wedding?"

"Corey?" His brows came together. "No. After the months he spent shut up in his lab, he acted like he had some right to blow up when we told him we were engaged. I'm not sure if that was the only reason he left, but the timing makes me think it was the biggest one." I tried to imagine Corey shutting himself away, desperately trying to figure out what had happened to me and how to get my memories back. Maybe he didn't see what was happening.

The baby let out a soft cry, and Damien began bouncing her up and down. The motion soothed both of them. It was only a moment before Damien's dimples appeared again. His natural charm apparently worked on females of all ages. After the eruption, had I been like this innocent baby, unable to choose who would hold me, rock me, and sway me?

Damien stepped away from the bed, and I examined his profile. He looked much less boyish than he had in Victor's office—when he had seemed like an abused animal. His face was narrower now and his dimples deeper, more like his father. I felt a familiar, acidic burning in my stomach.

Clutching my abdomen under the covers, my forearms came into contact with a gauze dressing that covered the incision below my gown. I pulled my arms away, hoping that I hadn't disturbed anything. I was so numb that the lower half of me didn't seem to be part of my body.

"What happened to your father? Where is Victor?"

Damien stepped toward me again, trying to read my face, but I couldn't look at him. "Are you in pain?"

"I need to know what happened to him."

Damien hesitated. "Nothing."

"Nothing?" I took a few deep breaths, but the image of Victor's cold eyes wouldn't leave my mind. His warm breath on my neck.

"You need to calm down, Jace. Try to focus on something else. We'll talk about this later."

The baby let out another loud cry.

"We're safe here because of your father," he continued. "But that nurse is going to come back expecting us to have a name for the birth record. We need to act normal. Focus on the baby. Don't worry about anything else." He continued to bounce the baby, but her cries only got louder.

Act normal? Did Damien understand the message on the tablet? *Stop Victor. Find answers how inside fruitful meadow. Mountain key.* Had Corey explained to Damien that I was the only one who could stop Victor? How was I supposed to act normal?

I'll never be safe while Victor's still out there.

"You should hold her," Damien said.

Me? I pushed myself up in bed. Before I could protest, Damien pulled one of the pillows from behind me around to my lap. The baby's arms and legs flailed until he put her into the crook of my arm. My other arm came up to keep her from sliding off the pillow. She instantly nestled against me, and her crying stopped. Damien's hand slid slowly across my arm, leaving a trail of goosebumps. His electrifying touch was more uncomfortable now than ever.

"I suggested naming her Bridget, after your mom."

I closed my eyes. The coffin. My mom's face morphing into the little girl's. Her glossy, golden curls against the satin pillow. Did my recurring dreams mean Victor would kill her like he had tried to kill me? *He's her grandfather.*

My eyes were moist when I opened them. Damien brushed the baby's open palm with his index finger and she grasped onto it, connecting us in an intimate pose that should have been beautiful, like a portrait captured in the soft light filtering through the window, but it felt more like an episode of the *Twilight Zone.*

"You liked the name Abigail."

Abigail. I pictured the little blonde girl again. Had that been her name? I waited for the déjà vu to start. That uncanny feeling—neck tingles and unfocused fishbowl vision that often came when I met someone for the first time.

Nothing.

"Abigail," I whispered. The feeling still didn't come when I verbalized it.

What was her name? I examined her tiny features. Flawless skin, soft round cheeks, delicate, full lips—she looked like the newborn pictures my parents had of me in the little pink album in my mom's cedar chest.

She hadn't been my choice. She was the product of a relationship that I had no part in. But she was obviously mine.

"I think it fits her," Damien said, leaning over my shoulder.

I touched the little striped cap on her head. "Abby," I called softly. She didn't respond. Her eyes were shut tight, and she had found her fist to suck on.

Damien touched the top of her head too. Pulling away the little cap, he exposed her full head of dark curls.

"It's a lovely name." Nurse Sophie's voice was muted by the ringing in my ears. She entered the name on her tablet screen. "I need to scan you both to link you to Abigail, then we'll have her chip ready to implant before you leave tomorrow morning."

A baby's hair color isn't permanent, I told myself.

"I think we've decided to delay," Damien said. I looked up from the baby, searching Damien's calm face. Delay what? *Her chip,* Nurse Sophie had said.

"Are you sure? She won't remember it, and it's less paperwork if you do it now."

"We're okay with the extra paperwork later."

"Do you have religious objections?"

"No, it's nothing like that. The chip is still voluntary here, and we're just not choosing to volunteer our baby until she's a little older." Damien stepped toward her and held out his palm.

"Most schools require it, but I guess as long as you have it done by then." Sophie's face registered blank annoyance as she passed the tablet over Damien's palm. Lights flashed on the tablet screen.

While Nurse Sophie looked over the information on the screen, Damien reached down and lifted the baby out of my arms. *The chip.* Forcing my eyes downward, I opened my palms, expecting to see a jagged scar in my left hand from the cut I had made with the broken bottle. Both were smooth and completely free of scars. Was the chip that Damien had implanted in my palm before we left for Mount Hood still active?

Sophie came toward me and positioned the tablet to read my chip. My right hand trembled as I lifted it above the screen. I looked to Damien for some kind of reassurance, but his eyes were on the baby.

The tablet buzzed and a red flashing light appeared on the screen.

I held my breath.

"No chip detected," Sophie read the error message aloud.

"She's a lefty." Damien's laugh sounded smooth.

Laughing unnaturally, I said, "I must be more out of it than I thought."

I took a deep breath and put my other hand over the scanner. The light flashed again, but this time my picture appeared on the screen with text on the side. *Jessica Peterson. Date of Birth: 4/8/1990. Place of Birth: Edmonton, Alberta, Canada. Verified User ID: 913740.*

Jessica Peterson? I glanced at Damien and he nodded. He wanted me to play along. Act normal.

Tucking the tablet under her arm, Sophie said, "It looks like you found the room controls." She pointed to the console attached to the rail of my bed. "If you need pain control before the repair treatments you can self-administer." She tapped an emoji face on the control panel, bringing up the same faces that appeared on the flat screen on the wall. "How would you rate your pain at the moment?"

I shrugged. "I'm still numb."

"Well, as soon as you feel any, touch the face that corresponds with your level of pain and a dose of medication will be administered automatically. Don't try to be a hero."

"When will the repair treatments start?" Damien asked.

"She's on the schedule for two treatments. The technician should be in soon for the first one, and she'll have a follow up before she's discharged in the morning." Sophie glanced at her tablet. "The second treatment is just cosmetic. The scar is usually completely healed by morning, but they'll treat it again with the laser to prevent bruising or discoloration."

My C-section scar. Healed by morning?

"Order your dinner when you're ready." Sophie moved on to the next subject, as if the repair treatment they were talking about was as typical as the chocolate pudding on the menu that came up when she touched the food service icon on the control pad.

"Great, thank you," Damien said.

"Are you ready for me to take Abigail back to the nursery?"

"We're planning to keep her with us," Damien answered.

"All night?" Sophie seemed surprised.

"Yes."

"You realize that her immune supplements can only be administered in the nursery. And babies always sleep better under the warming lamps."

"We'll manage." Damien's voice was firm.

Sophie stood looking at Damien for a moment.

"D'accord. If you're sure, I'll leave you alone then."

I was glad she was leaving, but I wished she would take Damien and the baby with her. I wanted to be completely alone.

She opened the door just as the technician was reaching to knock. He wore a long white lab coat and held a tablet identical to Sophie's.

"Jessica Peterson?" he asked.

"She's all ready for you." Sophie said, moving past the technician and his equipment.

"I'm Sean." The technician wheeled a small cart into the room. The Omnibus logo danced around on a black monitor screen. "How are you feeling? Are you in any pain?"

"I'm still pretty numb," I said.

"Perfect timing then. Sometimes the treatment can be a bit uncomfortable if the anesthesia has worn off completely." He stopped when the cart was near the head of the bed on the right side. "You've read the risk waiver?"

I looked to Damien. His eyes were focused on the sleeping baby in his arms.

The technician took my silence as a yes. "I just need to scan to confirm and we'll get started," he said.

Sean touched his tablet screen several times before holding it out. He wanted to scan my chip. Damien continued rocking the baby, seemingly unconcerned. I placed my palm over the screen.

"Great," Sean said. He handed me a pair of thick black glasses and put on an identical pair before pulling back my covers. "Let's see, it's been at least three hours since your surgery?" Sean lifted my hospital gown up, exposing my bare abdomen like he had done the same thing a million times. My face grew warm. *I'm being ridiculous. It's his job.*

I tried to breathe normally. Even though I wasn't ready to see my changed body—the physical evidence of what had happened to me—I couldn't help looking as the technician pulled away the light gauze dressing that covered the incision just below my belly button.

"No need to be nervous," he said. "You're not going to feel a thing."

"She's had the procedure before," Damien said. "Amazing results."

"I didn't see another C-section on her record." The technician raised his eyebrows.

"Not a C-section. She had a scar on her palm removed."

"Ah. How long ago was that?"

"Two years," Damien replied.

"You'll be surprised how much faster the process is now. The latest generation of hybrid cells has only been on the market for six months. She'll be up and around within the next few hours."

Sean touched the screen display above the cart. The machine came to life. A fan hummed. My head started pounding. Propped up enough to look at the incision site while the technician adjusted the machine's settings, I couldn't keep my eyes away from it. No blood. Between the sides of the open skin, a light pink colored foam filled the open wound. My head began to spin. Sean lifted a black wand and pressed a switch. Blurry red and green words flashed across the monitor screen. I closed my eyes, trying to regain focus.

* * *

Leaning against the stone archway, I let my backpack slide to the ground. The courtyard is full of students laughing and talking. Nobody looks like they're in a rush to get to their next class. Nobody looks nervous. They're all drinking Starbucks. Nobody notices me, so I take my schedule out and check the number against the one on the door again.

I wait to go in until a group of three girls opens the door. Surveying the classroom, I look for a comfortable place to sit. Not too close to the front. Somewhere in the middle, but on the end of the row near the door. Empty chairs on either side of me.

I place my laptop on the table and set my water bottle, pen, and notepad beside it.

"Welcome," Dr. Jenkins begins right on time and I breathe a small sigh of relief.

He starts by handing around course policies and the syllabus. I glance over it, and take out my highlighter to mark due dates.

"Make sure that you read all of chapters one through three before our next class," he says. "Today, I'd like to introduce myself to your writing. Give me a three-page essay telling me why you agree or disagree with gun control laws in the country. Turn it in at the back of the class. When you're finished, you're free to go."

The students around me groan and protest quietly, but I'm a little relieved. I prefer writing and editing at home, where I can go over it as many times as I like, but at least I have strong opinions about the subject. I pick up my pen and start working.

The classroom door squeaks and everyone turns to look. A tall, floppy-haired student steps inside, completely unapologetic about his late entrance, or the disruption it's causing. He looks like he just rolled out of bed in a wrinkled t-shirt.

I turn back to my essay. The topic sentence is strong, now I just need to decide which three points to focus on.

The student bumps my elbow as he shifts down the row.

"Excuse me," he whispers. I barely look up, annoyed that he's sitting next to me at all, but baffled that he chose the seat inside the row instead of the one on the end.

He drops his backpack and takes his time finding paper and a pen.

"I'm Corey Stein," he says, leaning toward me. "What are we doing?"

I raise my eyebrows and point at the whiteboard where the professor has written out the details of the assignment.

* * *

"—set the laser to five, but let me know if you feel anything at all. We'll be done before you know it." The technician's voice cut through the ringing in my ears.

What was happening to me? The courtyard, my freshman English class, and Dr. Jenkins were all very familiar. I could even remember writing the essay and the grade I had gotten on it, but that wasn't how I remembered meeting Corey for the first time. We had never spoken at Stanford. He had sat on the other end of the room all semester.

Sean touched a button on the wand, sending a bright blue beam directly into the gel that filled my wound. The beam moved across the length of the incision, leaving behind a slight tightening sensation.

The laser beeped and the fan turned off. "That's it," Sean said, setting the wand back on his cart. I looked down at the incision site again. The light pink foam had all but disappeared and the gap between my skin was fusing together. The left side of the incision was only a thin line now.

"The muscle tissue takes longer to regenerate, so they'll keep you in bed for a few more hours. Your nurse will let you know when you can get up and take a shower." Sean smiled at me, but didn't attempt to cover me up. He stood and pushed the cart back toward the door.

"Enjoy the rest of your stay."

"Thank you," Damien said.

I couldn't stop staring at the incision site. The final edge of pink foam disappeared, replaced by soft, brown flesh, leaving no trace of what had happened. How was it possible that medical technology had advanced so much in three years?

* * *

The natural light from the window was beginning to fade when Claire came back into the room. The numbness was beginning to wear off, but I didn't feel any pain. My fingers compulsively stroked the lines on my left palm.

Claire and Damien sat cooing and admiring the baby while I lay wrapped in a heavy brain fog. My mind was trying to untangle itself, but I didn't know which string to start with. I found myself pondering the flash of memory I'd experienced during the repair treatment. It was like the flashes I'd had on Mount Hood, but this wasn't a memory I was missing. Except for the part where Corey spoke to me.

Damien interrupted my train of thought, standing up and backing a few feet away from Claire, who sat with Abigail in a white gliding rocker. He took a thin, black phone out of his pocket and snapped a few pictures of them.

"I didn't get any pictures of you in the delivery room," he said, looking at me. "We should take a few now before dinner comes."

Claire stood slowly and brought the baby to me. Damien handed his phone to Claire, then sat on the bed. He wrapped his right arm around me, sliding the other under the baby. My body stiffened.

"Smile," Claire said.

I raised the corners of my mouth, but kept my eyes fixed on the sleeping baby.

"Lovely." Claire turned the screen toward us so we could see the moment she had captured. Damien's fair features contrasted my dark hair and skin. Both of our eyes seemed to jump out of the image—his deep blue, and mine luminescent green.

"I'll post it and tag both of you," Damien said when Claire handed him the phone and reclaimed the baby. Without moving off of the bed, Damien opened an application on his phone. A blue triangle icon turned into the word OmniSocial. My stomach tightened as the social networking site loaded, updates and pictures appearing at the top of the feed every few seconds like an old-fashioned news ticker. *Omnibus.*

"I don't understand," I said. "We have fake names and safe houses, but you're posting pictures on an Omnibus application?"

"We're hiding in plain sight," Damien said. "My father's looking for us off the grid. He thinks we're part of the underground like we were when Corey was with us in Edmonton."

"But with the chips, can't Victor hear everything we're saying?"

"Hearing 160 million verified users in North America makes it almost impossible for Omnibus to actually listen to what we're saying," Claire said, bouncing the baby softly. "We have people on the inside that would notify us if our conversations were flagged."

"And you're not worried about putting our faces up on an Omnibus networking site?"

"OmniSocial is the last place he would look for us. Posting pictures and updates regularly keeps us floating down the Omnibus river of information." Damien typed out a caption for the image. "We know the algorithms. As long as we stay within those, we won't draw any attention."

The nurse cleared me to get up and shower. Standing was awkward at first, but after hours of being at everyone's mercy, it gave me a sense of regained control. I immediately locked myself in the bathroom, relieved to finally be alone with my thoughts.

After stripping off the blue hospital gown, I stood waiting for water to warm up. Since I woke up in this hospital, each new piece of information about my changed life had been thrown at me like a bucket of ice water.

Victor was looking for me—for all of us—but Claire and Damien wanted me to believe that we were safe floating down the "Omnibus river of information." I touched my palm. His chip was inside me. He lurked in the uncontrolled flashes of memory I'd experienced on Mount Hood. How could I possibly feel safe when I couldn't even hide from him in my own mind?

Eventually, I put on a clean hospital gown, but I was in no hurry to leave the steam-filled bathroom. Standing near the door, the sounds of the television finally coaxed me to open it. They were watching CNN.

"Continuing outages in New Delhi have foreign employers questioning the feasibility of converting to Omnibus's verified user system." Anderson Cooper's familiar voice carried through the dim hospital room. "Omnibus CEO Victor Trent and top delegates from the

UN Cyber-Terrorism Task Force have been in talks with Indian Prime Minister, Pranab Mukherjee, for several days, offering aide as Hannaj Terrorists claim responsibility for the attacks." Footage of Victor shaking hands with the Prime Minister flashed onto the screen. My damp hair felt heavy and my temples began throbbing. I grabbed hold of the door frame. My eyes constricted, and the room began to spin.

* * *

Checking my reflection in the mirror next to the door, I reconsider one last time. I still have a reading assignment to finish for Monday. But it would be a shame to let the time I spent straightening my hair go to waste.

"C'mon, Jace," my roommate says, grabbing my arm. "I'm so glad you decided to come."

I follow her out the door into the humid night air. She links arms with me and our tall heels click against the cement walkway. Flashing lights and thumping music lead us to the apartment around the corner.

"You'll like these guys," she says, letting go of my arm and walking a few paces ahead when she sees one of her friends approaching from the other direction.

A door opens to my right and I step to the left, realizing I'm hugging the edge of the walkway, but my heel catches on a crack. My ankle rolls to the right and I stumble forward several small steps before a pair of arms stop me from crashing to the ground.

"Are you alright?" a familiar voice asks.

Trying to recompose myself, I tug the hem of my skirt toward my knees before looking at the face of the man who broke my fall. Corey Stein. The opinionated guy from my English class. He's still holding on to my waist awkwardly.

"Are you sure you have a license to drive those after dark? I pegged you as the sensible shoe type," he says, smirking. He's still touching my back, even though I'm fully upright and stable on my feet again. "They should sell an insurance policy with those."

"Jace," my roommate says. She must have doubled back when she realized she'd lost me. I twist myself out of Corey's arms before she reaches us. "Oh, hey. Who's this?"

"I don't know," I say. "I think he's in my English class."

"Oh really?" my roommate says, smiling flirtatiously at him. "Do you live here?"

"Home, sweet home," Corey replies.

"Are you heading to the party?" she asks.

He shakes his head.

"You should come!"

"Thanks, but I'm not dressed for it." He looks at my shoes. In the dark, I can't tell if his t-shirt is wrinkled, but based on every other time I've seen him, I'm willing to bet it is.

"You look fine," she presses.

"Not really my thing," he says, brushing past us. "You should be careful in those shoes. Make sure to call a cab if you're going to drink."

* * *

Sucking in a deep breath, I straightened my wobbly knees.

Damien's head turned toward the bathroom door. "I'm sorry. We'll change the station." He stood and reached for the control console attached to the side of the bed. "Or we can turn it off. You're probably ready for bed."

"No!" I said. "Leave it on."

Damien hesitated before moving away from the controls.

"Victor's working with the UN?" I asked.

"Yes," Claire said. "He always seems to be just a few steps behind the Hannaj, ready with exactly what's needed to clean up the aftermath. He's made himself indispensable to the UN." She touched the scar on her cheek softly before turning her attention back to the close-up of Victor's face on the screen.

"The attacks have helped push through his agenda," Damien said. "People will sell their souls to protect their information."

The footage shifted to Victor speaking to the UN The camera panned closer as he finished his speech. The delegates came to their feet, erupting in applause.

"Omnibus Chief Information Officer, Corey Stein also addressed the delegates, detailing Omnibus's five-year plan to convert less developed countries to the OmniNetwork." Anderson Cooper narrated as Corey stepped up to the podium. I took hold of the bedrail. Claire and Damien didn't react. The flashing light from the television cast strange shadows around the room.

"As citizens of the world, we are responsible for helping those who can't help themselves. It's unacceptable to leave others behind when we have the means to bring them with us into a safer world. Until we're all protected, no one is safe." Corey paused, reaching for a shiny object in his left suit coat pocket. He lowered the silver pocket watch on the chain slightly below his palm and let it swing back and forth like a pendulum three times before the camera switched back to Anderson Cooper.

The pocket watch. My heart slowed to a series of painful *thuds*. Corey's father—the CIA. It was their code. *Danger*.

Damien and Claire seemed completely unaware of what I had just seen. Why would they be aware? I was the only one who knew about Corey's pocket watch code. Did he know that I was back, or did he just take the opportunity to flash the watch whenever he was on camera in hopes that I would see the signal and know what it meant?

"You said Corey was in Washington with my father," I said. "What is he doing with Victor?"

Claire looked at me, seemingly surprised by my question. "The situation is complicated," she said, touching my arm lightly. "Are you sure you're feeling well?"

Even if I trusted Damien and Claire as implicitly as the other Jace seemed to, I couldn't tell them about the memories I'd recovered on Mount Hood or the flashes I was still having. I wanted to know why Corey was working for Victor.

"When can I talk to my father?" I demanded. He had the answers I needed.

"There are protocols that must be followed," Claire said. "But I'm working on contacting him."

"Does he know I'm in the hospital?"

"Of course," Damien replied. "He knows everything that happens at the safe house."

"It's getting late, and we're all tired. It will be much easier to explain everything tomorrow," Claire said. "I'm going to head back to the house so you two can try to get some rest."

Damien nodded. "It's been a long day."

A singular look passed between them, and she squeezed his arm before lightly brushing his cheek with a kiss. "I'll be back first thing in the morning," she said.

Claire came to my bedside and kissed me, too. I wasn't ready for her to leave. I wasn't ready to be alone with the baby and Damien again.

* * *

The flat screen near the door flashed on. The pain scale was gone now, replaced by my estimated discharge time and my new nurse's name.

Damien fed Abigail a bottle and changed her diaper before laying her down in the bassinet. He was completely preoccupied with her.

I could have been a passerby staring through the thick glass of a nursery window.

Out of habit, I reached out, touching the cold, wooden tray table beside the bed with my outstretched hand. I felt around before my eyes settled on the empty surface. I had no idea where my phone was or if I even still had one.

A few weeks after my mom's accident, I had dropped my phone on a run and shattered the screen. This felt much worse. The only thing that had helped me survive those two days without it was the technician's assurance that I would have it back on Monday at 8:30 a.m.

How many times had I reached for it that weekend? What had I been checking for? Pictures of my roommate's art project? I could walk into the other room to see it. Or updates on Kennedy Adam's European trip? She probably didn't even remember me. No. I would scroll through newsfeeds and like hundreds of strangers' pictures, but I could finally admit to myself now what I'd really been looking for. A missed call, a text message, an email—any kind of communication from my father. I thought his distance meant he didn't care about me. But with the return of some of my missing memories—the pictures I had drawn of the future, the plan we'd made in his office, the overwhelming need I had to forget—maybe I had been the one who had imposed the distance between us.

I closed my eyes and pretended to be resting. I was too exhausted to make sense of what it all meant. Damien must have believed I was asleep. Without talking to me, he finally turned the light off and stretched himself out on a roll-away bed. With my face turned away from him, my eyes reopened and I found myself staring at the strange shadows on the textured ceiling. I traced the lines in the texture with my eyes, trying to make a pattern appear. But I finally gave up. There was no pattern to be found. The design was completely random.

* * *

Thick mist rises from the green earth. It carries the sheer white layers of my dress upward in soft flutters.

Water trickles in the distance. I step in the direction the sound comes from, but my naked feet tear against the sharp volcanic rock, hidden at first by the mist and moss. A baby cries. She's near the water. She's alone. I can't abandon her. She needs me.

I try to run across the rocks, but each step leaves a bloody footprint. Finally, I see the waterfall, set back behind a luminous blue pool.

The baby's cries drown out the sound of the water, but I see now that she's not alone. Damien steps out of the mist, bouncing her. When he looks at me, his eyes are cold and black. Brushing his lips against the infant's blonde curls, he takes in a deep breath, flaring his nostrils. Another breath expands his chest, but it doesn't contract when he exhales. The eyes darken more. The hair fades away. The dimples deepen.

Victor has her now.

"No!" I reach out my arms and sprint toward them, but just before I touch the baby, a burst of steam blasts from a hole in the ground. I push my hand into the mist, reaching to take the baby, but they've both vanished.

* * *

"Take a deep breath. I'm here." Damien grasped my outstretched hand. "It was just a dream, J." The bed squeaked and my body slid toward the divot created by his weight. When my cheek bumped against his chest, he pulled our hands against him and slid his other arm around my heaving shoulders. I tried to catch my breath, but the scent of Damien's shirt was suffocating. In the dark, I didn't have his dimples and warm eyes to convince me that it was just a dream.

"Shhhh." His breath was like liquid nitrogen against my neck, instantly freezing my spine. I felt my body go rigid.

Twisting my hand to free it from his, I propelled myself into the rail on the opposite side of the bed.

Claire's scar, volcanoes, the girl in the coffin. They weren't like the flashes of memory, but they were more than just dreams.

I took a few deep breaths as my eyes adjusted.

"You can't get away from them, can you?" Damien's eyes reflected the soft blue lights from the monitors.

"Away from who?"

His dimple was a deep shadow on his face. "The nightmares."

"Did she have nightmares too?" I whispered.

"Who?"

"I mean, did I?"

He searched my face in the dim light, then nodded.

"What were they about?" I asked.

"You never remembered the details." He stood and my shoulders relaxed. "You were always trying to save someone, but you couldn't ever reach them in time."

* * *

The doctor's discharge instructions were surprisingly brief. The technician had already been in for my follow up treatment, but there had been very little for him to do. The scar had disappeared and the muscles underneath felt completely normal.

"Take it slowly, but you can resume whatever physical activity you've been doing as soon as you feel up to it." The doctor scanned my hand to verify my discharge, then Damien and I were left alone in the room to pack.

"Claire's on her way to pick us up. She'll meet us out front in about ten minutes."

I sat on the end of the bed, dressed in a comfortable grey sweat suit the other Jace must have packed for herself.

A blast of cold air hit as soon as we walked outside, and I pulled up the zipper of my sweatshirt. Claire stood waiting next to a pewter Volkswagen Passat. Piles of dirty, melting snow lined the sidewalks. Delivery trucks with motors running polluted the crisp morning air with exhaust.

"You look fantastic, Jace," Claire said. "Did you sleep well last night?"

"Thank you," I said, nodding.

"You look like you could use a shower," she said, turning to Damien.

"Good morning, Mother," Damien said as he opened the door and secured the baby's car seat. "We should have brought a heavier jacket for you." He came back to the curb for me, putting his arm around me to guide me to the other side of the car.

He held the door open, and I sat on the soft grey upholstery. This car was nothing like the Town Car Damien had fastened me into after carrying me out of the parking garage in New York, but I still watched to see if he would switch the child lock as he shut the door.

Outside the car, Claire said something that made Damien frown. His response to her was muffled, but I heard "your beloved protocol."

Claire's door clicked open. She shot Damien a look that silenced him instantly. "We're anxious to proceed with the plan. I've called a meeting with the entire Alliance."

"Alliance?" I asked.

"Your father and I hand selected a group of allies with the connections and resources we need." She smiled, full of strange exuberance. "You probably remember meeting some of them in New York."

Whatever was going on with this "alliance," I was glad the meeting would happen today. It meant my father was as anxious to see me as I was to see him.

Damien eased the car forward. We turned left out of the circular drive onto a busy street. Leafless trees rose up like old lady fingers out of the brown patches of grass. We passed plain red brick apartments and an enormous Greco-Roman building set back away from the street on a hill. French street signs. French business signs. More apartment buildings. A few houses.

"We're almost home," Damien said, turning the car off of the busy street onto a much narrower one. The apartments on my side of the car disappeared, replaced by a charming park. The car slowed, and Damien turned into the driveway of a large, grey stone house. He closed the garage door as soon as we were parked inside.

"Welcome home," Claire said.

walked up the steps slowly from the dark garage into an arched hallway with tall ceilings.

Claire stopped just short of the kitchen and set the car seat on the floor. She looked to her right, where a light grey marble basin was mounted to the wall, just above waist level. The marble was etched with an intricate pattern that hinted at a crucifix, with fleur-de-lis on three ends of a vine. Had the house been a church before?

Claire placed her hand just above the bowl and spread her fingers. I didn't see the glass plate above the basin until her palm touched it, activating a blue light that glowed beneath. Simultaneously, the metal wall mount slid forward until it covered her hand. It clicked softly when it locked into place. The box lit up and the blue light moved from her fingertips to her wrist, producing a soft spraying sound.

The light halted briefly before moving back toward her fingertips in one swift motion. Then the box reopened. Claire touched her forehead softly with her damp fingers.

"If you'll excuse me, I have a few things to do before the meeting." She disappeared into the kitchen, her footsteps echoing down a hallway until a door closed.

"Go ahead." Damien nodded toward the device.

"What does it do?" I asked.

"No need to wear tracking chips here. The safe house is exactly that—safe." He smiled and put his hand on the glass plate. "It doesn't hurt. The water warms and softens the adhesive." The device closed over his hand and the light appeared just as it had for Claire.

The chips weren't implanted? Relief rushed through me, but skepticism followed close behind. "What about the algorithms?"

"The chips are stored in water—which you might remember interferes with the signal. This device broadcasts pre-recorded house noises for anyone who might be listening to our ID's. It simulates the sounds of normal life much better than we could." The top opened and Damien removed his hand.

He moved aside and I placed my left hand over the plate. The top came down, and the spraying water started. The light warmed my palm, moving from fingertips to wrist, then returning before the box opened.

I examined my damp hand. It looked exactly the same. Damien lifted the car seat, and I followed him into the kitchen. Enormous white tiles on the floor met up with matt black cabinets and appliances. The countertops were stainless steel. The refrigerator had a small control panel built in that glowed light blue. It was all oddly modern for such an old-looking house.

I stood in the middle of the kitchen, paralyzed by the realization that this house was as unfamiliar as the hospital had been. I had no idea what was inside the cabinets. My instincts weren't telling me which drawer I would find the silverware in. I had lived in so many different houses since Sigonella, and none of them had felt completely unfamiliar like this. I held on to the cold metal counter top and took a deep breath in through my nose, then released it on a three count. After years of building a routine to minimize the anxiety my déjà vu caused, the lack of it should have been a relief instead of a trigger.

"Are you okay?" Damien asked.

"I'll be fine. I just need to get my bearings."

"Of course. I'm sorry I didn't think of it. Let me show you around." He lightly touched my elbow, guiding me away from the kitchen counter. "I should probably start by introducing you to Mirlande and Leon." He pressed a button on a black flat screen on the wall. After a short silence, the panel lit up.

"Yes? How can I help?" The deep voice had a thick accent.

"We're home with the baby, Leon."

"Be right there," the voice responded.

"Tell Mirlande."

"Right away."

Damien led me down a hallway. "Leon was secret service in Haiti before the coup in the 90's. He took care of Mirlande after her mother died in a refugee camp. He's the only parent she's ever known." The baby grunted and Damien stopped mid-hallway—a door on either side of him. He swayed the car seat gently until she was quiet again. "They've been with us since Edmonton."

I waited for him to continue.

"Laundry room and bathroom." He pointed to each. "Claire's room is at the end of the hall, and Mirlande's is on the right."

We turned back toward the kitchen. I heard footsteps coming up a staircase in the family room. He continued to hold onto my arm and lead me into the bright room. The white tile floor continued through the passageway, but an asymmetrical area rug with a block pattern in various shades of grey covered most of the floor under the smooth black leather sofa and loveseat.

Leon was the first to reach the top of the stairs. He was a very large man, with broad shoulders that looked like they might break out of the black suit coat he was still buttoning. His white shirt collar hung open, exposing a simple gold crucifix around his neck. His eyes, hair and skin were the darkest I had ever seen, contrasting the brilliant white smile that appeared when we locked eyes.

"You had us all so worried." He came straight to me and wrapped me up in a tight hug. "You look wonderful."

"Let's see this beautiful baby." Mirlande stepped into view. She was a stunning, natural beauty. Her unmade-up eyes glistened under perfectly arched eyebrows and her flawless chocolate skin glowed beneath the cornrow braids that fell at various lengths, framing her face. She didn't look at me, heading directly for Damien and the car seat. "How do I get her out of this contraption?"

Damien let go of my arm and set the seat on the floor, sliding Abigail out of the straps. "I'll let you hold her," Damien said with a mock stern face, "but you have to promise to give her back."

"I couldn't keep her if I wanted to. I have a lot of work to do still. Claire wants everything perfect for our visitors."

They both stood up to their full height as Damien passed the baby over to Mirlande. He was only slightly taller than her.

"She's perfect," Mirlande said. Kissing the top of Abby's head, she took in a deep sniff of new baby scent.

"I wish my mother would have waited," Damien said. "Give Jace a little time to adjust and settle in."

"She's just following the Admiral's protocol." Mirlande said.

Leon touched my shoulder. "Claire said something happened to you during delivery. You have amnesia again?" The fatherly concern in his voice drew me to him. "Don't worry. You'll work past it, just like the last time."

"Thank you," I said.

"Between monitoring everyone's travels and setting up a secure link for this afternoon, I have my hands full. I've got to get back to work. Come down later when you're all settled in."

Leon began his retreat back down the stairs. "Glad you're home safe and sound."

"Can we impose on you to hold her for a bit longer while I give Jace a quick tour of the place?" Damien asked Mirlande as soon as Leon was out of sight.

"Just throw the sheets on the beds while you're upstairs and I'll keep her all day for you." Mirlande poked her tongue out at Damien. *Playful. They seem almost like siblings*, I told myself. I smiled, but she still didn't make eye contact with me. Sitting down easily on the loveseat, Mirlande looked very natural with a baby in her arms. She had to be about our age. Did she have any children of her own? I would have asked her if I didn't feel like an observer rather than a participant in the conversation.

"C'mon." Damien touched the back of my arm again, guiding me through an arched doorway into an entry foyer with vaulted ceilings. The front door was solid. No windows. A freeform circular wood staircase filled up most of the room. Our footsteps echoed in the emptiness as we climbed to the second floor.

The upper story housed two moderate sized bedrooms, identically decorated in black, white and grey tones.

"Guest rooms," Damien said, stepping into the one closest to the stairs. Mirlande had stacked the clean linens on the bed. "They don't get much use. Mind helping?" he asked.

"Sure," I said.

Damien unfolded the sheets, tossing them into the air. He smiled at me as they billowed toward the side of the bed where I was standing. I reached for a corner and began smoothing, keeping my eyes focused on the sheets.

When I finished tucking a hospital corner, I glanced at Damien, who was just a step behind me, folding the corner exactly as I had. I froze.

"What?" he asked.

"Nothing," I said, stepping toward the door.

He looked down at his corner. "Doesn't it pass inspection? I can try again."

"Did I teach you to do the corners that way?"

"Yeah." He grinned. "It bothered you if I didn't do it right."

I didn't like the way Damien was looking at me. The other Jace had relearned how to walk and talk, but somehow she made a bed just like my mother had taught me. My shoulder bumped into the door as I backed out of the room. Embarrassed, I hurried into the next room and started unfolding the sheets myself.

Damien joined me, but kept silent as we worked.

After we finished the second guest room, Damien turned toward the double doors at the farthest end of the corridor. I followed him.

"This is our room," he said, opening the doors and walking inside.

The European style platform bed was already made up. Everything was black and white. Stark and modern. Nothing Damien would have chosen based on his house in St. Paul.

Damien sat down on a large black ottoman.

"Don't be shy," he said when I didn't follow him.

I hesitated, holding onto the door frame. It didn't feel right stepping into the bedroom of a man I'd only been on one date with.

"Maybe I should go check on the baby," I said.

"She's fine. Mirlande loves babies. She's been looking forward to this for a long time."

"Aren't you going to show me the basement?"

He untied his shoes. "Do you mind if I jump in the shower and shave first? It'll take less than ten minutes."

I looked over my shoulder toward the stairs, trying desperately to think of another excuse to run back down them.

"Why don't you get comfortable?" His smile was natural and he made it sound so easy, but getting comfortable had never been easy for me and it definitely wouldn't be now. He expected me to act like his wife. How could I make him understand that I might look and sound like her, but I didn't have the memories of their relationship?

Stumbling into the room, I let go of the doorframe and grabbed hold of a black desk to steady my shaking knees.

"I can't..." I stammered, trying to verbalize my thoughts. "I don't..."

He pulled off one shoe, then the other. "The bathroom and closet are through there. The desk is yours." He pulled his t-shirt off over his head. "Your photography stuff is in there."

I sat down at the desk so quickly I almost missed the chair. *In through the nose on a three count. Out through the mouth.*

He got up and walked toward the bathroom, unbuttoning his pants as he went. I spun my chair toward the wall, bumping my knee on the drawer. A pair of glasses with mirrored lenses dropped onto the carpet.

I heard Damien turn the shower on. *Why didn't he shut the door?*

Fumbling to reach for the glasses without looking down, I finally picked them up. A blue light flashed across the inside of the lenses when

I touched the corner of the frame. They fell out of my hands, back onto the desk.

Damien started singing.

The Omnibus logo appeared in the center of both lenses. Pain stabbed at my temples.

The room went dark.

* * *

"'Suffering is an ineradicable part of life, even as fate and death. Without suffering and death human life cannot be complete.'" Dr. Jenkins says. "Has anyone read Man's Search for Meaning *by Viktor Frankl?"*

It's one of my father's favorites, but I stop myself from raising my hand when, from the corner of my eye, I see Corey Stein's hand go up. By now, I'm not surprised. He's read every book Dr. Jenkins has mentioned. I brace myself to hear his strong opinion about this one.

"It's a nice thought," he begins, "and most religions teach something along those lines, but I don't think it's true. We always want to explain things we can't control. Frankl was just trying to give meaning to a senseless situation."

I sat up and looked at the ceiling. Was it really so terrible that Viktor Frankl found meaning and hope in the face of atrocity?

Dr. Jenkins nods slowly. "Okay, Mr. Stein. But be careful. You're sitting in a classroom full of Judeo-Christian believers. Even Eastern religions seek to find purpose and meaning in life. You're suggesting they'd rather believe in fairytales than accept the reality that bad things just happen?"

I glance at Corey. He smiles casually, like he didn't just insult most of the human race. My pen begins to tap softly against the desk.

"Not at all," Corey says. "Religion and science both recognize the problem. But religion tries to make people feel better about it instead of fixing it."

Because he thinks he's so much smarter than the rest of us.

"The opiate of the masses?" Dr. Jenkins suggests.

"Exactly," Corey says.

After almost a full semester of sitting next to my arrogant neighbor, I know he's blissfully unaware of the heat building up inside me.

He continues, "I prefer to be on the side that's trying to eradicate suffering instead of advocating for it, inflicting it, and even deifying it."

"Did you ever consider that being a believer and being a scientist aren't mutually exclusive," I say without raising my hand. Corey's head whips toward me, obviously surprised that I've broken my months of silence. "You're ignoring the fact that Viktor Frankl was a neurologist and a psychologist. He dedicated his whole life to easing suffering, both mental and physical."

Corey raises his eyebrows.

"But he also recognized that no matter how advanced we become as a race, humans will always encounter situations we can't control," I continue in one long breath. "Suffering and death will never be completely eliminated, but choosing to find meaning in them gives us power over our circumstances."

"So what you're saying is that the purpose of religion is to gain power?" He smirks.

* * *

The shower turned off, but Damien was still humming. I lifted my head off the desk, not waiting for it to clear before staggering out of the room.

When I reached the bottom of the stairs, I slowed down and took a few deep breaths, trying to sort out the emotions evoked by the memory I'd just experienced. I couldn't understand where the memory was coming from, and why it was coming back now. Were there more gaps in my memory than the one from kindergarten? The thought was very unsettling.

Mirlande hadn't moved from the couch. She stopped rocking the baby when I came into the room. Her almond shaped eyes narrowed.

"Back so soon?"

"Damien decided to shower." I sat down on the loveseat. My headache finally started to subside.

"Glad to be home?" she asked.

I shrugged.

"You really don't remember anything?"

I shook my head. "I don't remember the last three years."

She raised her eyebrows. "But you remember everything before the eruption?"

"Yes," I said.

"You remember Corey Stein?"

I was a little surprised. Was she testing me?

"Yes..."

"Were you in love with him?"

My face lit up, a flaming mixture of anger and embarrassment. I couldn't answer.

"You were, weren't you?" she accused. How could she be so presumptuous? She didn't even know me.

"I had bigger things to worry about." It was difficult to keep my expression neutral and my breathing normal.

She pushed her chin upward, as if acknowledging a point for me. "I wish he could hear you say that. He was convinced."

Her tone was venomous, but the words didn't poison me. *Corey was convinced that I loved him?*

"You don't like him," I said.

She shook her head, "What's not to like? He's America's darling...great hair and an amazing benefits package, I'm sure."

He was a traitor in her eyes. The thought would be devastating if I hadn't seen his signal. He somehow knew I was watching and was trying to warn me of danger. He might be working for Victor Trent, but there had to be some logical explanation why.

After what seemed to me like a calculated amount of time—just enough to make me extremely uncomfortable, Mirlande flipped a switch. "I like the name you chose. Is it okay if I call her Abby?"

She smiled when I made eye contact. Her dislike for Corey was obvious, but what had her relationship been like with the other Jace?

"Sure," I said awkwardly.

"I think it fits her."

The doorbell rang. Three distinct tones, followed by a robotic female voice: "Doctor Peter Watts, Verified ID 679123. Randall King, Verified ID 682590. The Omnibus robotic voice. The voice from the tablet.

The double doors upstairs clicked closed. Damien was coming down.

"I've got it," Damien called from the top of the stairs. I grasped my hands together tight on my lap. Should I stand up? Should I greet them at the door? What were they all expecting from me? Mirlande watched my face with intense scrutiny.

"Come on now, don't be shy. Get ready to bask in your moment of glory. You know you've always loved the limelight."

I stood up and moved toward the door, more to escape Mirlande's dripping sarcasm than to greet what was waiting for me.

Dr. Watts's eyes were misty when he embraced me.

"I'm so sorry this is happening again," he whispered in my ear before letting me go. He stepped back and looked me up and down like I was a specimen in a laboratory. "The baby was born yesterday?"

"Yes."

"Claire said you went in to be induced but something went wrong?"

"She didn't tolerate the Pitocin well." Damien stepped up from behind the doctor. "She blacked out and the baby was in distress. They decided it was too risky to continue and took her in for a C-section."

Randall King still stood by the door. I smiled at him, feeling awkward for both of us as we listened to my intimate medical history discussed like I wasn't even in the room. Randall smiled back, giving me a little tip of his grey, felt cowboy hat. How long had he been a part of this Alliance of people who knew about Victor, and time travel, and the plan that had been initiated by a six-year-old? Did he know about it at the UN dinner?

"Come inside. Come inside." Claire must have floated into the room, because her feet hadn't made any noise on the tiles. She had changed into a crisp white dress shirt with a flared, knee length skirt, accentuated at the waist with a wide red belt. She looked like she belonged on a fashion runway, even with the baby in her arms. She must have taken her from Mirlande. "It's so good to see you both."

She went to Randall King first. He looked at her with as much admiration as I felt. She gracefully leaned over the baby and kissed Randall's cheek.

"It's been too long, but you haven't changed. Someday I'm going to get you to tell me where you're hiding your fountain of youth so I can take a dip in it with you," he said.

She blushed, and it only illustrated his point.

"How were your travels? Any issues at the border?" Claire directed the question at Dr. Watts but I noticed the beautiful smile she gave Randall before looking away.

"The border was a mess. It's easier to travel to South America or India at the moment. But Parliament is voting next week."

"The patches worked beautifully in the hospital, but I'm still uneasy about traveling." Claire pivoted while keeping eye contact with Dr. Watts, stepping away from the door and toward the family room. We all followed. "Mirlande's putting out a light lunch for us. You're both hungry, I assume."

Randall looked at his wristwatch. "The call's scheduled for 2:00?"

"Yes," Claire answered, "Leon is securing the connections."

"Let me bring in the bags and I'll join you in a few minutes." Randall doubled back and left the rest of us to continue on to the kitchen where Mirlande had put out a colorful spread of delicious smelling food. Black beans were served next to a red rice dish garnished with colorful peppers, fresh bread, and some kind of fried round vegetable.

"I've missed these smells," Dr. Watts said, eyeing the food before he greeted Mirlande.

"I wish I could say the same." Mirlande punched Dr. Watts's arm softly, bringing her left forearm up to protect her face. Dr. Watts didn't even try to play along. He smiled, but looked uncomfortable until Mirlande moved past him.

I watched Damien and Dr. Watts dish up their food before getting some for myself. Claire sat at the end of the table with the baby.

"I'm going to take a plate down to Leon," Mirlande said, leaving the room.

Randall reappeared. "I checked the forum, and everyone has responded to your message. Everyone's ready."

Claire smiled. "Good."

"We've also secured funding pledges from five new silent partners on the West Coast," Randall added. "They don't want to know anything. They just want to be a part of stopping the madness." He filled up a plate and sat in the empty chair on Claire's right hand. "One of them was Elliot Lewis. Do you remember him? He ran the 400."

"Lewis?" Claire said. "Elliot Lewis. The name's vaguely familiar, but I can't picture him."

"Well, you probably never looked his direction because you only had eyes for me at the time, but he's done quite well for himself. He practically owns the State of Idaho. His drone combines are taking the farm industry by storm."

"I do remember him," Claire said.

"He despised Omnibus before he even knew anything about Victor. His first three patents were denied because they were almost identical to patents already filed by Omnibus."

Claire closed her eyes slowly.

"Stealing patents?" I muttered.

Randall raised his eyebrows. "Not just patents," he said. "Omnibus has had unprecedented timing with mergers and acquisitions, buying and selling stocks…a little bit of foreknowledge eliminates a lot of risk."

Patents and stock tips. I set my fork down.

Claire was watching me closely. As soon as my eyes met hers she took a deep breath and lifted her hand absently to the scar on her cheek. What was she thinking about?

"You said others," I said, "Other members of the Alliance have been affected by what Victor's done?"

"It would be hard to find someone who hasn't been affected," Damien said.

"But you're talking about those he has singled out." Claire looked at me as if we shared some secret knowledge. Had I told her something about this when I was a child?

"He's been playing with a stacked deck for so long that he thinks he'll always have the upper hand on us. He doesn't know what it's like when Vandy starts to fight." Randall winked at Claire.

"Down the field with blood to yield." Claire recited the words, annunciating like a Shakespearean actor.

I looked around the table, waiting for someone to tell me what I was missing.

"Vanderbilt University's fight song," Damien explained. "My mother and Randall were classmates."

"We're not really sure if it's a personal vendetta or just a coincidence that eight of our classmates have been targeted." Randall smiled at Claire.

"What will it take to convince you?" Claire asked softly.

"I'm counting on a personal interrogation—complete with flaming bamboo under the fingernails." Randall grinned. "Do you think the Admiral could work that into the plan?"

Claire didn't laugh. Damien didn't even look up from his plate. Randall seemed oblivious to the awkward silence.

Claire stroked her scar softly. "The plan doesn't serve us. We serve the plan."

Damien dropped his fork and made the sign of the cross. "All hail the plan."

Randall chuckled.

Claire shot a glare at both of them, but her expression softened before she turned her apologetic eyes toward me.

How much of the plan did my father tell you? I wondered, searching Claire's eyes.

I glanced at the digital clock above the stove. 1:30. Only thirty minutes until my father would enlighten the rest of us.

"Would you all excuse me? I want to change before the meeting," I said.

"Of course. Take a few minutes and rest too," Damien said. "You're supposed to be recovering."

"Take whatever time you need," Randall said. "The Alliance has been waiting for you patiently for years. We'll be here when you're ready, my dear." Randall and Damien both stood when I pushed my chair back. Dr. Watts held a hunk of bread in one hand and waved at me with the other before taking another bite of food.

I crossed paths with Mirlande near the stairs in the family room but kept walking. I didn't want to talk to her again.

She stopped. "Finished so soon?"

"I'm going to get ready for the call." I continued on past her.

"Where's Abby?" It felt accusatory. Did Mirlande hate the other Jace too? It seemed impossible that I could have earned so much animosity from her in such a short period of time. I didn't turn around.

"You'll have to fight Claire for her."

"It's fine that you don't want to look at me. It's pretty eerie looking into your eyes, you know. I can tell you don't remember me at all. I mean, you're her, but you're definitely not her."

I stopped at the spiral staircase. "I'm sorry. I wish I could remember."

"But it's all part of the plan?" Anger and a dash of bitterness.

I cleared my throat. "I wish I could tell you."

"Humph." Mirlande continued on to the kitchen. What had I done to make her hate me so much?

I reached the top of the stairs and nearly sprinted for the double doors at the end of the hall. I closed them firmly and leaned back against them. *Hold it together*. I would see my father's face soon. He was waiting for me. Would he be disappointed in me, or proud of the decisions I'd made on Mount Hood?

I wanted to touch up my makeup and change into something that made me feel powerful.

The bathroom was spotless white, with brushed nickel hardware. Beyond the vanity and double sinks, two closets were closed off by tempered glass. The brushed white pattern on the doors looked like a rain storm. Damien had left his closet open slightly, and I could see his rows of organized clothes. Opening the other side, I found a variety of colorful sundresses. Everything was mixed in together. No rhyme or reason on the color order. No length graduation.

It only took a second of shuffling through her clothes to realize that the other Jace wasn't a fan of suits. My professional options were very limited. Somewhere in the middle of her chaos, I came across a plain, black eyelet sundress with the tags still attached. It was reminiscent of the one I had worn on my first date with Damien.

After pulling the hanger off of the rack, I only hesitated a second before ripping the tags off and trading her sweat suit for something that at least looked like it was mine.

Only five minutes now. My palms were damp. *I shouldn't be nervous. I'm finally going to understand everything.*

The main floor was completely abandoned when I came down. They must have all gone to the basement.

I walked down to the basement cautiously. The windows were completely blacked out, and the only light came from the computer monitors around the perimeter of the large, open room. It took a few seconds for my eyes to adjust.

In the center of the room, Claire, Damien, and Randall surrounded a round, white table. A black, triangular device in the center of the table glowed with a soft red light.

"Perfect timing," Leon said. "Why don't you take a seat and we can make sure that the sound is working properly before we go live."

Dr. Watts sat down at one of the computers at the far end of the room. "Seattle and Munich are both set," he said.

"Who are we waiting on then?" Leon asked.

Dr. Watts touched the screen to toggle to a spreadsheet. "Just Nashville and DC."

My father wasn't ready yet. I sat down in a chair directly across the table from Claire. I purposely separated myself from Damien by putting one chair between us. He wasn't close enough to touch me, and I could only see his profile from the corner of my eye.

"Jace, can you say something to test the mic in front of you?" Leon asked.

I shrugged. "Test, test, test," I said, leaning in toward the device in the middle. I couldn't see anything that looked remotely like a microphone.

"It's picking her up just fine," Dr. Watts said.

"No need to lean in, Jace. You can get comfortable," said Randall. "Sit back and relax."

"DC is live." Dr. Watts's voice seemed full of the same nervous anticipation I was feeling.

"Let's get the visuals." Leon's fingers jumped across the keys. The black device in the center of the table responded by beaming holographic video feed into the air above the table. Face after face appeared, stacked on top of each other in boxes that reminded me of the Brady Bunch. I counted 23. The graphics were crystal clear. In the middle of the table, I smiled when Omar's slick, black hair appeared. Many of the other faces had been present that night at the UN as well. Had they already been part of this Alliance before the eruption?

The light stopped flashing. Was this everyone? Where was my father?

"Nashville's live," Dr. Watts said.

"Let's get started," Claire said. "Welcome. Veritas Omnia Vincit."

She paused while the Alliance chanted back in imperfect unison, "Veritas Omnia Vincit."

"I'm delighted to finally see all of you at the same time. It has been many years of watching and waiting, but I can tell you now that our efforts have not been in vain."

"We have reason to hope," Omar said, his eyes twinkling in my direction.

All eyes were now on me. I forced a smile. They said that DC was live, but after scanning the faces a second time, I knew my father wasn't one of them.

"We have ships strategically positioned to move on your command, Jace," Claire said. "We're ready to mobilize. We just need the location of the Point of Origin." She opened her palm, as if giving me permission to speak. My mouth seemed to be full of chalk. I had no idea what she was talking about. What did she expect me to say?

"Where is my father?" I asked.

Silence. Faces staring at me. Blinking. Like they didn't understand what I was asking.

"He couldn't make it." Claire cleared her throat. "He's in the middle of an international banking crisis."

I stared back at her blankly.

"Admiral Vega is the last pin Victor has to knock down before the President allows Omnibus Global Security to step into a military role in Washington," Randall said. "The U.S. armed forces are spread so thin trying to put out Hannaj fires that they don't have enough soldiers to keep the rioters under control in DC."

"I thought this meeting was to discuss the plan. How can we do that without my father?" I whispered the question to Damien, but by the reaction of the faces above the table, it was clear that they had all heard me.

Claire spoke calmly. "We know that another major event is coming, and Victor is planning to use the machine again. We need you to tell us which volcano is going to erupt so we can get there first and stop him. We need you to tell us what you know about the Point of Origin."

My vision began to blur slightly around the edges. *Point of Origin.* My eyes darted from Damien, to the faces above the table, to Claire, and back again. In the glow of the blue and green light their faces seemed changed. I had come into this room expecting to hear and understand the plan from my father's lips. I needed to see him. Did they think I had *all* of my memories back? *Point of Origin.*

The heart palpitations started and the room began to spin. What was I supposed to do? I looked to Claire again, trying with all my might to keep my composure. She kept her eyes fixed on me—willing me to answer her questions. In the uncomfortable silence, Dr. Watt's stepped away from his desk. His bright computer screen penetrated the darkness, blinding me.

* * *

Sitting in a bright corner of the library, I'm still stewing about English class and Corey Stein. My mental list of Judeo-Christian scientists and what they've done to diminish human suffering keeps taking me away from studying for my statistics final. I tap my fingernails against the long wooden table. What is it about his smug comments that always gets under my skin?

He comes around the corner from behind a bookshelf just as I'm reliving the whole conversation again—almost like my thoughts somehow summoned him. I shrink in my chair and attempt to cover my face with my hand. But when I look up again, he makes eye contact. There's no possibility of escaping without talking to him now.

"Jace," he says loudly as he approaches. "I almost didn't see you there." He drops his backpack across from me on the table and pulls out a chair.

I sit up tall and shuffle my notes around. My first instinct is to gather everything up and leave, but I just started working, and I only have twenty minutes until my next class. Where would I go?

"I had a feeling if I waited long enough, you'd say more than two words in Dr. Jenkins's class."

"I think a lot of us have been waiting patiently to get a word in edgewise, but sometimes you don't even pause to breathe."

"Ouch." Corey laughs. "I had no idea I was causing your selective mutism. I'll have to remind myself to breathe."

Turning back to my book, I pick up my pencil without responding.

"Your perspective today was articulate," he says, unzipping his backpack. "You must be passionate about your faith. What religion are you?"

Why can't he just go away and leave me alone? Discussing my religious beliefs isn't even something I do with close friends. "My father is Catholic," I say, looking down again immediately, hoping he'll get the hint that I'm not interested in continuing the conversation.

"That's nice for your father," he persists. "But what about you?"

"I respect all religions." I slam my text book shut. "I respect the rituals and traditions that help people like my father feel close to God."

He nods. "Traditions and rituals can be important culturally, but I've never understood how lighting a candle or wearing a special hat makes a person feel closer to God. My parents were Jewish and they took me to synagogue every Saturday. I didn't feel anything."

"They're not practicing anymore? Did you convince them that their religion was just made up to give them a false sense of control?"

"I guess you could say they're not practicing anymore," he says. But he doesn't laugh. "They died when I was twelve."

* * *

"Jace! Can you hear me?" Damien held both of my shoulders, shaking me.

"I'm sorry," I rasped.

"I told you it was too soon," Damien growled across the table at Claire. "I'm sorry for the inconvenience, but we're going to have to adjourn." Damien turned toward Leon. "Cut the feed."

Leon scrambled, touching the screen until all of the faces disappeared. Damien lifted me to my feet.

"Damien, give her a moment," Claire demanded. She came around the table. Damien wrapped his arm protectively around me and stood between us.

"We need to back off and give Jace time to rest," Damien said.

Claire ignored him. "Jace, if you can just—"

"I can't Claire. I don't remember everything. I need to talk to my father."

Claire's expression didn't change. "That may be very difficult. Since the eruption, communication from your father is rare. The protocols are very strict, and he doesn't always answer. Sometimes we have to trust his silence and do the best we can on our own."

T rust his silence. On our own. It felt like Claire had knocked the wind out of me. She didn't expect an answer from my father. But if he had been waiting for me to come back, why wouldn't he want to talk to me?

"How do we do it? What's the protocol for contacting him?" I asked.

"I'm the only one who is authorized to do it," Claire said. "I'll send another message tonight. Don't worry...I'll make it clear that you are more than anxious to talk to him."

Before I could question her further, Claire silently turned to go.

"Be sure to click your heels three times," Damien called after her. She didn't look back.

* * *

"I'm fine. I can walk," I said when Damien offered to carry me up the stairs.

"What happened to you back there? Your eyes glossed over and you went limp. It was just like in the delivery room." His lips were close to my ear.

"I don't know what's happening to me," I admitted. "They were expecting me to remember everything. I only have a handful of memories, and those are only small chunks. Flashes."

"Did you just have one now, when you blanked out?"

I nodded.

"What was it?" We reached the landing on the second floor. I stopped.

"A memory from college. But different."

"What do you mean?"

"It was a conversation with Corey I don't remember having."

He was silent, but I could see that he was trying to form a question. "You said you barely knew each other then, right?"

I nodded. "I don't remember ever speaking to him at school, but he was in my freshman English class."

It was so strange that these memories were coming to me now. My father and the Alliance were expecting me to remember significant information that would be key to stopping Victor. The tablet had said the answers were inside me. Were my feelings for Corey causing my brain to search for memories related to him instead?

"You said you've had a few flashes," he said. "Was I in any of them?"

I hesitated. "Not in any of them since the eruption. You were in some of my memories from kindergarten."

Damien ran a hand through his hair.

"I'm sorry I let this happen," he said. "I should have made them wait. This could have been avoided."

"You didn't know."

He touched my chin, bringing my face up gently until I met his eyes. He searched mine for a second. Was he looking to see what I was holding back from him? "We've been through worse. We'll figure this out together."

I couldn't agree with him, couldn't reassure him. I wanted it to be true for his sake. I couldn't remember what we had been through or what was yet to come, but my gut instinct was telling me that he was wrong.

* * *

I didn't come down for dinner. I could smell it cooking and I was starving now, but I couldn't face all of them yet. I pretended to be asleep when Damien knocked softly on the door. He didn't try to wake me after saying my name. He just stood watching me for a few moments before leaving me alone again.

I thought about walking down the stairs, and right out the front door. My father was the CNO. If I found the American Consulate, they could contact him for me. But that wasn't even remotely rational. If I tried to contact my father on my own and Victor was watching him closely, I would put everyone in danger.

I had to give Claire time to hear from my father before I tried to contact him. I couldn't leave, but while I was stuck in Montreal, I could try to find out as much as possible about the Alliance and the past three years. I pushed the covers off and stood up, moving toward the black desk near the door. Maybe the other Jace left something that could help.

Even though Damien had given me permission to look earlier, I hesitated momentarily before opening the top drawer. Inside I found a digital camera with three professional quality lenses. I'd always wanted something like this. I shut the drawer without picking it up.

Opening the smaller drawer on the right side, I found flash drives and a silver-trimmed photo album. I'd never made prints of any of my pictures before.

The album cover was a stunning black and white photo—a wedding photo taken from the bride's perspective, looking down at a simple slip dress. The bride's arm was outstretched, holding the sheer overlay away from her skirt with her left hand crossing over the groom's so that both rings were showcased against his black pant leg.

You're her, but you're definitely not her. The other Jace knew how to make hospital corners and she liked to take pictures, but she wasn't me. If she had been, Corey would have recognized her. He would have fought for her instead of leaving.

I bit the inside of my cheek and flipped the album open. The other Jace didn't take the picture on the first page. Still dressed in wedding clothes, she and Damien were locked in an embrace that made my cheeks warm. The soft pink light of sunset wrapped around them. Damien's hands were resting naturally on the small of her back. Her eyes were closed, her fingers touching the back of his neck and hairline and her thumb barely touching his ear. His forehead rested against hers, and his eyes were closed too. I imagined he was holding his breath. Savoring the moment. Almost praying it wouldn't end.

The next four were portraits. Claire wearing a large shade hat, digging in the garden. Leon pushing up the glasses on his nose—light on his face from a computer screen. Mirlande. Her raw beauty was jaw-dropping. The braids undone, her face surrounded by tight, wild curls. Her eyes sparkled with more than just tolerance for the photographer. They must have been friends.

I turned the page. Damien was without a shirt, in a pair of satin boxing shorts with a dragon on the front. He didn't have gloves on, but his hands were taped up. Was he a fighter? He'd never mentioned it before.

The rest of the photos were artistic shots of interesting subjects—all of them developed in black and white. An abandoned house surrounded by weeping willows with the branches reaching down to touch the dilapidated roof. A close up of the veins on a leaf. Several photos of a wildflower garden.

Footsteps sounded on the stairs outside the door. I snapped the album shut and closed the drawer. Almost sprinting to the bed, I lay down and curled into a ball. I closed my eyes, waiting for the door to open.

The baby was fussing. The noise came closer and closer until the door opened softly.

"Jace, are you awake?"

The baby's wails suddenly stopped.

I could pretend to be asleep, but he wasn't going to leave me alone in here forever. This was his bedroom. He would want to sleep eventually.

"I'm awake." I sat up and turned toward the door.

"She's been fed and changed, but she just won't quiet down. Claire offered to keep her tonight so we can both sleep, but I don't know. It doesn't feel right. I think she needs you."

He looked exhausted. If the other Jace had been here, the full burden of caring for the baby wouldn't have rested on his shoulders. I held my arms out reluctantly.

He transferred Abby into my arms. It was smooth and easy. Abby looked up at me with her steely grey eyes and poked out her dark red tongue like a little snake.

"Are you hungry?" he asked. "You've hardly eaten anything today."

"It's late. I should have come down earlier."

"You needed the rest. And I don't blame you if you didn't want to come down." He smiled faintly. "Claire shouldn't have called that meeting before talking to you. She just assumed you remembered everything."

"I wish I did."

Abby stopped sucking on her hand and reached up, touching the bare skin just below my collar bone. Warmth rushed through me. She moved her hand back and forth, like she was trying to comfort me the only way she could.

"The Alliance can wait." Damien turned back toward the door. "I'll be back in a second."

I let out a small sigh as soon as he was out the door, touching the baby's soft curls with my free hand. She smelled so fresh, almost like an afternoon rain shower, with a hint of powder and a flowery perfume. Probably Claire's.

"I'm sorry," I whispered. "I should be giving you what you need." My voice was thick. Her eyes didn't even seem to be focused on me. Abby's caresses became more frenzied and she stiffened and wiggled uncomfortably before opening her palm and grabbing the skin just below my collarbone—closing her fist around it and digging in her sharp fingernails.

The pain was startling. "Ouch, ouch, ouch!" I touched her hand. "Let go."

She only seemed to grip it tighter. Tears filled up my eyes and spilled over. *She's not trying to hurt you. It's just a reflex. She can't control herself yet.* She began fussing again. At first, soft, grunting cries—but within seconds she was wailing.

I couldn't think about how to comfort her until I found a way to extricate myself. Brushing the back of her fist as calmly as I could, I reached my finger underneath and pushed it into the small space between my skin and her hand. Her grip loosened until I could slide my finger completely inside.

"Your magic didn't last as long as I hoped it would." Damien came back in carrying a bassinet and a sandwich on a small plate. "Maybe I should have taken Claire up on her offer. We might not be getting much sleep tonight."

I bounced Abby softly until she calmed down again. Damien set the black and silver bassinet next to the bed before bringing the sandwich to me.

"Did we pick that out together?" I asked, still staring at the bassinet. It was as modern as all of the other furnishings in the house. A silver metal rocking base, with a thick black oval cushion for the baby.

"It was a gift from Claire." He looked at the double doors. "Someday we'll have our own house, and we can pick out our own furniture." Did he know he was whispering? Who did he think was listening?

He lifted the baby out of my arms so that I could eat the sandwich.

"Thanks," I said, taking the plate.

"You're bleeding."

I looked down at the stinging scratch on my chest. Three tiny, red gashes marred my skin.

"It's just a little scratch," I said.

"She did this?" Damien touched her hands, gently forcing her fist open to look at the nails. "I'll look for her nail kit. We don't want her scratching herself."

Damien disappeared into the bathroom with Abby. I heard a cabinet open and close, then he started talking to her in a sing-song voice.

"This isn't going to hurt a bit. Shh. Shh. Daddy's going to be so careful."

I took a bite of the sandwich.

"Why don't you get comfortable?" he called to me. "Your pajamas are in the top drawer."

I took another bite of sandwich, but my mouth was dry and I could barely swallow it. Suddenly, I was happy that Abby wouldn't be sleeping with Claire. If I thought of her as our miniature chaperone, I could keep my anxiety at bay. I had no intention of picking up with Damien where the other Jace had left off.

When I finished the sandwich, I stood up and opened the top drawer of the shiny white dresser. The stack of colorful, plaid pajama bottoms almost forced me to slam the door shut. *Definitely not me.* I sifted through the stack of t-shirts that must have been meant to go with the colorful bottoms. They were all quirky screen-prints. Some with funny sayings, others with random pictures. The strangest had a drawing of Vincent Van Gogh, smoking a pipe with a huge bandage wrapped around his face and ear.

At the bottom of the stack, below the t-shirts I felt something smooth and satiny. I pulled it out of the drawer before I saw what it was. A white satin pajama top, almost identical to the one I had worn in New York. The fold creases were deep and the tags were still attached. I held it against me, wondering how long ago he had bought it for her.

"There…much better," I heard him say. He'd finished her manicure. I would wait until he came back with the baby, then go change in the bathroom. Damien came around the corner with Abby over his shoulder. He stopped short when he saw me with the shirt pressed against my chest.

"Oh good," he said, trying to cover his slight hesitation. "You found something."

I slipped into the bathroom and closed the door behind me, changing out of the black sundress and into the satin pajama top.

Looking through the drawers and medicine cabinet, I found everything I needed to keep up the other Jace's skin care routine. After applying moisturizer, I stood staring at the pewter toothbrush holder, trying to decide which one was mine.

I finally gave up. "Red or green?" I called.

He chuckled. "Green."

When I came out, Damien was just laying the baby in her bassinet. He lifted his finger to his lips, then walked softly into the bathroom.

"You can turn the lights out. I'll only be a minute."

My pulse began pounding against the perimeter of my vision. Our chaperone was already sleeping. I hurried back to the bed and climbed under the covers. Damien turned the sink on and hummed softly while brushing his teeth. The same song as earlier. My hands were clammy and my stomach was churning. I closed my eyes and pictured the other Jace's wedding photo. I wanted a love that looked like that someday, but I wanted it to be mine. I wanted to start at the beginning, not the middle of the story.

I took a deep breath in through my nose, but I didn't release it. Instead I bit my cheek until the pain was stronger than the urge to cry.

Damien shut off the sink. He switched the bathroom light off and stopped humming as soon as he came into the room in a pair of plaid pajama bottoms. Where is his stupid screen print shirt? I hadn't turned the lights off as he'd suggested and now I wished I had. I didn't know where to look.

He paused. "You used to be a lefty." Both of his dimples appeared as he walked around to the left side of the bed. My heart raced. *His side of the bed. Should I ask him if he wants to trade?* I didn't want to get out of bed. Was it too late to suggest that one of us sleep on a couch? He took one last peek in the bassinet before flipping the light switch.

The wooden platform creaked slightly when he sat down but the mattress didn't move. I lay on my back, completely still with the blankets pulled up tight around my neck. Damien moved around for a few minutes, trying to get comfortable. Finally, he turned on his side and held still, staring at my profile in the dim light. I tried to make my heart slow down, but without my breathing exercises, it was impossible.

"Tomorrow's going to be better. I promise," he said.

"Do you think I'll be able to talk to my father?"

He shrugged. "Claire says she's working on it."

I was silent for a few moments. "What's going to happen if I can't get those memories back? I don't know anything about the Point of Origin."

"I don't know," he whispered. "It will be hard for some of them to accept that."

I swallowed. My throat was so dry.

"Try not to worry about it." He reached his arm out and draped it across me. I stiffened. "I'm not going to let them do anything to you."

"What do you mean?" I asked.

"Nothing. I shouldn't have mentioned it. I already told them it's out of the question."

"What do they want to do to me?"

"If the memories come back on their own, that's one thing, but we're not going to risk any procedures that might set you back—no matter how safe Peter claims they are."

"Dr. Watts has a procedure that he thinks can help me?"

"This won't be the first time he's tried, Jace. I don't want to watch you go through all that again. It's very invasive." He felt for my hand and pulled it to his lips. "You've got to trust me, J. I want what's best for all of us."

"Does my father know about it? What does he say?" I sat up in bed, forcing Damien's arm off of me. "It might work, Damien."

He shook his head. "It's too risky."

A chill ran down my spine. I slowly sank back down against the pillows, but I immediately turned my back to Damien.

"I love you," he said, scooting closer to me until he was pressed against my back. He lifted the hair off of my neck and kissed it softly.

"I can't do this," I said. "I can't just step into someone else's life and pick up where they left off."

"This isn't someone else's life, J, it's yours."

"It doesn't feel like it."

"What can I do to convince you? You're forgetting something important—or maybe you don't realize it—I didn't start falling in love with you after the eruption. It hasn't been just three years for me. I've always loved you. Since kindergarten."

The hairs on my arms stood on end and the ringing in my ears blocked out all other sound.

"I can't even remember kindergarten." My distorted voice boomed in my ears.

"I know. It's okay, I'm here. It doesn't matter." He touched my arm.

"I need some time."

"I'll give it to you. That's what I want," he whispered, kissing my ear softly, "that's what I promised. To honor and cherish you. To give you everything you need."

My shudder paused his breathing. *I never promised him anything.*

He cleared his throat.

"I don't think you can give back what's been taken from me."

Silence.

Rolling off of the bed, he grabbed his pillow and the black and white comforter, leaving me with the sheet and a white blanket.

"There aren't many guys I know who've had to convince the same girl to fall in love with them three separate times." He dropped the pillow and comforter on the floor at the foot of the bed. "I'm up for the challenge."

There was nothing left for me to say. A long time passed before my heart settled back to normal. Damien's breathing became slow and rhythmic long before I even tried closing my eyes.

I 'm standing at a sink, washing dishes, looking out a window. The greenery is minimal in the tiny backyard that is framed in by the other plain, white row houses. There's nothing fancy about it, but I love it. I'm humming "I'll Be There for You" by Bon Jovi.

A little girl skips across the grass. The little girl from the tablet. The little girl from the coffin. My little girl. Silky blonde curls bounce up and down. She looks to the window and waves at me. I blow her a kiss.

My breath comes out unnaturally strong. It fogs up the window and freezes the glass.

Darkness comes quickly. Something is covering the sun and I can't see her anymore. I panic. When I tap my finger against the glass, it cracks. The cracks expand outward from my finger. I pound my fist against the glass until it shatters and falls from the frame.

But it has all changed. The little girl is gone. The row houses are gone. The grass and bushes have been swept away by a river of glowing lava.

* * *

I was breathing fast when I woke up. The bassinet was empty and the comforter was spread across the bed. I was alone. Whipping around, I looked at the alarm clock. 5:15 a.m.

The doctor had said I could resume exercising as soon as I felt ready. I needed to run.

Searching the drawers for the other Jace's workout clothes, I found what I was looking for in the bottom drawer. She had several pairs of knee length tights, and one pair of purple satin boxing style shorts with the same dragon logo printed on the front that I had seen Damien wearing in the photograph. I looked them over before setting them back in the drawer. Was she a fighter too? Did she have her own personality, or did she just do whatever Damien did, and like whatever Damien liked?

After putting on a grey pair of tights and a blue tank top, I found a pair of cross trainers in the closet. Dr. Watts and Randall's bedroom doors were closed when I passed. The house was completely quiet. I crept down the stairs and peered around the corner into the family room. I expected to find Damien sleeping with the baby on the couch, but the room was empty.

I needed to get out to reclaim my routine, but I also wanted to get my bearings. I turned back toward the front door. Hopefully, I could go out and come back before anyone even knew I was gone.

I reached for the door handle and tried to turn it, but it wouldn't budge. There was no deadbolt to unlock. The flat glass control panel to the right of the door mimicked the color of the paint on the wall. The locks were electronic. My shoulders dropped. I was afraid to touch the screen. With my luck I would probably set off the alarms.

A cupboard door opened and closed. Someone was awake in the kitchen. I turned and made my way there. Leon sat at the kitchen table, eating a bowl of hot cereal.

"Good morning." He smiled when I came into the room. "Did you get enough rest?" He surveyed my outfit.

"Thank you. I'm feeling much better. In fact, I wanted to go for a run, but I don't know how to open the front door."

"You run?"

"Compulsively." I smiled. "Is there a code to open the door? Can I have it?"

He ate a mouthful of cereal. "I'm afraid you'll have to take somebody with you. We have rules for our safety. The buddy system."

My heart sank like a rock. "I saw the big park across the street. What if I just run the perimeter?"

"It might seem over cautious, but your father's protocols keep us all safe." He pushed his chair away from the table. "Mirlande will be happy to go with you. She and Damien are in the gym. Want me to ask her?"

Did Damien and Mirlande always work out together? Leon mentioned it so casually that it sounded like a daily ritual.

"I'll ask her," I said.

"Maybe you'll decide to join them instead. There's a treadmill down there."

I smiled but shook my head. Maybe the other Jace had worked out in the basement, but I wasn't her. I hated working out in an enclosed space. I wanted the freedom and fresh air of an outdoor run, not a metered, monitored, controlled run on a treadmill. Nothing in the world sounded worse to me than running and running without making any progress—without going anywhere.

* * *

The basement was dark, except for a crack of light coming from under one of the doors on the far side of the great room with the conference table. I paused outside the door. The impact of gloved fists sounded against pads—two softer thuds, then a louder one was interlaced with the rhythmic hiss of breath being exhaled. The pattern was repeated over and over. I finally made myself open the door.

It was a wide, open room with mirrors on the wall to my right. A square mat covered the center of the floor, acting as a boxing ring for Damien and Mirlande.

Mirlande saw me right away but didn't acknowledge me. Dressed in black shorts and a white sports bra, every rippling muscle glistened with sweat. She had her braids pulled up in a high ponytail, with a few loose braids framing her face. Damien's back was to me. He was throwing the punches. Two jabs, then a roundhouse kick. Mirlande held her hands up to receive the strikes with red and black pads strapped to her hands. Matching pads were strapped to her waist and shins.

She deftly dodged and blocked his punches and kicks. They moved together in smooth synchronization—like ballroom dancers. Damien was shirtless in the satin shorts from the picture. Watching him strike with focused determination, I wondered if he was taking out his frustrations on the pads.

Between sets of the combination, Mirlande slowly shifted around until the doorway was in Damien's peripheral vision. He dropped his fists to his side as soon as he saw me standing there. A wide smile spread across his face and he immediately came to me. Mirlande smiled watching him.

He wrapped me up in a hug, lifting me off the ground like he'd completely forgotten our conversation.

"It's great that you want to get back at it so soon," he said, setting me back on my feet. My skin was a little sticky with the sweat he had transferred to me. I wiped it off, trying not to cringe.

"I didn't want to disturb you. I was just hoping to borrow Mirlande when you finish."

Damien raised his eyebrows.

"Leon said I need a running buddy."

"Running?" Damien sounded as surprised as Leon had been. He hadn't known me well enough before the eruption to be familiar with my habits. Maybe the other Jace didn't run. Maybe she even hated it.

Mirlande's head tilted toward the treadmill in the corner. "We're almost finished. You could warm up over there. Or your gloves are ready if you want to join us." She nodded toward a black box just to the right of the door.

"I'll just watch."

Damien backed up a few steps. "Sure?"

I nodded.

Mirlande brought her pads back up. Damien shook out his arms and shuffled back and forth a few times before starting a new combination. Now the pattern was two jabs, two elbows, and an uppercut followed by a knee to the midsection. This glimpse into the other Jace's daily life felt like voyeurism. Unfamiliar. Still no episodes of déjà vu.

I pressed my back against the wall, watching awkwardly for about five more minutes.

"That's good," Damien said, nodding toward me. "Why don't you two go. I'll finish up on the heavy bag."

Mirlande pulled the Velcro away on her padding and threw everything in the black box. She punched Damien's shoulder as she passed him. "Don't slack off."

She didn't make eye contact, brushing past me on her way out the door.

I followed her up the stairs. She was already standing with her hand inside the marble basin.

"Mirlande Magloire," she said. Applying the chip took a few seconds longer than removing it had, and the machine didn't produce a spraying sound. The light grew brighter momentarily, but didn't move from fingers to wrist. Within seconds, the shiny metal slid back and Mirlande removed her hand.

I placed my hand inside the basin and spoke the name "Jessica Peterson." While the machine was working, Mirlande touched the control pad next to the door and it flashed from the neutral tan paint color to the same bright blue screen as the one in the kitchen. Touching a lock icon, she entered the numbers so quickly when the keypad appeared that I only saw the first two and the last. It was eight digits.

She stepped outside just before the machine finished with my chip. I realized my mistake as soon as I stepped out onto the front porch. A gust of frigid air encircled my body, but Mirlande was already half-way down the drive. The door clicked closed behind me. I blew a breath of warm air into my hands and took off sprinting to catch up. Mirlande was already across the street, jogging in place until I reached her.

"What kind of run are you looking for?" she asked.

I looked left and right, wondering which direction was likely to have businesses. I could only see houses. "Three miles or so? Not too fast."

She smiled mischievously and took off running to the right. I followed a few paces behind. If she thought it would bother me that she was running faster than I was, she was wrong. I was happy to pretend I was running alone. I only wished that I had my phone and running playlist. A little Van Halen would drown out the thoughts that were weighing me down. We passed the street signs at the corner of the park. Avenue Bloomfield. So unfamiliar. I repeated it a few times in my head so I would remember.

It wasn't cold enough to see my breath, but my lungs burned after a few minutes at Mirlande's pace. My body was different. I could feel it. The other Jace may have kept up workouts during the pregnancy, but running didn't feel natural for my muscles. I had to think about the motion. I would be sore tomorrow.

We ran several blocks separated and silent. The safe house seemed to be the only single family home in the area. We passed endless red brick townhouses with wrought iron rails and balconies. At some of the intersections, small shops lined the first story of the buildings. We were running too fast to see what kinds of businesses. This area would be beautiful in another month when the buds on the old trees lining the street turned into a leafy canopy. Now, it was all a bit drab.

Mirlande glanced over her shoulder periodically to make sure I was still there. Each time she seemed to pick up the pace slightly. I tried not to care. If she lost me, I could do an out and back.

The next time she looked back I was half a block behind her. She gave me a smug smile. "Not a competitive runner, I see," she yelled back, then picked up her pace again. Something snapped inside me. I wanted to wipe the smile off of her face.

Pushing myself to my limit, I closed the gap until I was only a few paces behind her. She must have heard me because she began sprinting too. I pumped my arms and legs with every ounce of energy I had in me. The words to my power song, "Welcome to the Jungle," played in my brain. Within seconds, I was running alongside her.

Her face was determined. She wasn't going to let me pass her. She didn't even want me keeping up. I couldn't hold her pace forever—her legs were much longer—but I wasn't going to give up. *Not a competitive runner*. She didn't know who I was.

Finally, Mirlande came to a jarring halt. I ran a few feet beyond her and stopped too. We both panted for breath. The chilly breeze felt good now.

"Not bad, J. You managed to surprise me," Mirlande said, finally making eye contact.

"I get the idea that the other Jace wasn't much of a runner."

"The other Jace?" Mirlande smiled. "Hmm. I guess you could put it that way."

"I saw the boxing shorts in her drawer. Did she box with you?"

"You were a decent opponent before the belly got in the way. I was looking forward to having you back." Without warning, she began running again. I wasn't completely recovered, but her pace was more moderate now. She kept her eyes on the road ahead.

We came to a busy intersection. Avenue Van Horne. Mirlande cut to the left. We ran in silence for a few minutes.

I was right—Mirlande and the other Jace had been friends. Maybe I could use that to my advantage. Of all of the people in the safe house, she was the most logical choice to press for answers about the Alliance and my missing three years. It would be much less awkward asking her about Corey than trying to find a way to ask Claire or Damien why he had gone to work for Victor.

"You don't seem to like Corey," I finally said.

"Does anyone?"

"You believe he's a traitor?"

She didn't answer.

"Do you know why he left?"

She hesitated. "A whole lot of nonsense about the signal, and splinters, and loops, and the Point of Origin. He's the one who started this madness—the race to find it."

Corey knew about the Point of Origin before he left. Was whatever he was trying to tell me with the pocket watch related to it? "Do you know what it is?"

"He thinks it's where this whole mess started. He read about it in the notes from Victor's laboratory. From the pictures on your phone." *The signal.* She knew about the notes Victor had taken from the shortwave. Corey took pictures of the dated entries from Victor's notebook with my phone just before the eruption.

We passed a row of rental bikes parked in front of a metro station. I made a mental note, repeating the cross streets several times in my head. *Van Horne and Wiseman.*

"So everyone's looking for the place this all started…the time travel? Do they have a short list of possibilities?"

"1500 active volcanoes on earth…not exactly a short list."

The park came into view. We were on the opposite side of it now. The safe house was visible through the barren trees. I only had a few more minutes of freedom.

I looked over at Mirlande. When I decided what to do, she would be my ticket out of the house. "You and I were good friends, weren't we?"

"More like sisters, I'd say."

"I know I'm different now, but I could use a friend."

She looked me straight in the eyes. "That'll all depend." Mirlande took off and I raced to catch up. My legs burned, but I pushed myself until I was beside her again.

"Depend on what?" I panted.

"On who you decide to hurt."

I stopped pushing. She left me behind in the park, sprinting across the street and disappearing into the house while I tried to recover. She was right. No matter what I decided to do, people were going to get hurt.

Mirlande was nowhere in sight when I came through the doors, but the marble basin was still illuminated. I placed my hand on the plate of glass. The cold sweat from the run stung, but the water on my hand warmed me and slowed my heart rate. When the top retracted, I walked quietly to the family room and peeked around the corner.

Rays of morning light streamed through the opaque window shades, washing out the subtle pink hues of a large abstract painting hanging next to the window. A series of shade and texture changes formed a perfect circle in the center of the canvas. Claire sat below the painting, her head crowned by the circle, wearing a blue silk robe. Her loose waves fell around Abby like a golden blanket, and her glowing cheek rested on Abby's dark curls.

I couldn't tell if her downcast eyes were closed. The scene was too beautiful to disturb. The other Jace would have hurried up the stairs to get the camera. But I couldn't go get it. The camera wasn't mine.

"Come in, Jace." Claire's face stayed pressed against the baby, but she raised her eyes, somehow managing to look even more angelic.

I wiped my palms against my tights and stepped through the doorway.

"I want to apologize to you about yesterday," she said. "I know it's a poor excuse, but I had visualized your return so many times that I lost track of reality."

"I'm sorry I disappointed you."

"It was my fault." Claire touched her scar absently.

"How did it happen, Claire?" The question hung in the air, painful and awkward.

"The scar?"

I nodded.

"I was in the wrong place when the tower was hit." Claire put the baby gently up over her shoulder and began to stroke her back.

"You went, even though you knew what would happen?" The crayon drawings, the World Trade Center towers on fire. Why hadn't she listened to me?

"I had to."

Because of the plan? I sank into the black leather chair opposite Claire.

"We needed video evidence that I had entered the building," Claire continued. "He had to think I was dead. It was terrifying, but I trusted that your father could get me out of there alive."

"You had to be inside the building when it was hit?" I sat forward, pushing my hand against my chest to try to keep my heart inside.

"No, your father knew exactly when I had to be out of there. The plan was perfect, but the players weren't." Claire stared at the wall behind me.

"I only remember tiny pieces, but I know you left Sigonella before my father knew anything about my drawings. When did he tell you the plan?"

She swallowed hard. "I knew something wasn't right, even before I met you. Before you warned me about the signal. I could hear him at night, tuning my father's old radio. I heard the beeping. I heard him scratching away in his notebook. I didn't know what he was doing, but it made me sick to my stomach." Claire stroked the baby's hair.

Had she been afraid of him even before I had warned her?

"The signal?" I asked.

"The funny part is that I don't think you really knew what it was. After you started drawing the pictures, I kept a close eye on you. You always seemed to be searching the house for something."

I nodded. "I knew he had sent himself messages, but I wasn't sure what he was receiving them on."

"Your warning shook me. It forced me to open my eyes." She blinked hard several times and glanced up at the ceiling.

"But you didn't leave. You stayed with him even though you knew what he was doing?"

Claire didn't look at me. "I didn't know everything immediately. I put together the pieces little by little with your father's help." The baby grunted softly. "Shhh. It's very strange living with someone that you think you know intimately, then learning that they are not who you thought they were at all."

Like being married to a stranger. I thought about what Damien had told me about Claire and Victor's relationship after Sigonella. Victor had been cold and distant. Claire had been depressed. But things changed when they moved to New York. Damien thought that his parents had reconciled there.

"What happened when you moved to New York?" I posed the question softly.

Claire frowned. "Everything was in place to execute the plan. Damien's trust fund was in order. I thought I was ready. But then something changed." I didn't interrupt her when she paused. "It was subtle at first. He looked at me differently. He said nice things. I didn't realize how much I craved his attention until I had it back."

She cleared her throat lightly.

"Victor's timing was perfect. I was confused. He didn't tell me about the new office in the World Trade Center until the night before. He'd arranged an evening at the opera. They were rehearsing *Lakmé.* 'The Flower Duet' was exquisite. He held my hand during the whole performance, and I saw tears in his eyes." Her hand stopped moving on Abby's back. "Suddenly, I was full of hope. Maybe there would be no reason for me to go into the building. Maybe my nightmare would end. The date would pass and we could move forward and forget everything."

I understood, to a degree, what she felt. Victor had enticed all of us to come to him on Mount Hood, dangling whatever fruit in front of us he knew we couldn't resist. He exploited my moments of weakness to bind me down so he could use me for his purposes.

Claire's eyes seemed unfocused. "It was such a beautiful evening, almost like a dream." She turned to me, her pupils fully dilated. "He told me about the appointment in the dark with the same sweet tone of voice he'd used all evening.

"I met his designer inside the partially decorated office at 8:15 a.m. as planned. 96th floor." She looked at me meaningfully, "I was to leave the radio in Victor's office and excuse myself to use the ladies room at 8:30. "

I squeezed my hands together in front of me. "That didn't leave you much time. Didn't the first plane strike around 8:45?"

She touched her scar. "It would have been enough. I was almost to the stairwell, right on schedule, when my phone rang." She closed her eyes, but not before I saw the regret. "It wasn't part of the plan. I didn't expect to have to talk to him again. I shouldn't have answered."

"What did he say?" I went back to holding my breath as soon as I asked the question.

"He told me that he couldn't explain why, but I had to get out of the building immediately."

"He sent you there, and then he changed his mind?"

She nodded. "It was a detail I wasn't prepared for. I couldn't make a decision. Strangers brushed past me—not knowing what was about to happen to them." She was silent for a moment. "They haunt me, Jace. I could have saved some of them."

"Victor wanted to save you?" I tried to mask the doubt in my voice.

"Or he saw the radio on the security cameras." Her words were cold. She opened her mouth again, but hesitated. "I was in the stairwell when the plane hit. I should have been out of the building. Instead I was on the 89th floor. Falling debris knocked me to the ground." She touched her face. "I was lucky it wasn't worse."

"I'm sorry," I whispered.

"I've been living with this burden for a long time, Jace. I want to make it right. I've done my best to gather allies and resources to help you, but it hasn't been easy keeping them at bay. They want answers and they want action, especially now that you're back. We can't wait forever, Jace. Victor is preparing for something big."

"You want me to have the procedure." The words almost stuck in my throat.

Claire's eyes shifted, then refocused on mine. "Damien told you about it?"

I nodded. "I don't know why I had to forget, Claire, but I don't think it was meant to be permanent. My father and Dr. Watts expected my memories to come back fully before the eruption, didn't they?"

Claire nodded. "You told your father that you needed to forget so that your life would progress naturally."

I cast my eyes down. Victor was just as powerful now as the images on the tablet had shown him. Forgetting hadn't changed anything.

"But it didn't work," I said.

A door opened and closed upstairs and Damien's humming floated down. Claire and I both straightened our postures and looked up.

"It isn't over yet. We can still fix this," Claire said in a low voice. Damien's humming moved swiftly toward us, his footsteps sounding in the entryway. I stood before he entered the room. Claire had cleared all emotion from her face, but the strange tension of unfinished conversation lingered.

"How was your run?" Damien asked. His light kiss on my cheek raised the hair on my arms and I recoiled.

"Sorry," he whispered, moving past me. Claire raised an eyebrow. "You're both so serious. What did I miss?"

I cleared my throat. "Claire was telling me about 9/11."

Damien stopped in front of his mother, looking down at Abby.

"I'll take her now."

Claire smiled, lifting her arms to hand the baby over to Damien. "She's an angel."

"In the arms of her resurrected grandmother," he said before taking the baby to the chair next to mine.

"I was never really gone."

"For me you were." He didn't look up from the baby's face.

"None of us understand why it had to be this way," Claire said, looking at me. "But we can have the answers now."

"You know how I feel about the procedure," Damien said. "I'm not going to stop Jace from making her own decision, but she needs full disclosure first."

Claire nodded turning toward her bedroom. "Of course. Doctor Watts can answer all of your questions about the procedure whenever you're ready, Jace."

I had a feeling that the flashes of memory I'd already recovered were just the tip of the iceberg. They seemed so insignificant, but I had no way of knowing what could be lurking underneath.

* * *

After I showered and changed, I found Doctor Watts working on his computer at the far end of the basement conference room. An empty dentist style chair in partially reclined position was connected to his computer through a tangled web of cords and wires. I froze next to the conference table. Going to the doctor and dentist's office had always triggered panic attacks, but instead of making a scene when I was a child, I used my breathing exercises, hiding my fear from my mother.

"Hello," Dr. Watts said, typing a few more words before swiveling his chair toward me.

"Hello," I replied.

"You want to know about the procedure." He didn't waste time with small talk. "Have a seat and I'll explain how it all works," He pushed his glasses up on his nose, then pointed at the chair with the wires.

My temples began to pulse. The chair was nothing like Victor's gurney in the laboratory—Dr. Watts and the Alliance weren't going to strap me down, but I still felt uneasy. Pulling out a chair from the conference table, I sat down.

"The procedure is simple, You'll have six electrodes placed on your scalp," Dr. Watts began, reaching for one of the electrodes. "They're painless. You won't feel anything."

He replaced the electrode on the chair. Picking up a tiny object from a metal tray with his tweezers, he held it in the air. "This device will be injected into the space between your hippocampus and your amygdala. It's used to stimulate your neurotransmitters. The electrical activity from your brain will be recorded, then sent to my computer and converted to images."

"And then what?"

"—and then I'll prompt you with a series of questions. You may not immediately know the answers, but we will establish a visual pathway—a connection to your long-term memories. If you know what the Point of Origin is, we'll be able to see the memories related to it."

See the memories? Was I prepared for a room full of people to see what had been hidden away in my mind? A chill ran down my spine.

"What are the risks?" I asked

Dr. Watts hesitated. His round eyes shifted behind his wire rimmed glasses.

"When we tried the procedure before, it caused small lapses in your short term memory, but I'm confident it will work this time."

"Why didn't it work before?" I asked.

"How do I put this?" he said. "I don't believe your memories were physically present to be retrieved."

I tried to wrap my mind around what he was saying. "The memories weren't physically present? So it was more than amnesia after Mount Hood?"

"Yes. I think we've proven that Victor's machine sent your consciousness forward in time. Your body continued to function, but your personality, your memories—you weren't there at all."

The other Jace. She really wasn't me. "But now that I'm back, why don't I remember everything?"

"You understand that my brother, Jason, helped you repress some of your memories." He waited for me to nod my acknowledgement before continuing. "The process involved weakening synaptic connections by superimposing an entirely new neural network using a combination of chemical and sensory stimulation and hypnotic suggestion."

I sat forward on my chair. *Chemical and sensory stimulation and hypnosis.* I nodded, waiting for him to continue.

"Jason never intended for us to try to reverse the process. Your memories were programmed to reconnect on their own. You were already experiencing reconnections before the eruption."

"My brain is still trying to reconnect, Dr. Watts. You saw what happened during the teleconference...I was reliving a memory."

"Yes," he said. "I wondered about that. What was the memory?"

"I've been remembering my freshman year of college, but the memories are...strange. Different."

"Really?" he asked. "How so?"

"Conversations with Corey that I never had."

"Hmmm." Dr. Watts stood up. "You must be remembering another splinter."

"Splinter?" I asked. Mirlande had said something about splinters too.

"One of the hazards of traveling," he said. "Even the tiniest divergence from what was done the first time can create a splintered timeline."

My head began to pound. "How many splinters are we talking about?"

"We don't know. Everything I'm telling you is based off of what Corey and I were able to deduce from Victor's notes and the little Claire has learned from your father. Hopefully you'll be able to tell us more after the procedure."

"But if my memories are coming back on their own, shouldn't we just wait for it to happen naturally?"

Dr. Watts looked over his shoulder toward the stairway. "I wish we had that luxury, but our sources tell us Victor is expecting an event at the Point of Origin in three days. If it takes longer than that to recover your memories, are you comfortable living with the consequences?"

"Why would Victor send himself all of this information about the Point of Origin, but forget to tell himself where it is?"

"He didn't forget." Dr. Watts shook his head. "Someone on another splinter who knew the significance of the Point of Origin must have had access to the radio too."

"Who?" I asked. "Why do you say that?"

"Corey and I each had our own theories. Someone sent hundreds of messages predicting different eruptions on the same date. They must have been trying to muddy the waters." He paused. "Omnibus has narrowed down the possible locations to a dozen that have the right conditions, but he can't be in all of those places at the same time."

I nodded. "What's so special about the Point of Origin?" I asked. "What is Victor planning to do there?"

"You know about Victor's successful experiments in Manila...most of his research there was on young test subjects. Children. And he was only sending their memories back a few days or weeks at most."

I nodded. "He wanted to know why it worked for me, when it had failed with his adult test subjects."

"You do seem to be the only exception to the rule. You have his genetic researchers baffled."

"He's been testing my genes?"

"Yes. But the viability of the subject is only one half of the equation. To send someone back any significant amount of time, he needs an eruption big enough to cause the necessary disturbance in the electromagnetic field."

"So the Point of Origin is a big eruption?"

"At least a six on the Volcanic Explosivity Index."

I rubbed my temples lightly. "So he's trying to send someone else back to deliver his message."

"We're not sure of his motivations, but he's clearly trying to duplicate his results in Manilla over a greater distance in time," he said. "The only way to stop him is to get there first."

"Then it sounds like I have no other choice."

"I'm sorry now that I never had any of my own," I heard Randall say softly.

"I wonder if you would have if things had been different," Claire replied.

They stopped talking when they heard us coming. As I came back up the stairs with Dr. Watts, Randall was seated on the sofa with his arm draped lightly around Claire and the baby. Abby was awake, her tiny fist grasping Randall's enormous pinky finger.

Mirlande and Damien's voices and the sound of dishes clinking carried into the room. Even when the world was falling apart, the dishes still needed to be done.

"There you are," Claire said when we reached the top of the stairs. Her eyes moved quickly from mine to Dr. Watts's. She wanted to know if he had convinced me. Had I agreed to the procedure?

We stood on the edge of the room for an awkward moment before Dr. Watts excused himself. "Jace is fully briefed. I have a few things to attend to, if you don't need me."

"Thank you, Peter," Claire said. She watched him disappear before returning her attention to me. "Did he answer your questions?" she asked.

"Yes," I said. She knew that there was no real time for me to think about it. No time for me to make a rational decision.

A burst of laughter rolled out of the kitchen.

"What would you have done if I hadn't come back now?" I asked. "What were you planning to do about the Point of Origin without my help?"

"We always seem to be two steps behind him. We're keeping track of his movements, but without knowing the location, we would probably just have to clean up the aftermath again." Randall uncrossed his legs and pulled his hand carefully away from Abby.

"But you *are* here," Claire said. "And you have the answers we need to stop this."

The water turned off in the kitchen. Damien laughed again and his footsteps sounded on the tile, coming toward us.

"I'll do it," I said.

"Atta girl," Randall said under his breath.

"Tomorrow?" Claire asked Dr. Watts.

"I'll have everything ready by early afternoon," he assured her.

"You all might want to turn on the television." Leon's voice crackled over the PA system next to the kitchen door just before Damien walked through.

"What is it?" Damien asked.

"The Summit meeting is starting."

Randall reached for the remote control. I took a seat on the black leather chair across from Claire. Damien sat down next to me.

"...United Nations Information Reclamation Summit. We'll hear from French President Petain and other world leaders. It's part of an emergency assembly meeting happening all this week in New York." The announcer's voice was dry and emotionless.

Reclamation Summit. The image from the tablet. Banners that read "Reclamation Day" flying over the Potomac. It was all still happening on this splinter, even without me there taking pictures.

Broadcast from the United Nations General Assembly, the screen was filled with a view of the golden backdrop with its iconic fig leaf emblem above the heads of the Secretary General and the other speakers, seated high above everyone else on the podium. A steady hum of voices came from the delegates on the floor, many of whom were still milling around. The jumbotrons to the right and left of the backdrop focused on the Secretary General as he adjusted his suit jacket, glasses and microphone. The audience made no indication of attention as the camera panned in on the stand.

I spotted Victor's shiny scalp, just below and to the left of the podium. He sat alone, but four men in dark suits with the Omnibus triangle emblazoned on their left shoulders stood behind him, all wearing thin framed, mirrored glasses.

"Are those the same as the glasses on the desk upstairs?" I asked.

"OmniGlasses," Damien answered. "They work like a smart phone, only they're more intuitive and hands free."

The Secretary General leaned over and whispered something to the French President before clearing his throat. "Your excellencies. Distinguished heads of state and government. Honorable ministers. Distinguished delegates. Ladies and Gentlemen. I declare open this special Summit on Information Reclamation." He struck his gavel against the podium. "Allow me to extend to all of you a very warm welcome to this summit meeting. Let me also welcome the president of the 72nd session of the General Assembly, his excellency Vit Hajek, and invite him to say a few words."

"Well, this is something," Randall said, dropping back into his seat on the couch next to Claire. "I would have thought they would wait to make a move at the UN until the House and Senate voted." I glanced at Randall before refocusing on the screen. Mirlande had come into the room and stood at the side of the couch.

"Thank you," said the assembly president. "For years we have been plagued by acts of information terrorism perpetrated by the Hannaj organization. Billions of dollars have been siphoned electronically from our banks despite supposedly secure firewalls. Hannaj operatives have stolen the identities of millions of innocent civilians. The classified information of multiple governments has been breached, manipulated, and leaked online. Too many lives have been lost trying to hunt down cyber terrorists. Even the smallest attacks on the most helpless countries affect all of us. We cannot afford to let these terrorists win." He paused, glancing up at the assembly. "Only through this international forum, that consists of all the countries in the world, rich and poor, can we effectively deal with this pressing issue."

Mirlande moved around the couch and stood behind my chair. I moved forward slightly.

"Are you sure you're looking for a geothermal event?" Damien asked. "He seems to have his hands full this week."

"Shhh," Claire commanded. "This week is pivotal in more ways than one." She glanced at me. "But tomorrow the tables will start to turn."

Damien clutched my forearm. "Did you agree to the procedure?"

I cleared my throat and kept my eyes fixed on the television screen. "There isn't time to wait," I said softly. "Look what's at stake."

"This was going to happen no matter what," he whispered. "You saw the pictures on the tablet. You're not responsible for the future."

"We're all responsible for it, Damien," Claire interjected, turning back to the television. "All of us have been given something special. We're all here—we've been given a second chance for a reason."

"You don't really know why you've been given a second chance, and that's what bothers you." Damien stood up and came toward Claire, reaching his hands down toward Abby. "If you have so much faith in the Admiral and his plan, don't you think you should wait for instructions from him? Where are the official orders? Why hasn't he answered you, Claire?"

"That's enough," Claire said, coming to her feet to meet Damien. "The Admiral and I have worked together for years. He's aware of us. I told him what we want to do. If he didn't want us to go ahead with the procedure, he would have let us know. His silence is a yes."

"Why is his silence always whatever you want it to be?" He lifted the baby out of Claire's arms.

"Be reasonable."

"I can't be reasonable about what you're asking us to risk," he roared.

"We're not asking her to do anything except give us a location."

Damien shook his head and turned his back, walking toward the entryway. "But you don't know what it might take away from her." He looked over his shoulder at me. "She's a person, not just a pawn in your plan."

Claire's face reddened. "If you'll all excuse me." Her voice broke and she covered her mouth. Turning toward the kitchen, she walked out of the room.

Damien hesitated in the doorway. He still didn't understand. Even if I didn't remember all of it, I knew I was the one who had made the plan.

Trying to refocus my eyes on the television, I let him walk out of the room without protesting. His shoes clunked against the tiles in the entry and continued up the stairs. I took a deep breath and loosened my jaw.

Randall pointed the remote control at the television and turned it up three notches.

President Hajek's speech filled the awkwardness. "Omnibus offers us a solution that will starve out the Hannaj terrorists. A fast track plan that will put the world on the secure OmniNetwork at very little cost to consumers." A close up of Victor's face filled the screen. I gripped the arms of the chair.

Mirlande slid into Damien's seat, reminding me of her silent presence in the room. I didn't look at her. I could only imagine what she must be thinking about me and the decision that I had made without Damien's approval.

"…turn the floor over to Victor Trent." The speaker stepped back from the microphone and the delegates applauded. Mirlande waited in awkward anticipation.

"Ladies and Gentlemen, thank you." Victor's thick voice cut through the applause, but the thunderous clapping only increased. My head started throbbing.

* * *

The awkward silence stretches between us like a trench, but I can't think of any words to fill it. What do you say to someone who lost both of his parents? I'm sorry? I don't want to instantly let go of my aversion to Corey Stein and his arrogance, but I can't help trying to cover up my insensitivity.

"Are you an only child?" I blunder. "I mean, do you have other family?"

"You're wondering if I was raised by wolves after they died?" Corey lifts one corner of his mouth. "Would that explain a few things?"

I can't help laughing. Corey's smile broadens until he's laughing too.

"I am an only child," Corey says, taking a breath. "But my aunt took me in. My cousin is like a sister, but she's pretty quiet—maybe she couldn't get a word in edgewise either."

"Listen, I'm sorry about that." I feel my face grow warm. "We kind of got off on the wrong foot."

"Don't apologize." He takes a thick book out of his backpack. "I can't learn from my mistakes if nobody points out what they are."

He sounds sincere, and his words are refreshingly humble. He opens the book and scans the page with his finger, apparently finding where he had left off. At risk of seeming nosy, I try to see the title of the book. It doesn't look like it's in English.

"What are you reading?" I finally ask.

He flips the book over and shows me the cover. À la Recherche du Temps Perdu. Marcel Proust.

"What is that? French?"

He shrugs like it's no big deal. "In Search of Lost Time," he translates for me. "You would probably find this interesting. Proust wasn't especially religious, but he had some unique theories about the meaning of life."

"Maybe I'll look for a copy to read over the break." I reopen my statistics book. "In English."

"As luck would have it, I own the English version too." Corey smiles. "I'll bring it to class on Thursday. And maybe we can discuss it over dinner...after the break."

"**Y**OU look like you could use a bit of fresh air," Mirlande said.

Victor was still on the screen, lifting his hands like he was soaking up the energy of the crowd. "We come together at this historic summit as nations truly united in our purpose." More applause. "Information terrorism reaches its tentacles far and wide across the globe—strangling the economies of countries, rich and poor."

"I need a few things from the market," she said. "Want to come with me?"

My head was still throbbing, and I couldn't relax my grip on the arms of the chair. My relationship with Corey had obviously developed very differently on the splinter I was remembering. And even though the memories themselves weren't unpleasant, not knowing when they were going to happen was unsettling.

"Since the death of my wife on 9/11," Victor continued, "I have dedicated my life to developing technology that will give us the advantage over these terrorists—these organizations who hold no regard for the sanctity of human life."

"Randall," Mirlande spoke up over the television, "Tell Claire that we've gone to the market." She touched my arm and stood up. My arms relaxed slightly, but my heart was still pounding.

"Fortunately, Omnibus Global Security has been able to shut the Hannaj out in countries that can afford to convert to the Verified User System, but in a global community, increasingly connected by our information, we cannot afford to leave anyone vulnerable."

Mirlande touched my shoulder from behind. "J," she whispered, "You don't need to watch this."

Still feeling unsteady, I rose up slowly from my chair. "Okay."

"It will do you good to get out," Mirlande said.

"I'd ask to come along, but I suppose someone should stay here to hold down the fort," Randall drawled without looking away from the television.

Mirlande was already in the entryway. I followed her tentatively.

"You'll want a jacket," she said, opening a coat closet to the left of the doorway. She tossed a grey leather jacket at me before slipping on a black one herself.

By the time I placed my hand in the basin, I was feeling almost normal. When the box reopened, I shoved my hand into the pocket of my jacket.

Heavy clouds hung in the sky as I walked beside Mirlande. It wasn't too cold—the light jacket was just enough. The hum of car engines and horns in the distance brought everything into focus for me. We walked in the same direction we had gone that morning, toward the metro station on Van Horne.

"Have you ever been to an open air market?"

I nodded. "My mom and I used to go to the farmer's market in downtown Corpus Christi. They had live music sometimes."

We continued walking in silence until we passed a truck with workers trimming the branches of one of the mature trees.

"Jean Talon was one of the other Jace's favorite places to go," Mirlande said. "It's great for taking photos—very European."

I nodded. "I saw some of her photos in an album. She was really talented."

"You like to take pictures too, don't you?"

I looked at her. "How did you know?" I asked.

Mirlande stopped dead in her tracks. "I made a mistake, J." She made eye contact, grabbing both of my hands. "I promised Corey that I would give something to you as soon as you came back. It was before the wedding and the baby. I didn't know what to do. I thought I was protecting the other Jace by holding onto it. I'm sorry."

"What is it?"

"Your phone." She pulled it out of her purse.

My heart stopped.

"I don't know why. It doesn't have service, and he deleted almost everything from the memory. Maybe it was so you'd have a way to contact your father." She paused. "He said you'd know what to do with it."

"Is it charged?" I asked.

Mirlande nodded.

My hands trembled as I pressed the power button and waited for it to turn on. It felt good to hold it. The home screen was almost empty. My Gmail and Instagram apps were the only things he hadn't deleted.

Instagram. Prickly goose bumps covered me when I saw it.

I took a deep breath. Corey had trusted Mirlande enough to give her the phone, and I needed her help. I had to trust her too. "I need to check Instagram. I think Corey's trying to send me a message there."

"On Instagram?"

I nodded. "We had a system. I'll show you. I just need access to the internet."

She grabbed my upper arm, "I'll help you. But you can't keep anything from me, J. I can't stick my neck out for you unless you promise to tell me everything." Her eyes were wide and clear.

"Okay," I said.

As we entered the metro station, Mirlande guided me to the turnstiles. A long line of people waited to enter through a single turnstile marked "Unverified," while passengers moved quickly through the other four turnstiles. Mirlande let go of me and scanned her palm. A red "x" on the top of the turnstile changed to a green "o."

Walking toward the trains, I touched the seamless patch on my left hand while I watched the line of people ahead of me who had all passed through easily because they had Victor's chips implanted in their palms.

The tapping of shoes against the tile floor echoed through the station, but as we descended to the platform, the whoosh of an incoming train below drowned out all other noises. While we stood among the crowd of waiting passengers, I studied a map of the city and the metro system that hung on the red brick wall. Montreal was an oddly shaped island, not unlike New York City, but it was surrounded on all sides by the Saint Lawrence Seaway instead of ocean. The metro system wasn't nearly as complex as New York's, only three lines—blue, green, and orange, covered the city. We were on the blue line at a station called Outremont.

"The market is here at Jean-Talon." Mirlande pointed to a dot on the map that was only two stops down the line. "There's a small electronics shop that still has a free Wi-Fi signal. You won't be able to connect for long."

"What made you decide to help me?" I asked.

Mirlande stepped away slightly. "I agree with Damien. If your father wanted you to have the procedure, don't you think he'd find a way to tell you himself?"

"You don't believe that my father would approve of this procedure?" I asked. "Do you believe that Claire really contacted him?"

"I don't know what to believe." Mirlande leaned her head over and peered into the black tunnel. "It's hard to have faith in someone that you've only heard about. Leon's worked for him for more than ten years and we've never seen him. Orders and protocols have always come through Claire."

My vision began to blur and black spots flashed in synchronization with my heart. A blast of air pushed out of the tunnel and we heard our train approaching. I squinted, watching Mirlande's braids blow away from her face. I stood close to her as our train pulled into the station. When the doors opened, only a few people exited. The train was packed with standing passengers and the platform was full of people waiting to board. We pushed our way in, filling up a tiny empty space near the doors. Three tones chimed and the doors slid closed. As the train rushed forward into the dark tunnel, I reached for a bar to the left of the door to steady myself. Pressed against the bodies of two complete strangers, I felt like I was suffocating. *In through the nose on a three count, out through the mouth.*

I peered out at the walls of the tunnel as they rushed past. Bright, florescent lights filled up the darkness at steady intervals. I was mesmerized by the alternating colors that passed—first a green blur, then a round, blinding blue light. Stabbing pain struck my temples. I tried to close my eyes or avert them from the harsh light, but I couldn't.

* * *

"I have to be honest with you." I hand the book over. "I couldn't finish it."

"Really?" he asks, looking sincerely baffled. "How far did you get? I know the translation isn't perfect, but once you get going it's much easier."

I shake my head. "It wasn't the translation. I've read Tolstoy. I just couldn't keep reading it. I hated it."

He looks like I just shot his puppy. "Do you still want to have dinner?" He opens the door a little wider. "Su Hong already delivered."

"I thought you were cooking something." I step through the door and see the white take out boxes next to the delivery bag on the table. Our texts over the break gave me the impression that this was a date, but now I'm not sure. He didn't bother to spread out a tablecloth, and he isn't wearing shoes.

"Cooking isn't really my thing," he says, walking toward the table. "And eating is really only something I do to stay alive." He pulls out the chair he wants me to sit in.

I glance around the apartment before sitting. I have to admit that the more I get to know Corey, the more curious I become. The lack of decor fits with what I've learned about him. What you see is what you get.

Against one wall he has a black futon, facing a large book shelf where you'd expect to see a television. The shelves are packed with books—most older looking, all hardbound without dust jackets. He's probably read all of them.

"Here you go," he says, handing me a set of chopsticks. "So really? You hated it, or you're just saying that to start a debate?"

He opens the top of one of the boxes and lifts out a bite of noodles with his chopsticks.

"No. I really hated it," I say. "Do you have plates?"

Corey looks from me, to the table. "Oh, sure." He stands up and disappears into the kitchen. "What did you hate?"

"What did you like?" I say. "I tried to find something, but I couldn't. It was a series of disjointed, overly descriptive memories."

"Overly descriptive?" Corey brings back two plates. "I'm surprised you didn't appreciate that. He's finding meaning in the small things."

"What meaning?" I ask. "I stopped reading at page 234 when I realized he was never going to get to the point."

* * *

I felt something shaking my arms before the ringing in my ears subsided.

"J, are you feeling alright?" Mirlande's voice called me back to the train just as it came out of the tunnel into the full light of the next station.

"Station Acadie," a soothing female voice announced.

"What happened?" Mirlande asked, stepping closer to me, allowing even more passengers onto the train.

"I'm not sure," I told her. "The lights gave me a headache."

"Yes. I can see that. Your eyes glossed over for a few seconds and I thought you were going to pass out, just like back at the house before we left."

The doors chimed again and closed.

"I had a flash of memory." I closed my eyes, still able to see the colors from the lights in the tunnel. What if I didn't need anyone's help to get the memories back? What if I had control?

"Just now?" She sounded a bit breathless. "What memory?"

The train began moving again and I grasped the handle tighter.

"Sensory stimulation," I muttered to myself. "Can you hang onto me? I want to try something," I said, already watching the lights in the tunnel as the train accelerated. Mirlande grabbed my arm and nodded, watching me intently. I focused my eyes on the lights in the tunnel and waited for a flash to begin. The train jostled slightly and the heavy man next to me bumped into my shoulder.

"Je m'excuse!" he said. I smiled, waving him off, then returned my focus to the lights. I took a deep breath, unfocusing my eyes, forcing them to become blurry. With my heart beating slow and steady I focused on my temples waiting to feel the stabbing pain that would come with each pulse. Nothing happened. The slight screeching of the brakes began as we approached the next stop.

"Station Parc," the voice announced. I let out a slow breath.

"You think the lights in the tunnel triggered the memory?" Mirlande asked. The train came to a halt and some of the passengers exited. I was relieved that we didn't pick up any new ones.

"I don't know how it works," I admitted, "but I think the lights have something to do with it."

Mirlande nodded, holding my arm again as we pushed forward into the tunnel. I focused on the lights. They began moving faster and faster past the train window. How had it happened before? *Red, green, red, green.* My eyes stayed focused while I waited. I didn't want to give up the idea that I might be able to control this, but when we approached the next station, my disappointment was overwhelming.

"Anything?" Mirlande asked.

I shook my head. I had to bite my cheek to keep my emotions at bay. I just wanted answers.

"The next stop is ours." She rubbed my arm softly before breaking contact with me. "Don't be discouraged. Maybe the message you have waiting from Corey will tell you how to get the memories back without the procedure."

I didn't say anything, but I hoped she was right.

"We'll get the groceries first, then I'll show you the shop where you can access the internet. The less time you stay connected the better. As soon as you log in, refresh your Instagram, then disconnect. We can look at your feed when we're back on the train."

"But what if I need to respond?"

Mirlande shook her head emphatically. "Absolutely not. It's risky enough connecting, even for a short period of time. If someone is watching those accounts, responding would lead them right to us."

The open air farmer's market was only a short distance from the metro station. The sky had clouded over and huge, fluffy snowflakes fell, floating on the breeze and melting as soon as they touched the wet pavement. The faint, grinding melody of an accordion grew louder as we approached the bustling center of the market. Most of the vendors were under the cover of a large industrial roof. Colorful awnings kept some of the wind and snow away from shoppers. With all of the street and shop signs in French, I felt like I could have been walking down a street in Paris.

"The weather changes quickly here in the springtime. You never know what you're going to get," Mirlande said, moving under the canopy and out of the falling snow. She led me through the center of the market, down a row of vendors with colorful fruits and vegetables displayed on bright green shelves and baskets. The smell of fresh bread and unfamiliar spices hung in the air.

Despite the barrage of beautiful scenery, my mind was still occupied with my experience on the train. Would these memories about Corey on the other splinter eventually connect with the memory of him in the lab with the numbers? I should have been more focused on trying to recover my memories about the Point of Origin, but I couldn't help wanting to know where these memories would lead.

I stopped walking and looked around. One of the photographs in the black and white album had been taken from almost this exact location. I moved toward a display of flowers and bent down. She'd taken the picture from below with the flowers in focus in the foreground and the unfocused sign behind.

For a moment, I envied the other Jace. She had been able to look at life through a different lens, with no foreknowledge of the future or regrets from the past. She'd been able to live in the present.

When I caught up with her, Mirlande was chatting with one of the vendors in French while he rang up her purchases. His salt and pepper hair was mostly hidden under a hound's tooth hat, and his thick, grey moustache and exaggerated hand gestures made him seem cartoonish. I couldn't help smiling watching the scene. Mirlande's eyes sparkled as she talked. Her accent was charming. The vendor kissed her hand after he gave her change.

"Et pour toi, Madame?" The man smiled at me. I smiled awkwardly back. The other Jace had probably spoken enough French to at least get by. Maybe she'd even met this man when she'd come here with Mirlande before.

"Merci," I said, feeling stupid as I backed away.

"Bon apès midi," Mirlande jumped in, waving at the man as she pulled me away. We wandered through the vendors for several more minutes until finally, she led me back out of the market toward the metro station.

We were just passing a store with bright yellow, red, and blue signage. *Electrotel.* Telephones and faxes. Mirlande slowed down and looked in the windows. I gripped the phone in my jacket pocket.

Old fashioned bells jingled as Mirlande opened the doors. "They have a lot of vintage computer accessories here," she said. "I'm rebuilding a 2005 Gateway desktop with Leon. I've been looking for a mouse with a chord. Remember when everybody used those?"

I nodded.

"While we're here, I might check to see if one came in."

We were the only customers in the shop, and the clerk was on the far end of one of the isles, stocking shelves. Mirlande passed by the counter, pointing out a sign on the wall that gave a Wi-Fi username and password. *Electrotel1995*.

Mirlande approached the clerk and asked a question, leaving me alone at the front of the store. My hands trembled slightly as I turned my phone on. It only took a second to enter the information into my settings. I held my breath until the check mark appeared next to the username, indicating that I was connected. After pressing the home button, I touched the Instagram app.

I pulled down the first picture on the screen to make sure that my feed had refreshed. Mirlande wanted me to load the pictures and wait to look at them until we were safely on the train, but I couldn't help myself. My skin tingled when I saw the first picture in my feed—it was from one of Corey's fake accounts. I glanced at the first four pictures with trembling fingers—all from Corey's accounts. My heart started pounding. I took a few deep breaths and continued scrolling down. The first ten pictures in my feed were all from Corey's accounts. I clicked away from the news feed to the icon that brought up my profile. The last picture posted was the collage I had made of Mount Hood and Mount St. Helens the morning of the eruption. My eyes jumped to the account statistics. 563 posts, 439 followers, and only following six accounts. I clicked to see the five fake accounts and one more that I didn't recognize. @badauss. I clicked on the link to the profile. My Minnesota roommate, Sheila's account came up. She looked different in her profile picture. Her hair was platinum blonde instead of burgundy. I glanced at her pictures, and quickly clicked on the most recent one to see when it had been posted. Eighteen weeks ago. She was posed with her scruffy boyfriend, Josh, in front of the Lincoln Memorial. Did she live in DC now, or was she just visiting? I didn't have time to investigate.

Mirlande was slowly making her way back toward me from the other end of the store. "They don't have what I'm looking for," she said. "Ready?"

"Yes," I replied. I clicked back over to my feed, refreshing one more time to make sure that all of the pictures had loaded. I turned off the screen, then put the phone back in my pocket and followed Mirlande out of the shop.

Mirlande didn't say anything on the short walk to the metro, and I couldn't stop thinking about the pictures on my phone. How long had Corey's message been waiting for me to find it?

We waited almost five minutes before our train came. The car wasn't crowded like it had been on the way to the market. Mirlande and I sat next to each other, facing the back.

"Is there a message?" she asked as soon as the train started moving.

"I think so," I said, turning the screen back on. "He deleted all of my friends so I would only see his fake accounts."

"Well—" She leaned in. "Let's have a look."

The Instagram app was still open. The first picture in my feed was of the Minnesota frat boy, @bridger_fa, and twelve other guys drinking shots in smoky, low lighting. No caption. Geotagged at the University of Minnesota. Posted two weeks ago. I searched the image closely.

"Cute," Mirlande said. "What does it mean?"

It didn't mean anything to me. Maybe Corey had made a mistake with this one. "I'm not sure. Give me a minute." I studied the picture for a second, then moved on. Maybe I had to see more to make a connection.

The second, an image of two aged leather wingback chairs, had been posted by the antique dealer @stpaulvintage. The caption was also blank. It couldn't be a coincidence. I scrolled quickly past an image posted by @staciberi90 of three girls in high heeled shoes walking miniature schnauzers. Also without a caption. My heart began pounding. The captions had made Corey's messages easy to understand in New York. What was he expecting me to see in these pictures? What if I couldn't decipher his message? My temples throbbed.

"Station De Castlenau," the voice announced. I glanced up just long enough to see the faux wood paneling on the walls of the metro station.

I scrolled back to the beginning and started again. What did shots, wingback chairs, and schnauzers have in common? I was at a complete loss. Maybe I needed to see all of the images for it to make sense.

I continued on to an obscure quote by Maya Angelou on a picture of a purple sunset posted on @stpaulvintage's account. "Try to be a rainbow in someone's cloud."

Next came an image posted by @biyu773, the Asian model that I had been unreasonably jealous of.

"Oh wow!" Mirlande reacted to the image. The dark haired beauty looked breathtaking in an off-white eyelet lace gown. It was an outtake from a fashion shoot, with the professional lights and cameras in the background, but whoever had taken Biyu's picture must have been professional too. The angle of her chin cast a perfect shadow on her neck and her dramatic eyes in a sideways glance made the picture a work of art.

"It looks like one of yours," Mirlande said. She meant one of the other Jace's photos, but I didn't correct her. The picture evoked intense emotion. It didn't have a caption, but the subject seemed relevant at least. Had my wedding been on Corey's mind?

I tried to focus. Corey had always intuitively known how to send messages that I understood. Taking a deep breath, I continued looking.

Next came a Lou Holtz quote. Another meme from @stpaulvintange. "I never learn anything by talking. I only learn things when I ask questions." I didn't stop to analyze the quote because the next image caught my eyes. The saturated bright green in the photograph under @bluegirl900's name forced me to scroll down. It was a headstone in a grassy cemetery. Megan's grave. No amount of cheek biting could stop the tears that filled my eyes. I'd never met her before, but it hit me again that Corey's friend had been a real person. She had died because she was trying to help us.

"What does it mean?" Mirlande asked.

"I don't know," I whispered, blinking the tears out of my eyes.

"Station Parc," the train's voice interrupted us. We slowed, coming out of the tunnel. A single passenger sat waiting on a bench. Behind the bench, the wall was lined with cylindrical panels that changed from blue to green as the train passed, revealing a hidden picture that looked like a snake slithering through the station. The man boarded the train. The three tones chimed and we were underway again. Only one more station before we would get off.

My heart was pounding. I scrolled down until the headstone was completely off of my screen. The colorful rug posted by @stpaulvintage was blurry through my tears. No caption. Meaningless. What was Corey trying to do? A beach picture of @briger_fa and a blonde girl in a purple bikini. Another meme posted by @stpaulvintage was a quote by Frank Herbert, "There is no real ending. It's just the place where you stop the story."

The next ten pictures were all posted by @badauss—Sheila. First the one with her boyfriend in DC, then the quirky history of her life since late 2017 when she had joined Instagram. Her very first post had been a picture of the side of a U-Haul van. She must have opened the account when she moved to DC.

And then came the picture of @bridger_fa's running shoe with Corey's invitation to meet him for a run. Posted 136 weeks ago. It had been so simple and easy to understand.

That was it. I had seen all of Corey's new pictures and I didn't understand the message at all.

"Not what you were expecting?" Mirlande must have sensed my frustration.

"No," I replied. My eyes became unfocused, staring out the window into the darkness. Green light. White light. Green light. Blue light. Green, white, green, blue. The pattern repeated over and over.

"Station Acadie." No one entered or exited the train. Strange red lights shone down on the red tile floor and a blue panel lined the center of the wall. Someone had gone out of their way to make each individual station unique. The design had probably seemed futuristic when they built it, but now it was completely dated.

I looked again through the pictures, scrolling backward. The beach picture had been posted 12 weeks ago. For whatever reason, Corey had decided to space the pieces of the puzzle out over 12 weeks. Ten pictures.

I looked at all of them again, mentally noting the subject of the picture and the number it was in the lineup.

Ten pictures. What if this wasn't about the pictures at all? What if they served a double purpose, like the ten images in the Omnibus folder on the tablet?

The train accelerated into the dark tunnel again.

"We get off at the next stop," Mirlande said. Her voice seemed urgent. She wanted me to understand the message before we got back almost as much as I did.

My heart began to pound and my vision blurred. *Green, white, green, blue.* The colored lights passed in blinding flashes. What if I couldn't interpret the message? The stabbing pain struck my temples, forcing my eyes closed.

* * *

"I don't have any makeup on," I protest.

"You don't need any." He looks mischievous. "It's dark outside."

I look over my shoulder at the books on the table. This is the fifth night in a row of strange excuses to see me. Running out of fig butter hardly seems like an emergency, but I already know I'll say yes. Arguing with Corey is much more fun than my Communication Theory book.

"Come in while I put on my shoes."

He smiles and comes inside. "I can finish your homework while I'm waiting."

"Don't touch anything. I won't be that long." Shutting the door to my bedroom, I walk to the closet. I consider putting on something nicer, but quickly change my mind, reaching for my running shoes. Corey's obvious non-concern about appearances makes me completely at ease around him. He's much more interested in my mind than what I'm wearing.

"How late is Trader Joe's open?"

"We might need to hurry a little." Corey takes an ornate silver pocket watch out of his pants pocket. "They close in 15 minutes."

The evening air is crisp and humid. Lingering clouds from a rainstorm earlier in the day block out most of the light from the moon and stars.

"You carry a pocket watch?" I ask.

"I haven't shown you this?" He hands me the watch. "It's a family heirloom. My grandfather handed it down to my father." He pauses briefly. "And my father left it to me."

"It's beautiful." I turn the watch over in my hands and press the button that unlatches it. This is the first time Corey has mentioned his parents since the library. I've wondered about them, but felt awkward bringing up the subject.

Our neighborhood is quiet, but Corey steps around me so he is walking on the outside of the sidewalk. "It has a lot of history. My father never left home without it. It's been all over the world."

"Did he travel with his job? What did your father do?" I ask.

"I'm not exactly sure, it was all very hush-hush." We crossed the street onto Emerson, heading toward campus. "But based on the survivor benefits and the brass that showed up at the funeral, I'm pretty sure he worked for the CIA."

"CIA!" I say. "Was your father a spy?"

"I don't know exactly what he did for them, but It wasn't a desk job." Corey reaches for my arm as a group of students crosses the sidewalk in front of us.

"Did he die in the line of duty?"

"I found them dead in bed the morning after a state dinner. Both dead." Corey shrugged. "He was very protective of us and it was rare that my mother was invited to anything work related." His voice trembles slightly. "The autopsy results were never released." I feel the uncharacteristic emotion in the silence that follows.

I stop walking and turn toward him, searching his face in the dim light of a street lamp. "I'm so sorry." I take his hand and squeeze it.

"You can see why it's hard for me to look for meaning in the situation—I can't even get straight answers about what happened."

* * *

The ringing in my ears diminished just as the voice announced Outremont station. Slight screeching from the brakes brought me fully back to my current reality. Mirlande's dark eyes were the first thing I saw when my vision came into focus.

"It happened again, didn't it?"

I nodded. The phone in my hands suddenly felt heavy as my brain tried to unscramble itself.

Reliving the memories on this splinter with Corey felt like coming home. I longed to feel that comfortable and normal again.

"What did you see?" Mirlande prompted when I was silent.

Pushing away from her slightly, I closed my eyes.

The train squeaked to a halt. Mirlande didn't stand up right away but nodded toward the doors and picked up her sack of groceries from the floor. I glanced at my illuminated phone screen, intending to shut it off, but my eyes fell on the blue geotag above the beach picture, "Spring break at Daytona Beach 430414..."

The deep breath I sucked in was masked by the whoosh of the doors sliding open, and Mirlande was already standing. I turned the screen off and pushed the phone into the other Jace's jacket pocket before Mirlande could ask me about my reaction, but she wasn't even watching me. She had already stepped out onto the platform.

I followed Mirlande through the bland, red brick station, trying to remember if each of the ten pictures had the blue geotag. I had used Instagram enough to know that these locations could either be added automatically by the phone's GPS, or manually by the user. The mention of Spring Break in @bridger_fa's beach picture tag had been added manually. I touched my temple lightly. They all would have been added manually. It wasn't rational to think that Corey would have traveled to all of those locations just to post a meaningless picture for me to find.

The message had to be in the geotags.

The silence of the house absorbed the echo of our steps in the entry. Mirlande motioned for me to follow her into the kitchen, where we unloaded the bag of produce she had carried home.

"Where is everyone?" I whispered. "Do you think Damien and Claire are still angry?"

"There will always be tension in that relationship. But it will blow over."

Her optimistic view of the situation pacified me, but it was much more difficult to believe her when everyone gathered for dinner that night. Claire and Damien didn't speak a word to each other. Randall made several congenial attempts to lighten the mood, but during dessert, he gave up.

"If anyone's interested to know…the house voted today. The Reclamation Bill passed with a 74 margin," Randall said.

Claire cleared her throat and looked directly at Damien.

"I'm going to bed," Damien said, pushing his chair away from the table. "It's been a long day."

His eyes only stopped for a second on mine before he stood up and moved toward Abby's bassinet. Mirlande nodded her head toward the door, telling me that I should go with him, but acting like a normal wife was the last thing I wanted to do. I stood up anyway.

Acting like a normal mother seemed much less daunting. "Why don't you leave her down here," I blurted out just as he was reaching down to pick up the baby. "Get some rest, and I'll bring her up after I help Mirlande with the dishes."

Damien turned on his heels. "Are you sure?"

"Get some rest, Damien," Claire urged. "We'll all have clearer perspective in the morning."

Damien hesitated before retreating to the door. Mirlande pushed her chair back slightly, but stopped herself from standing up.

"Ya'll missed most of Victor's speech at the Reclamation Summit, too," Randall said. "Omnibus is going to fund mandatory conversion in underdeveloped countries for the first five years, then the United Nations will take over maintenance."

Claire picked up her fork and began eating again.

"It still amazes me that everyone is so willing to go along with it." Dr. Watts spoke up for the first time.

Randall shook his head. "It shouldn't surprise anyone. He's spent years building up dependence on technology in nations that couldn't afford it. Information terrorism wouldn't have had much of an impact on them without the help of Omnibus and the benevolent Mr. Trent."

"I don't think we should be overly concerned about that at the moment," Claire said. "None of it will matter if he gets to the Point of Origin first."

I could feel Claire's eyes on me. Setting my fork down, I looked up at her.

"Did you hear from my father today?" I asked.

She shook her head. "And I'm sure you can see why, with everything going on in Washington. It's all happening much sooner than any of us expected. Perhaps to try to distract us from what he is really trying to accomplish."

She was searching my eyes for any signs of doubt. Had I changed my mind about the procedure? Had Damien's blatant disapproval swayed my decision?

I let Claire's comment go without a response. When Abby began fussing softly a few minutes later, I used it as an opportunity to excuse myself.

"It's probably about time I took a turn feeding and changing her," I said, approaching the bassinet.

"There's a bottle already made up in the refrigerator. It just needs to go in the warmer for a minute," Claire said, standing up to retrieve it.

"Don't worry. I can manage," I said. I scooped Abby up and she stopped fussing instantly. I opened the refrigerator, fully aware that everyone was watching me from the table. I took out the bottle and glanced around the kitchen until I saw the bottle warmer. Placing the bottle inside, I pressed a green button. Utensils began clinking behind me again.

When the bottle was warm, I carried it and the baby out of the room.

The curtains were drawn and Damien was just a lump under the covers on the bed when I opened the bedroom door. I tiptoed in and shut the door softly behind me. He couldn't have been asleep long, and I didn't want to disturb him. I stood at the door for a moment, listening to his deep breathing.

My eyes adjusted to the dim light, and I moved carefully to the chair at the desk. Abby wasn't overly anxious for her bottle, but I wanted to get her back to sleep as quickly as possible. The phone in my pocket silently beckoned me to look at it again.

Her diaper was dry and she was already dressed in a sleeper, so I offered her the warm bottle and sat back in the office chair. She nestled against me in the dark, emptying the bottle slowly. Contented grunts and sighs accented Damien's rhythmic breathing.

When she finally finished, I let her suck on the nipple for a few minutes before slowly lifting the bottle away. Her cheeks continued their motion in the dark. Silently, I rose up out of the chair, and slowly moved toward her bassinet. Transferring her from my arms to the little mattress was natural—automatic. I kept my hand on her chest for a few seconds after lifting my arm out from under her. She only stirred slightly and was completely relaxed again within seconds.

Damien rolled over just as I passed him on my way to the bathroom. His breathing was silent now and I could feel his eyes on me in the dark. I didn't wait for him to say something. Instead, I picked up my speed and closed and locked the bathroom door firmly behind me. I switched on the light when my heart resumed beating. Moving farther into the bathroom, I lifted my phone out of my pocket.

When I touched the power button and unlocked the screen, it opened directly to the picture on Instagram that I had been looking at earlier—the girl in the purple bikini. *Spring Break at Daytona Beach 430414*. I clicked on the blue geotag and held my breath, hoping the location was already stored in the phone's memory.

I heard Damien shuffling around on the other side of the door. His footsteps stopped just outside the bathroom. Would he knock? I turned on the sink full blast, hoping he would go back to bed. I didn't hear his footsteps, but he didn't knock either.

I turned my attention back to the phone, but it was difficult to focus my eyes now and my hands trembled. The full name of the location had loaded, and it included two more digits on the number after Daytona Beach. 43041413. I couldn't tell if other pictures were trying to load under "Top Posts" for this location—@bridger_fa's was the only picture below the red pin on a blank map. My finger hovered over the pin for a second before I touched it. At the bottom of the screen, my phone gave me the option of opening the location in maps or canceling the request. I touched cancel. It wouldn't load without a connection. I took a screenshot of the full location name.

I turned off the sink and clinked the toothbrushes around in the pewter cup. I couldn't hear Damien anymore. Was he still standing outside the door? I took a deep breath. The previous post had a geotag too. @stpaulvintage's colorful rug was tagged "Item number 01012908." Corey had posted 10 pictures. 10 images in the Omnibus file on the tablet. He had shown me in the library with the blue sticky notes. Eight digit numbers on each picture. The first two digits were the book. Second two, chapter. Third, verse. Fourth, word. Corey's signal with the pocket watch left no doubt about what it all meant. I took screenshots of all ten geotags. I needed access to a Bible.

I pushed the phone back into my pocket and moved to the door. A floorboard creaked as Damien got back in bed. I waited a second after hearing it before opening the door.

He switched on the lamp next to the bed just as I walked out.

"I'm sorry," he said. "I didn't think you would come up here so soon. Can I get you anything before I bed down for the night?"

I shook my head. He pulled the comforter to the floor and snatched his pillow with the other hand. It didn't make sense for him to sleep on the floor when I wasn't going to sleep at all.

"I'm sure you're exhausted," I said. "Why don't you take the bed, and I'll sleep on the couch downstairs."

"Don't worry about it," he said, already spreading the comforter on the floor. "You have a big day tomorrow." Lying down, he moved his pillow around, trying to get comfortable.

"This isn't easy for me," I said.

He took a deep breath. "It doesn't have to be like this, J. You don't have to do what they want."

"Why are you so angry at Claire?" I asked. "Look at everything she's been through. Look at everything that's been taken away from her."

He propped himself up on his elbow. "Nothing has been taken from her, J. She gave it all away—voluntarily." He watched me in silence. I didn't move. "I can guess how you feel. You probably feel some responsibility for what's happened to her. Actually, I think you feel responsible for what's happened to all of us. But you shouldn't."

My eyes welled up with tears. "I am responsible for it."

"You told them about a plan, but the Admiral and my mother executed it. And she probably told you that it wasn't executed perfectly. Things have gone wrong at every turn. We're lucky to be alive after Mount Hood, and my mother barely escaped the World Trade Center." He cracked his neck against his open palm. "Maybe it would have been better if she hadn't."

"How can you say that?" My voice cut through the empty space between us. "You think it would have been better if she died that day?"

"That came out wrong." He sat up. "Of course I don't mean that. But if she was only going to carry out half of the plan, it would have been better if she'd gone down with it instead of bringing it out with her."

"What are you talking about?"

"The short-wave." The inflection in his voice indicated that I should already know what he meant.

"But she left it sitting on the desk in Victor's office."

"Did she tell you that?" He shook his head in disbelief. "She did take it with her to the towers, but I don't know if she ever planned to leave it there. She claims he called her and she panicked." Damien stood up. "That's why she almost didn't make it out. She went back to his office to get it. Even after being hit in the stairwell, when she was barely conscious…she managed to find it in the rubble and carry it down with her."

My heart was beating a million miles per hour. Victor hadn't been bluffing. He knew Claire was alive, and he knew she had the radio.

"Does my father know she has it?"

He didn't answer, looking at the wall behind me while he contemplated. "I have no idea what your father knows. I haven't seen or talked to him since the eruption. I am going entirely on what my mother has told me about the plan." He paused. "And as much as I wanted to trust her in the beginning, it's become impossible to ignore my doubts."

"Did Corey know about the radio?"

Damien recoiled slightly. "Yes. He knew." He took a deep breath. "He was the one who discovered that it could still receive messages."

I felt like the wind had been knocked out of me.

When I didn't say anything, he continued, "They received and copied down hundreds of short Morse Code messages. They looked like random gibberish to me, but Corey wanted to read all kinds of meaning into them."

Corey and Claire had been listening to the radio for messages?

"What did he think they meant?" I asked.

"I've looked over them and I don't understand the significance. They are short and disjointed. To me they seem like journal entries. Corey and Claire agreed that the messages are similar enough that they were most likely composed by a single author, but they still disagree about who that author is."

"Claire believes that Victor sent the messages?" I asked.

Damien nodded.

"Who does Corey think sent them?"

"He thinks he did."

I tried to keep my voice from trembling. "I need to see them."

Damien took my hand when we reached the bottom of the spiral staircase, leading the way through the dark house, down the stairs to the basement. When we reached a desk in the corner of the conference room, he pulled out the chair and flipped on a small reading lamp.

"Don't worry," he said, responding to the coldness of my hand. "Leon is a heavy sleeper." He rubbed it gently between his palms for a few seconds before I pulled it away.

I hadn't paid attention to this desk before. It was against the wall on the opposite side of the room from Dr. Watt's desk, its empty surface collecting dust.

Damien opened the top drawer. The wire organizer inside kept pencils, pens, ruler and paper clips neatly separated. *Blue sticky notes.* It must have been Corey's desk. I picked up the pad and flipped from the front to the back, remembering that day in the library when he had shown me the Bible message from the tablet.

"It must be on the other side," Damien whispered, waiting for me to replace the sticky notes and close the drawer before he opened the other. The dark blue notebook was the only item inside. The plastic covered, five subject notebook with dog-eared pages had a single word written on the cover in black magic marker: Memories.

Damien picked it up, hesitating slightly before placing it in my outstretched hands. "Are you sure you want to see this, J?"

My heart and head were both pounding. If whatever Corey had seen in the messages had convinced him that he should go to Victor Trent, I had to know what they said. What was it that had convinced Corey that he had sent them?

I nodded. "I need as much information as possible, Damien. Everything depends on me."

He finally relinquished his hold. I sat in the chair and placed the notebook under the dim lamp, turning to the first page. The messages were recorded first in Morse Code, then interpreted below, with a double space between.

My eyes scanned the first set of dots and dashes. Below, the message began with a date.

October 15, 2023 Still no change.

More dots and dashes.

October 17, 2023, She's gone. Knew it was a risk, but hoped for better outcome.

October 18, 2023 Still in shock. Service was small.

The pounding in my head became louder. I thought about the date on the password protected "J" file on the tablet. October 18, 2023. He was talking about me. *My death.*

My eyes had difficulty keeping focus as I scanned through the random entries. Most of them were labeled as memories.

October 23, 2023 Memory: learned to ride a bike.

October 31, 2023 Memory: didn't feel like dressing up, but made her go with me to the work party.

December 23, 2023 Memory: spending holidays with the Admiral.

I flipped through the pages again. There were hundreds of entries marked as memories, and they all seemed to be about Abby. I began looking for the ones without the label.

January 4, 2024 making progress with splicing

June 6, 2024 cells still rejecting mutation

June 25, 2024 found N3 Series tablet

"Do you see why it drove him insane?" Damien whispered. "There's no rhyme or reason. No complete thoughts. And honestly, it's just as possible that I sent these messages back, especially the ones about Abby."

Soft ringing started in my ears.

I continued searching the pages. There were so many entries. My head began pounding and the yellow light from the reading lamp suddenly seemed to brighten, contrasting the darkness sharply. My page flipping became frenzied.

"Don't do this, J," Damien said, putting his hand on top of mine to stop me from turning the pages.

Looking up at him, I couldn't ignore the anguish in his eyes.

"What did Corey see here? Did he find answers?" I asked.

Damien shrugged. "I don't know what he saw, but…" His voice trailed off.

"But what?"

He hesitated. "It was like looking into a crystal ball—it was distorted and it clouded his judgment."

"What do you mean?"

He squeezed my hand. "He was so convinced that he was the author of these messages, and that they meant that he was going to be with you in the future. He thought it would all just fall into his lap. But it didn't happen that way. You didn't choose him."

I broke eye contact. The throbbing intensified. I wanted him to take his hand away. I wanted to keep searching, but Damien's touch was electric, connecting us with the uncontrollable heat that had simultaneously drawn me toward him and pushed me away since our first meeting at my desk in St. Paul.

What could I say? What could I do that wouldn't betray my emotions? It wasn't just these messages that gave a glimpse of a different future. My mind was a crystal ball too. "Why did you bring me down here? Why did you show me this?"

With his hand still enveloping mine, our quickened pulses became synchronized. He waited to answer until I looked in his eyes.

"Because I want you to choose me again."

Burning, pulsing, pounding. Damien's face came in and out of focus until the darkness swallowed up the light from the small lamp, snuffing it out, leaving me completely cold.

* * *

We all rise. My hand is locked inside the grip of my mom's cold palm. I didn't want to come, but I couldn't refuse when my father suggested that mom needed our support.

Following the long line of black clad mourners after the casket, I catch soft whispers of conversation once we leave the confines of the church. The men near the statue of St. Sebastian are talking about the score of the Redskins game.

"Did you give him your number?" a girl in a skirt much too short asks her overly-made-up friend.

"Dana! It's a funeral." She giggles. "I told him to find me on Facebook."

"How's school this semester?" my mom whispers. "We hardly hear from you."

"It's good. I've just been busy." She always seems to sense when something is going on with me, but I'm not ready to tell her about Corey yet, especially with my father listening. Anyway, there's really nothing to tell.

It strikes me as cruel that life goes on for the rest of us when I see the tearstained face of my mom's friend, Claire Trent. She's on one side of the casket embracing people and shaking hands. Her husband stands behind the casket, effectively separating himself from the masses.

At the cemetery, a solemn procession of sailors, clad in full dress uniform, escort the casket. When each stops to remove the golden SEAL Trident from his uniform, slapping it onto the casket and pounding it with his fist, I can't stop the tears from falling onto my cheeks.

My mom pulls out her handkerchief and starts sniffling again. "I can't believe he's gone," she cries.

"No parent should have to bury their child," my father says, patting her shoulder softly.

* * *

Tears were cascading down my cheeks when the dark basement came spinning back into focus. Damien cradled me in his arms on the floor beneath the desk. Stroking the hair off of my forehead, he kissed me softly.

"What is it?" he asked. "What did you see?"

I couldn't speak. I didn't understand. I didn't know what to say. *Damien's funeral, but I didn't know him.* The timing was all wrong. *Before my mom's death. Before the baby.*

My mind rushed back to the first evening I had spent with Damien. At the Italian restaurant, where we had shared chunks of our past with each other like bread dipped in oil and vinegar, he'd said something about a stint in the Navy right after high school.

I sat up, pushing myself away from his warmth. "A long time ago you told me that you left the Navy because your father had other plans for you. Were you a SEAL?"

Damien searched my face. "I was part way through the training program."

"What happened?"

"A rare condition showed up on my blood work...just long enough to get me discharged."

I scrambled to my feet. None of this made sense. The more I remembered, the farther away the truth seemed from my grasp. Had Corey been able to piece it together?

"You saw something about my time in the Navy? What was it, J?"

I pulled my hand away. "You're right. Maybe we shouldn't be looking." I started back toward the stairs, but Damien stopped me short, pulling me by the arm into the gym and closing the door behind us before flicking on the lights. When the fluorescent bulbs buzzed to life, I pinched my eyes closed. I didn't want to look at him. Damien's face was only inches from mine and he was still holding my arm.

"Please don't do this to me, J," he begged, tipping my face up. I stepped back, but he came with me until there was no farther back for me to go. Pressed against the mirror, I finally opened my eyes.

Looking at him was like a direct window into a soul as lost as mine.

"We don't belong here," I whispered. "You must feel that."

"Until three days ago, I belonged wherever you were."

The heat from his body contrasted the cold from the mirror so sharply that it became painful to be in the middle.

"I don't know where I belong, Damien, but we both know that wasn't me."

He winced and dropped my arm, but pressed his hands against the mirror on either side of me.

"Because you don't remember? Look around you, Jace. Let yourself feel. Try as hard to remember what we had as you are trying to remember the Point of Origin."

The heat was unbearable. I was suffocating. I had to be free. Lifting my arms in the narrow space between Damien and the mirrors, I put my left hand on his outer elbow and brought my palm up to his chin with my fingertips on his cheek.

"This is bigger than us," I grunted. In one swift motion, I pulled inward on his elbow while twisting his jaw away. The back of his head smacked against the mirror. I gasped for air and stumbled away on the padded floor.

Heart pounding, I brought my fists up, but when I turned back toward Damien, I was perplexed by the triumphant smile on his face.

"You do remember," he said.

My eyes darted back and forth from Damien's face to my unruly, pajama clad reflection in the mirror. The woman staring back at me was powerful and strong, ready to strike.

"I taught you that move."

The electricity in the room flowed through me. *No, you taught her that. I'm her, but I'm definitely not her.*

With the lights turned out and Damien in his makeshift bed on the floor, the noises of the city seemed strangely amplified. Exhaustion and adrenaline fought to control my mind.

1:05 a.m. 1:14 a.m. 1:25 a.m. My eyes finally drifted closed after what seemed like hours of staring at the flashing colon between the numbers on the alarm clock.

* * *

Black rocks. Mist. Bright blue water. The little girl's sparkling blue eyes. She's laughing—running over the black sand inside the cave with crystal walls.

"Echo!" she calls.

The cave rumbles in response.

"No!" My mouth forms the words, but the sound is drowned out by another rumble.

"It's coming," the little girl drops her arms to her sides and turns around.

"It's coming," Corey echoes, standing to my right.

"It's coming." Victor slurs the "s". To my left, he forms a triangle with Cory and the little girl.

A tremendous tremor starts somewhere farther into the cave. The noise grows louder as it rolls toward us. Abby is directly in its path. It will hit her first.

"I'm coming," I call. "Hold on, Abby!" Running toward her, my feet begin to sink into the black sand.

The blue walls of the cave pick up a soft orange glow that slowly changes to red. Corey doesn't move. He and Victor stand with arms to their sides, staring blankly at each other.

"Abby!"

Slow moving, rumbling lava turns the corner of the cave, melting the ice on all sides as it burns. The flow of melt water comes first, enveloping our feet, then ankles, then knees. Why won't she come to me? I'm trudging through the water toward her, but she doesn't move.

"Abby! Run! Meet me halfway."

She reaches her arms toward me, blue eyes swimming in tears.

"I'm not Abby!" she cries.

The lava reaches her, but she doesn't cry out in pain. Her eyes roll back and drift closed, then she collapses into the burning flow, instantly becoming part of it.

I scream. The heat moves toward me, burning my face.

* * *

I sat up straight in bed, realizing that the wails were real and they were coming from Abby. I scrambled to get to her, but Damien's shadow moved in front of the bassinet before I could reach it.

"It's okay, Shhh," he soothed. He lifted her softly over his shoulder, then turned toward me. "Sorry I didn't get to her before she woke you. You've got a big day tomorrow." He rubbed my arm lightly as he passed. "You need to sleep."

I pushed my wild hair away from my face and stumbled back to the big empty bed. Damien opened and closed the door quietly, disappearing into the hall. He must have done this last night too, but I had been completely unaware. He'd gotten to her before she'd woken me.

It only took me a few seconds to shake the disorientation, but the low, sinking feeling in the pit of my stomach lingered. The little girl from the pictures on the tablet wasn't Abby. Damien wasn't her father. But all of my dreams had somehow been related to her. She was in danger in all of them. Or in a coffin.

110

I waited in the dark listening for a few seconds. My heart rate was still elevated. I took a deep breath in through the nose, and released it slowly through my mouth.

The house was still—no hint of Damien coming back up the stairs. I reached for the phone under my pillow. I dimmed the screen completely before taking screenshots of each of the remaining geotags. Now I just needed access to a Bible.

The minutes ticked away slowly. 2:40 a.m. If I waited until morning, Mirlande could look up the references for me on the OmniNetwork. But the more I thought about it, the more I wanted to see the message alone before showing it to anyone.

There was no sign of Damien coming back. It occurred to me that he had gotten up to feed the baby last night and had opted to stay downstairs on the couch after she went back to sleep. It would be more comfortable than the floor but wouldn't raise any eyebrows since he had gone to bed with me first. I let fifteen minutes pass before I considered my suspicion confirmed.

Double checking to make sure that the door was completely closed, I moved over to the other Jace's desk. The OmniGlasses hadn't been moved from where I'd dropped them. I didn't know if using an online Bible would send up any red flags with the algorithm people at Omnibus, but I had to take the risk.

Folding open the frames, I slid them over my ears. I'd expected them to take a moment to power up, but I was surprised to see OmniSocial already scrolling down the lenses. The glasses had adjusted themselves automatically to the dark bedroom, giving me a soft yellow font. My eyes darted back and forth, reading the information in front of me. A news article about a plane crash over the Pacific Ocean. The rate of speed was just slightly too fast to be comfortable. It forced me to skip words. The article disappeared before I'd finished reading it. Four picture boxes appeared on the screen—a field of wildflowers, a close up of a woman wearing a t-shirt with a motivational saying, a 3D globe, and a baby's pacifier.

The 3D globe increased in size as my eyes lingered on it. After less than a second the pictures disappeared and the information feed continued. Four news headlines were at the top of the feed with small pictures depicting the content of the story. My eyes went directly to the one in the middle about the Reclamation Summit. Victor Trent's name was in the title.

The story opened automatically and I skimmed through the details. The first day of proceedings had been successful. Every nation was represented and all agreed that change needed to happen. While I skimmed the text it moved slowly to the right, making way for related articles in red text to the left. I thought I'd quickly returned my focus to the article, but some of the red letters on the left changed to blue. I sat up stiff in my chair, realizing that Victor Trent's name was highlighted repeatedly. My eyes were drawn automatically to the long list of stories about him.

I blinked my eyes. The text all vanished, and a video flashed across the lenses. An interview Victor had given after the day's proceedings at the UN My heart began beating hard.

"I won't rest until the world has access to the protection that the OmniNetwork provides. The Hannaj have no respect for the sanctity of identity. I abhor how they've stolen it from both the living and the dead."

The ringing in my ears drown out Victor's voice and I pressed my palms to my temples.

* * *

Corey stops abruptly. The bronze figures, lit from below, dot the courtyard to our right.

"This is it," he says. "We're here."

"The Rodin Garden? I thought you wanted to show me something I hadn't seen before." I walk past the Cantor Art Center almost every day.

"You've seen it, but have you really looked?"

Laughing, I let go of his hand. "It's one of my favorite places," I say, walking toward the Three Shades sculpture in the center of the path. "But I find it much easier to look at in the light."

"So does everyone else," he says, catching up with me. "That's why I like to come at night—so I don't end up in the background of a stranger's Facebook post."

The faces of the Three Shades look sinister instead of tortured like they do during the daytime. They're inspired by Michelangelo's Creation of Adam, *but Rodin's sculptures look hopeless, with necks contorted until the top of each head almost touches the face of the next shade in the circle. And instead of pointing toward God, their extended index fingers point limply downward.*

"Come to think of it, I'm not surprised you brought me here," I say, ready to pick a fight. "You and Rodin have a similar outlook on humanity."

"'Abandon all hope, ye who enter here,'" Corey recites the Dante quote from Inferno, taking me by the hand and leading me toward the Gates of Hell sculpture. A smaller version of the Three Shades stands above the Thinker at the top of the gate.

I examine the gate in the dim light, trying to see it through Corey's eyes. The hundreds of emaciated figures twist around and pile on top of each other, embodying every form of suffering—frozen in the most exquisite moment of torture. My Catholic roots and what I know about Inferno influences me to see the depicted suffering as the result of human weakness. Sins that the figures are being punished for. But Corey doesn't believe any of that. He believes that suffering is random and meaningless. Arbitrary.

"So..." I say, turning to him after an unusually long period of silence. "Go ahead."

He doesn't respond immediately, keeping his eyes on the lower portion of the sculpture. I expect him to look up with his mischievous left eyebrow raised, but when he finally meets my eyes, his expression is serious.

"I had to bring you here at night," he whispered.

"Afraid I was going to Facebook a picture of you?"

"No," he said, squeezing my hand lightly. "Because I want to tell you. You're the 34th Canto for me. I see things differently because of you."

My skin tingles. He isn't joking. He didn't bring me here to start a debate.

"The 34th Canto?" I repeat. I know what it is. The final verses of Inferno, where Dante climbs out of the underworld after seeing the devil in the ninth circle—the depths of hell. But I'm short of breath, waiting for him to complete the thought.

"'From there we came outside and saw the stars.'" His eyes move slowly up toward the clear night sky.

"Are you trying to tell me that I've converted you? Are you finally going to admit that all of this might mean something?"

He steps closer to me, "You mean something."

His lips are only inches from mine. He lets go of my hand and cradles my face, examining it like he's trying to cement every nuance in his memory.

"You mean something..." I whisper, his lips moving even closer, "too."

* * *

"Omnibus will bring the world safely into the future." Victor's voice jerked me back into the dark.

Reaching up for the glasses with sweaty palms and trembling fingers, I pulled them away from my face. The sound of Victor's voice cut off immediately.

I wanted to go back. I wanted to be close to Corey again. I wanted to hear him say it all again.

Squeezing my eyes shut, I slid the glasses back over my ears.

"Bible," I said softly.

I opened my eyes slowly and found the search results waiting for me. Scanning the list, my eyes lingered on one that mentioned King James Version. A list of King James Bibles popped up in my left peripheral vision. I let my eyes rest on the first option. *Bible Gateway.*

The landing page included a table of content and search field. I turned my phone on to look for the first number. The brightness of the OmniGlasses automatically adjusted to contrast the light from my phone screen. 02352222. The second book was the book of Exodus.

The book opened and I looked at chapter 35. My eyes traveled down the verses. They scrolled up automatically when I reached the bottom of the screen.

22 And they came, both men and women, as many as were willing hearted, and brought bracelets, and earrings, and rings, and tablets, all jewels of gold: and every man that offered an offering of gold unto the Lord.

The 22nd word was "tablets."

07 16 10 14 "lies."

08 02 12 26 "trust."

01 06 05 25 "only."

01 02 24 07 "father."

01 12 09 06 "still."

43 15 13 02…43 15 13 02. I recognized the numbers instantly. In the flash of memory I'd had on Mount Hood, it was one of the sets of numbers that Corey had given me to memorize before he sent me back. One of the numbers we had entered on the machine.

I took a few deep breaths before looking at the word Menu in the upper left hand corner of the glasses. Counting down 43 books, I came to John:

13 Greater love hath no man than this, that a man lay down his life for his friends.

"Love." My head began spinning. "Still love…" I almost didn't need to look up the final verses, but the burning in my chest demanded it.

01 01 29 08 "you."

43 04 14 13 "never."

01 35 02 27 "change."

How did he know? Goosebumps from head to toe left me with teary eyes. They were almost the exact words he had said to me in that white room—strapped to that other gurney. *"I still love you, that's never going to change."*

I was more convinced than ever that at some point, on another splinter, I had been strapped to a gurney, ready to have my memories sent back in time, only it hadn't been forced. It was my decision, and Corey had been the one at the controls.

I set the phone down in my lap while I tried to understand. Corey was telling me not to trust Claire and the Alliance. What did he know about them? Was all of this coming from the messages he had received on the shortwave?

But Damien didn't trust Claire, either.

My father was the only one who could answer my questions, but how could I get to him? My temples began to throb with my accelerated heart.

I reached up to remove the glasses but stopped myself. *43 03 07 11.* The second set of numbers I had given Corey came into my mind. I went back to the menu one more time and located the chapter and verse: John 3:7

7 Marvel not that I said unto thee, Ye must be born again.

The light from the phone in my lap disappeared when the screen timed out and turned itself off and I was left looking at the words of the verse, which had dimmed automatically to compensate for the loss of light in the room. My eyes focused hard on the word born and a list of related verses in the Bible appeared in red text in my left peripheral vision. I couldn't breathe. Entering the numbers on Mount Hood had propelled me forward to the birth of Abby. My eyes shifted to the red words. *Born again. Born of the spirit. Born of water.* Suddenly, the key word turned blue, sparking my tunnel vision.

* * *

Corey turns off the engine but doesn't take the keys out of the ignition.

"Ready?" I ask before pushing my door open.

"Is it too late to postpone?" He smiles like he's joking. But I know he's nervous. He's hardly spoken to me all day.

I look up at the house. My mom's standing in the front room window. She smiles and waves.

"They already know we're here." I laugh. "Just relax. They're going to love you."

"I don't know," Corey says, pulling the keys out of the ignition. "After six months of watching your dad's interviews on C-Span, I'm not sure if he loves anyone."

"Don't let him intimidate you."

Tired of waiting, my mom has already opened the front door and is waving us inside. I get out and run to embrace her.

"How are you?" she asks, backing away to examine me. "You are absolutely glowing!" She kisses my cheek before looking at Corey, who is coming tentatively up the path behind me. "And you must be Corey. I've heard so much about you!"

She greets him with a hug and a kiss on both cheeks. I try not to laugh at his awkward response—almost like he's never been hugged before. "Good to meet...you too, Mrs. Vega."

"How was the traffic?" she asks. We chat about the drive as we make our way inside. She leads us straight to the kitchen and offers Corey a drink. Her iPod is on the dock near the sink, playing Bon Jovi loud enough that we have to raise our voices to hear each other. She was probably singing along before we got here.

"Can we turn that off, Bridgett?" my father asks, coming into the room from his office. "Welcome home, mija."

* * *

The dark room pulled me back, but the happy and carefree feelings from the memory hung in the air. But these memories weren't helping me understand anything. Snatching the glasses from my face, I folded them and put them back against the wall.

The Alliance was expecting an event in three days. I looked at the clock. Only two days now. How was I supposed to stop it? I needed to talk to my father. I needed to remember the plan.

Sitting alone in the dark, all I could hear was the slow pounding of my heart. What was I going to do? How was I going to contact my father without Claire? I felt utterly alone—trapped inside someone else's life and a house that felt anything but safe.

Finally, I moved back to the bed and put my phone under my pillow. My body needed sleep, but my mind was running in a million different directions, trying to put together the pieces of the puzzle, but I couldn't. I was still missing too many. Instead of counting sheep, the numbers began repeating in my head over and over 43 04 14 13, 43 03 07 11...I

117

closed my eyes and visualized the numbers on the geotags. *The tablet is a lie. Trust only my father. Corey loves me.* I needed to find a way to contact my father. How could I do it? I might be able to find my father's contact information on the OmniGlasses, but I was certain that any kind of communication I tried to send through them would be monitored.

I slid my hand under the pillow and touched the phone. Jean-Talon market and the underground internet seemed like the only safe means of contact with the outside world. Claire and the Alliance didn't know that I had access to it. Mirlande was the only one who did, and I doubted she would want everyone to know how I'd gotten it.

No one would question another early morning run. Mirlande could get me out the front door, but I knew she wouldn't agree to what I wanted to do. Once we were running, I would have to get away and go to the market alone.

At 5:00 a.m., the house was silent. I stopped trying to sleep and got dressed to go running. This time I opted for a plain black V-neck T-shirt and matching black tights with reflective stripes down the sides. I powered down my phone before zipping it into the pocket of the other Jace's fitted, black Nike jacket.

When I went downstairs, I found Damien sleeping on the couch with Abby on his chest. I crept through the dark room and tiptoed down the hall to Mirlande's bedroom. It only took her a moment to answer the door.

She squinted her eyes. "Are you okay? You don't look like you slept well."

"Can we go for a run?" I asked. "I'm nervous about the procedure. I need to clear my head."

Mirlande nodded. "Just let me get dressed."

Waiting outside the door, I reviewed what I had to do again. I hoped that Mirlande's competitive nature would buy me the time I needed. The metro station was along Avenue Van Horne. I could picture it with the rental bikes parked out front. I would wait until they came into view, then challenge Mirlande to race to the next light. Within a few seconds, she would be far ahead of me. I was counting on her not looking back until she reached the goal. By then, I would have disappeared into the metro station. All I had to do was get off at Jean-Talon. I knew my way back to the Electrotel.

When Mirlande came out, I avoided eye contact. We made our way quietly to the front door. Placing my hand in the basin first, I tried not to tap my foot while waiting for the chip to be applied. I moved to the door when the machine had finished, feeling Mirlande's eyes on my back while her hand was in the machine. Could she sense my deception? Could she anticipate what was going to happen?

The soft spraying sound halted, and Mirlande entered the code. The door unlocked and we stepped out onto the dark porch. My breath seemed to freeze and fall to the ground as soon as it left my body. It would be another hour before the sun came up.

We set out at a reasonable pace in the same direction we had gone yesterday. We were both silent, and I avoided looking at her. I rehearsed the words I planned to say over and over in my mind, but my tension only increased. Soon, we were only a block away from the metro station on Avenue Van Horne. It was almost time.

We rounded the corner.

"Mirlande," I said. "Was I a good fighter?"

She looked over at me, but I kept my eyes on the path ahead. "That's a random question. Why do you ask?"

"Just wondering." I paused. "Last night I used a move on Damien that made me think I was pretty good."

She raised her eyebrows. "You could hold your own. I don't know if I'd say you were 'good,'" she replied, glancing out of the corner of her eye at me to see what kind of reaction she would get.

I laughed slightly. "Something like you and running, I guess."

"Ha!"

"Don't feel bad," I said. "It's just like fighting—it takes years of training to get the proper form."

"Oh really?" Her smile disappeared. "Proper form?" She was taking the bait.

I tried to keep my smile contained. "Yeah. Like yesterday, your height let you keep up for a little while, but endurance takes time to build."

"You trying to say that I couldn't beat you for distance?"

I shrugged my shoulders.

"Let's go," she said, taking off at a sprint just before the light at Wiseman. Adrenaline rushed to my extremities. I wouldn't have to backtrack at all. Mirlande passed the metro station without looking back. I followed her at a sprint, but she was already half a block ahead of me. If she kept focused forward, she probably wouldn't realize that my footsteps had disappeared until I was safely in the station. She would follow me when she realized what happened, but I prayed that the train would arrive before she did.

I cut hard to my left but slowed to a fast walk when I entered the metro. A lone worker sat inside the booth. I didn't make eye contact with him when I scanned my chip and pushed through the turnstiles. The rushing sound of a train filled the station. Was it coming or going? I didn't wait until the ticket booth was out of sight to hit a sprint again. The squeal of brakes muted the noise of the train. Glancing up at the sign, I made sure I was headed toward Saint-Michel before bounding down the stairs to the platform.

Three passengers stepped onto the train. The doors chimed, signaling that they were going to close, just as I jumped onto the last car. My vision blurred, and I was barely able to see the rail in the center of the car before I grabbed hold of it. The three tones chimed and the train moved slowly into the tunnel. My pulse sent tiny black dots swirling around in my peripheral vision.

Sinking down onto a hard plastic bench, I faced away from the window. I couldn't risk seeing the lights that might trigger a flash. This was no time to lose control of my senses. Where was Mirlande now? Would she have reached the platform at the station? Was there any chance she would miss the next train? She would be confused, but it wouldn't take her long to figure out what I was doing. I could only count on the time between trains to get to the store to connect to the internet.

We came out of the tunnel at Parc station. My heartbeat slowed painfully. Had Mirlande boarded the next train yet?

Unzipping the small pocket on the back of my tights with shaking fingers, I pulled out my phone and opened my Gmail app. The message would need to be short. My thumbs hovered over the keyboard. Would he have kept his old email account or was he floating down the Omnibus river of information with everyone else? I had to hope that he would get my message and reply to it before Mirlande could drag me away. Passengers exited and entered the train, and we started moving again.

What did I want to say to him? I needed to ask about the procedure. *And the Alliance...the Point of Origin...Victor Trent and Global Security.* Soft buzzing in my ears got progressively louder, drowning out the voices of the other passengers. *Corey. Damien. Claire. The baby. The plan.*

My eyes lost focus and I couldn't help seeing the green and white and blue lights flash in the tunnel. My temples began to throb. Throbbing in the exact place where the pins from Victor's halo had been bolted to my head.

* * *

It isn't like him to be late. I got the text to meet him at the Rodin garden during study group. Glancing at my phone, I reread his text.

Meet me in thirty minutes—delivered forty-five minutes ago. As much as I love an evening in the garden, I have finals to study for.

I'm just getting ready to compose a snarky text when I hear his shoes crunching against the gravel behind me.

"Sorry," he says. "There was an accident on El Camino."

"You couldn't have texted to tell me that?"

"My phone died. I left the charger in my suitcase. This isn't exactly how I'd planned on—" He interrupts himself, touching his lips to mine. The kiss starts out full of exasperation, but turns unexpectedly tender.

"I'm sorry," he repeats.

"It's okay," I say, my mood completely altered. "How did the interview go?"

A slow smile spreads across his face. "I'd say it went well."

"Really?" Taking his hand, I pull him toward one of the benches facing the Gates of Hell sculpture.

"Really," he says. Dropping his briefcase next to the bench, he sits down, then pulls me onto his lap. "They're going to offer me a position on the research team. They'll pay my living expenses, and they'll give me whatever time I need to write my thesis."

I'm overwhelmed. "Congratulations! That's amazing news." I close my eyes and kiss him again, trying to hide my emotions.

"Are you okay?" he asks, pulling away to look into my eyes.

"Of course," I say. "I'm so happy for you. I'm just a little tired." I am happy for him, but this forces me to think about my uncertain future. I have no idea what I'll be doing a year from now. I can't help being sad that he won't be able to stop by my apartment at odd hours, or text me to meet him like this. We'll probably still communicate every day, but it won't be the same from a distance. Shrinking down, I press my cheek against his white dress shirt.

"I told them I couldn't accept the position yet," he whispers.

"You did? Why?" I ask, listening to the accelerated beating of his heart.

"Because," he replies, hesitating before nudging me away from his chest. He tries to reach into his briefcase, but can't. "Your father said you would want me to get down on one knee anyway," he says, sliding me onto the bench beside him.

Before my mind can catch up with what's happening, he's kneeling in front of me with a little black box. When he opens it, the simple emerald cut diamond sparkles, even in the dim light.

* * *

"Station De Castlenau." The screeching of the brakes shook away the remnants of my flash, but I didn't want to come back. I wanted to feel his shirt against my face and his arms around me again.

I stared out the window at the flashing lights when the train resumed, purposely blurring my focus, but I couldn't go back.

Daddy, I typed, *I need to talk to you. I need to know you're there. Please answer me.*

I clicked on the message but I couldn't see it anymore. My eyes were blurry from the tears filling them. I turned off the screen.

123

"Prochaine station, Jean-Talon." The train's voice was loud in the emptiness. *Why am I doing this?* How could I expect my father to answer me on an email address from three years ago when he hadn't answered Claire's messages using the protocols he had set up?

"Station Jean-Talon," the voice announced. I stood up and held onto the rail near the doors. Though I wanted to sprint as soon as the doors opened, I somehow kept my pace at a fast walk until I reached the street outside the station. The fiery rising sun sent waves across the dark blue sky. Taillights of cars and produce trucks heading toward the market were blurred in my peripheral vision, my focus locked on the yellow sign in the distance. I clutched my phone, and the weight of it gave me momentum as I swung my arms.

I skidded to a stop in front of the Electrotel. Turning my phone on, I waited for it to automatically reconnect to the Wi-Fi. Someone across the street honked and I looked up at the long line of cars waiting at Tim Hortons. Were they honking at me? I moved to the corner of the building and hid in the shadows.

Three bars. I reopened my Gmail app and typed my father's name in the "to" field on the email I had composed. Relief flooded through me when his address auto populated. I shook my head. It didn't mean that he still used the account. It just meant that my Gmail remembered him.

With a deep breath, I pasted my message, clicking send before I could reconsider. For the first time, I looked over my shoulder toward the metro station. The street was empty, except for a cat who was only half visible, poking its head into a trash can near a bus stop.

Walking around in a small circle, I pressed myself against the window again. *This is crazy.* I couldn't expect him to answer me immediately. What if he didn't answer at all? Would I go back and let them insert the probe to extract my memories? What did I really know about what the Alliance would do with the location of the Point of Origin?

I looked at my phone, running in place to try to warm myself. Less than two minutes had passed. How long did I have? Five minutes would be generous unless Mirlande had missed the next train.

I hit refresh on my email. "Please, please, please," I begged.

A reply loaded, but it hit me like a punch in the gut. An automated response—out of office. *He's not available.* I blew out a long breath to keep my eyes from filling up with stinging tears. *I guess some things never change.* Why had I wasted my time coming here? Why had I set myself up for disappointment? I looked down at the message again. Maybe he didn't check this email at all anymore. Maybe he had put the out of office assistant on permanently when he changed over to the OmniNetwork. I clicked on the email to read the details.

I am currently out of the office. If you need immediate assistance, contact my administrative assistant, Sheila Linehan 555-367-2956.

"Sheila!" Sheila was living in DC. Were she and Corey both working for my father? Maybe that was why Corey had followed her Instagram account. But how did he expect me to call her without service? I took a screenshot of her phone number so I'd have access to it later.

Or what if he was telling me something else? I had dismissed Sheila's Instagram pictures because they weren't part of the message with the geotags, but even without looking closely, I'd noticed that they were all taken in Washington DC, except for the very first picture with the moving van. What if he was trying to tell me to go there?

I knew I didn't have much time, but I touched the Instagram icon again to take another look at Sheila's pictures. I was greeted by the grey dial spinning against a blank white screen as the application automatically refreshed. I expected to see @bridger_fa and his shot drinking buddies, but instead a picture of Corey's shiny, silver pocket watch appeared. This one had a caption that simply read *Run.* My heart stopped, and my eyes darted to the geotag. *4910 Jean Talon Street West.*

My arms dropped to my sides as my eyes rose to the street number posted on the Electrotel building. They knew where I was.

The ringing in my ears started again. I looked down at my palm. I had compromised us. With trembling fingers, I held the button on the top of my phone until the screen asked me if I wanted to power down.

"What are you trying to do? Get us all killed?" Mirlande's shrill voice cut through the ringing just before her hand jerked me away from the store window. "Who did you contact?"

"They know where we are, Mirlande," I said.

Mirlande pushed the metro door open and the rush of air took my already short breath completely away. We scanned our palms at the turnstiles and ran toward the escalators. Mirlande stopped under the signs pointing in different directions for the blue and orange lines. The noise of a train entering the station ricocheted off of the brick walls from the platforms below.

"Why did I leave without telling anyone?" Mirlande said. "We have to get back to warn them."

"This is my fault."

Mirlande glared at me. "I don't have time to be angry at you now. Corey's message was obviously a trap and we both fell right into it. We need to focus on fixing our mistake. We have to get back to the safe house."

Mirlande was right. Someone had to go back to the safe house to warn everyone. But the chip had lead them to me. I touched my left palm. Wouldn't it lead Omnibus straight there with us?

"Can we remove the chips without the machine?" I asked.

Mirlande's eyes darted back and forth between her palm and mine. "We need hot water." Her voice seemed amplified after the noise of the train exiting the station faded away.

"Where's the restroom?"

"The metros don't have any," she replied.

No restrooms. Where else could we find hot water close by? I took a few steps away from the railing, my eyes searching the station. The small green circle was almost hidden behind a newspaper stand, but Mirlande and I both saw it at the same time: a small Starbucks kiosk. Mirlande moved toward it without speaking, but I was only a heartbeat behind.

"It should work," Mirlande said, racing toward it. "Could I get a cup of hot water?" she asked before she had even reached the counter.

The barista nodded. "Anything else?" She filled a foam cup with the steaming liquid, then reached for a lid in what seemed like exaggerated slow motion.

"Thanks," said Mirlande, snatching the cup as soon as she could reach it. "How much?" She held out her palm to be scanned, but the barista waved her off.

"No charge."

"Merci." Mirlande started back toward the escalator, but instead of descending, she stood against a glass railing that overlooked the platform. Before I reached her, she had already removed the lid from the cup and was carefully pouring a few drops of the water onto her palm. She didn't flinch, even though the water was steaming hot. She placed the bottom of the cup over her palm for a few seconds before handing it to me.

"I just need to find a corner," she said, digging around the edge of the softened plastic with her fingernail. It only took her a second to separate the edge near a wrinkle between her thumb and index finger. Then she peeled back the rest of the flesh colored patch. Before I could examine it closely, she dropped it inside the cup of water.

"I'm off the grid now. You're next."

Off the grid. My spine tingled. Without the chip, there would be no way for Omnibus or the Alliance to track my movements. If Corey wanted me to go to DC, this was my best chance.

I held out my palm and she dropped the hot water on it, just like she had her own. I waited until my chip was safely inside the cup before telling her.

"I'm not going back to the safe house, Mirlande."

"What do you mean? We have to. They have your chip ID. They'll run a reverse on you as soon as they realize what's happened. They'll be able to see everywhere you've been. We'll only be a few steps ahead of them, but we have to warn everyone."

"I can't go back."

Mirlande pushed me toward the tiled wall as the crowd of disembarking passengers came up the escalator. "Why?"

Without waiting for the voices and footsteps to fade into the distance, I moved closer to Mirlande and spoke directly into her ear. "I can't go through with the procedure. I can't give the Alliance anything until I talk to my father."

"Your father?" Her tone was dripping with disbelief. "And how exactly are you planning to do that?"

"I'm going to go to him."

"In Washington? Are you crazy?"

Maybe I was, but I didn't care. My father and Corey were both beckoning me to come to them. I had to go. It wasn't just Corey's message that was telling me so; my flashes of memory were telling me that he was my future.

"Flying is probably out of the question with airport security." My mind began searching alternatives. "What about a bus? How closely are they monitored? Can I ride a bus without a chip?"

Mirlande backed away from me, stunned. She looked around the station with desperate eyes. "You're serious about this."

I nodded.

"You don't even know how the system works, and you're going to try to do this on your own? You won't make it out of the city. Forget about getting out of the country."

The doors on the train below us chimed again before they clapped closed and it departed. My heart accelerated with the train. Mirlande had no idea what I was capable of, she could only be judging me based on what she had been told, or on her experience with the other Jace, but her complete disbelief in my abilities still stung.

A bus must have just unloaded outside of the metro station, because a wave of people pushed through the doors. I felt the rush of air, but my back was turned. Mirlande froze, watching as the scanners began to beep. Her eyes widened and she grabbed my arm.

"Don't turn around. Just follow me."

The hair on the back of my neck stood on end. "They're here already?"

She nodded, turning toward the escalator. Following her, I resisted the urge to look back.

"They must be confused that they lost our signals so suddenly," she said when we were standing on the escalators. "We'll be ok if we can get on a train before they scan us."

When we finally reached the bottom of the escalator, I glanced over my shoulder and saw four men dressed in dark suits through the glass and metal railing above us. They were all wearing OmniGlasses. The noise of an incoming train drowned out the pounding of my heart.

"C'mon," Mirlande said, pulling me through the stream of people headed to the platform. "It's headed toward Cote-Vertu. It's not the most direct route, but it will take us to Berri-UQAM. That's a central station, so it will at least give us some options."

I followed her, trying to focus on the train ahead of me, but the sea of disembarking passengers seemed to push me backward. Mirlande dodged and weaved through them without much effort, reaching the last car on the train several steps before I did. I tried to mentally calculate how far behind me Victor's men were. Would they have reached the bottom of the escalator yet?

I jumped across the threshold into the crowded car, and pushed my way toward a pole in the middle of the train where Mirlande stood. The three tones chimed and the doors closed. I held my breath. Had they reached the platform? Had they seen us?

The train lurched forward, and I took a deep breath in through my nose and released it on a three count before looking back. Two of the men in suits had just reached the platform, their eyes barely scanning the packed train before one of them touched his glasses. He looked up at the platform sign and said something, then disappeared from my view when the train went into the tunnel.

"Prochaine station Beaubien." My eyes jumped to the metro map mounted on the back wall of the train. It took me a second to trace the orange line with my eyes until I found Jean-Talon and Beaubien. The orange line was U-shaped, connecting with the blue and green lines on both sides of the U as they spanned the length of the city. There would be no quick way to get back to the safe house if we continued in this direction.

The car jostled slightly and I touched Mirlande's back to steady myself. She turned toward me, still clutching the Starbucks cup that contained our chips. "What now?" she asked.

It probably seemed impossible to Mirlande that I could make it out of the city on my own, let alone the country. *Maybe she's right.* It would be a miracle if I could even make it out of the metro. With no money and no verification, how would I cross the border? The pounding of my heart was deafening. I closed my eyes, pushing off a wave of nausea.

"You don't have a plan, do you?" Mirlande muttered. The ringing started in my ears as the colored lights passed by in the dark tunnel. Red, green, and white were barely distinguishable, they blurred together in one long strip of bright light.

* * *

His face is completely drained of color when I answer the door. Something's wrong.

"What is it?" I ask. "Come inside."

He shakes his head. "Get your purse. Your father asked me to bring you to Monterey."

My arms drop to my sides. "My father," I stammer. "Why? What is it?"

Corey touches my arm softly. "There's been an accident."

* * *

Smack! Mirlande's hand was close to my face, ready to strike again. The train car jerked back into focus. "You've got to be kidding me, J. This is not the time to flashback. Now that they've lost our signals, they'll shift their attention to where you've been today. It won't take those suits long to track down the safe house. We have to decide what to do."

The end of the tunnel was quickly approaching. The ringing in my ears had almost disappeared when the brakes started screeching. I had to do something.

Despite Mirlande's lack of confidence, I would find a way to get us both out of the metro and myself out of the country. I only wished that my déjà vu would come back. If I could see ahead, even just a little bit, I would have an advantage.

"You've got to go back," I said. "It's the only way."

"Snap out of it Jace. You can't just waltz into DC. You can't just go talk to your father. Don't you think Damien and I would have done that already if it was an option?"

I searched her face for a moment. Damien and I? What about the other Jace? Would she have gone too? I shook off the question. "I'll find a way."

"You'll get us all killed."

"They don't want you," I realized out loud. "You have to get off here. Go back and warn Claire and Damien and the others." I grabbed the cup out of her hands. She glared at me with her mouth gaping open.

"What are you going to do?"

"I'm going to put myself back on the grid. Hopefully they'll get so excited about trying to catch up with me that they'll forget about running the reverse for a little while. At least long enough for you to get back."

She blinked several times. The train slowed to a crawl. The platform at Beaubien was packed. There wasn't time to come up with a better plan. She knew I was right. Someone had to go back to warn everyone, and she knew she couldn't count on me going there. It had to be her.

"What will I tell Damien? I can't lie to him. I'm going to tell him that you're going to DC. He'll follow you there."

"Don't let him," I begged. "Tell him to stay with the baby and Claire. My father will contact them when we know what we have to do at the Point of Origin."

Lifting off the lid of the cup, I fished out the lighter colored patch. Water dripped through my fingers. Glancing at the metro map again, I took a deep breath. "Didn't you say that Berri-UQAM is a central station?"

Mirlande raised her eyebrows, then nodded. "The orange, green and yellow lines meet up there."

"Is it a bus station too?"

Mirlande nodded. "If you get there before the suits do, you might be able to leave the city on a bus, but you won't make it through at the border without verification."

"I'll worry about that when I get there."

The train halted, the three tones chiming. Mirlande stood frozen as passengers exited.

"Go," I mouthed.

"I can't let you do this J, you have no idea what you're up against."

She was right. No one was going to *let* me.

The tones chimed. The doors were about to close. I pressed my right shoulder against Mirlande's arm, pushing her with all my force toward the open door. She lost her balance and stumbled out onto the platform, but dropping into fight position, she sprang back at the doors. It was too late. The doors closed.

I know exactly what I'm up against.

"Go," I mouthed again.

She clenched her jaw, glaring at me. The window slid past her open palm.

We watched each other until just before the train passed into the tunnel. Finally, she turned and ran after the crowd of passengers headed toward the exit.

It took a second for my heart to start beating again. I glanced around at the people in my vicinity. The dark haired girl and her boyfriend on the bench next to me didn't look up. They were laughing at something they were watching on her phone. I spun in a small circle. No one made eye contact. Every single person was engaged with a phone, tablet screen, or their OmniGlasses. They were completely oblivious.

Except for the two girls at the far end of the car. The taller one held open a Tim Horton's bag and offered a donut to the other. I gripped the pole, trying to calm my breathing. They hadn't noticed either. They looked like they were in their early twenties or even late teens, but they weren't dressed the part. The coats they wore were very plain. My eyes dropped to their stockings and shoes. The taller of the two girls wore white tights and black Mary Janes with thick soles that looked like they had seen better days. The shorter girl, with honey blonde hair, also wore flat dress shoes.

I looked away from them, back up to the metro map on the wall. Berri-UQAM was five stops down the line. That would give me roughly 15 minutes to fill in the details of the plan that was forming in my mind. With my chip transmitting a signal again, I assumed that the suits would arrive at the station just after I did. I wouldn't have access to money as soon as I got rid of the patches, so I needed to keep them until I bought a bus ticket. The station was a central hub, and I was counting on it being crowded during rush hour. I gripped the Starbucks cup a little tighter. My best hope would be to create as much confusion as possible.

The train slowed as we entered Rosemont station. I glanced over my shoulder at the crowd of waiting commuters. The new passengers packed themselves in around me.

"Excuse me," a soft voice behind me said. I turned my head sharply. It was the taller of the two girls from the other side of the car. She was standing next to me now.

"What?" I asked.

Now that she was closer, I noticed a tag on her lapel: *Sister Swanson, the Church of Jesus Christ of Latter-day Saints.* It was engraved in plain white print. She didn't look like any nun I had ever seen.

"You just look a little lost, and I was wondering if I could help?" She had a distinct Southern drawl.

"Thanks," I said dismissively. "I'm fine."

"You're not from around here, are you?"

The doors closed again and the train began moving forward. I gripped the pole a little tighter and shook my head.

"You're not either," I said.

She smiled. "Nope. You're right about that. I'm from Georgia. But I've lived here for over a year, so if you need directions, I'm pretty sure I can help."

"Thanks. I'm fine," I repeated. I looked away toward the window as we entered the tunnel but closed my eyes and turned back when the first white light passed.

"You seem a little jumpy. Are you sure you're alright?"

"Positive," I said, reopening my eyes just as the other girl pushed her way toward the center pole that I was now gripping with white knuckles.

"I'm Sister Allphin," the girl said, stretching out her hand toward me.

I was still clutching my patch in my right hand, so I didn't have a free hand for her to shake.

"Are you nuns?" I asked.

Sister Swanson laughed. "Not exactly. We're missionaries."

"Oh," I said.

"Sure you're not lost?" Sister Swanson asked again. Her eyes were kind and sincerely concerned.

"I'm not lost," I said, forcing a smile. "This is just my first time traveling alone on the metro."

"I know how you feel," Sister Allphin said. "I've only been here for two weeks. I'm from Utah." She seemed unreasonably happy to tell me this.

"Oh," I said. The train shook slightly. We would be coming into the next station soon. I squeezed the patch a little tighter in my hand. There was still a very real possibility that the suits would be waiting for me at any one of the stops along the line.

"Prochain station, Laurier," the voice announced.

The butterflies in my stomach made me light headed as the train pulled into the station. The platform wasn't as full as at Rosemont. Nobody waiting was dressed in a suit.

"Are you looking for someone?" Sister Allphin asked.

I didn't respond. My mind was trying to play out what would happen when I got to Berri-UQAM. I couldn't just buy a single bus ticket to the border. The suits would link Mirlande's ID to mine soon enough, and I would be easy to track down.

And how was I going to use the chip now that it was detached? I didn't need to draw any more attention to myself. I looked around the train. It wasn't especially cold outside, but people were still wearing light jackets. I needed a pair of gloves. I looked back at the two missionaries—long coats and backpacks. There was a decent chance that one of them had a pair of gloves.

"The next stop is ours," Sister Swanson said, pulling on the straps below her backpack to tighten them.

The train began moving again. They were getting off—I had to hurry. "I know you were probably just being polite when you asked to help me, but could I ask a favor?"

Sister Allphin's exaggerated smile beamed so bright that I had to take a step backward. Why was she so excited that I was asking for her help?

"Sure," Sister Swanson said. "That's why we're here. What can we do for you?"

"Do either of you have a pair of gloves you could just give to me? I don't have any way to pay you."

"Sure. I have a pair," Sister Swanson said. She pulled her backpack off her shoulder and unzipped it, then began shuffling around inside one of the front pockets.

"While she's looking for the gloves, can I give you something too?" Sister Allphin asked all in one frenzied breath.

"What is it?"

The train's brakes began to whistle softly as we exited the tunnel. Another train was entering the station from the opposite direction, the sound drowning out Sister Allphin's voice. She was in a hurry to tell me something before they got off of the train. Her mouth moved quickly, and her hands were a little bit shaky as she used them to illustrate what she was saying. I strained to hear, but only a few of the words were discernible. "Book…ancient America…translated…"

I smiled like I could understand.

Sister Swanson finally produced a pair of black gloves. They were as utilitarian as everything else she was wearing, but they would work. She smiled at me and handed them over while Sister Allphin continued talking. The train finally came to a stop.

"It's meant a lot to me and my family, and I know that if you'll read it, you can find answers that will bring you happiness in your life." She continued to shout, even though the noise from the other train stopped when she was halfway through her sentence.

Several of the passengers standing by the doors turned their heads to look at her, most of them with smug expressions. "Will you take it and read it and pray about whether it's true or not?" Sister Allphin slurred the entire question into one long word. I caught Sister Swanson's eye roll as she stepped toward the doors. "Take it. I promise it will make your life better."

The three tones chimed and the doors slid open.

She pushed the book toward me and I was forced to let go of the pole to take it.

"We need to get off," Sister Swanson reached for Sister Allphin and pulled her toward the door. "It was nice to meet you. Good luck."

I didn't see how a prayer book would help my situation. I was about to hand it back to them, when I suddenly realized that this was my opportunity. This book might buy me a little more time.

Opening my palm, I dropped my patch onto a page in the middle of the book. It was thin enough that no one should notice it. I took a deep breath and snapped the book shut.

"Wait!" I called just as Sister Allphin stepped out of the car. "I can't take this." I pushed the book out the door and into the hands of the instantly deflated girl. "Thanks anyway. And thank you for the gloves."

The passengers waiting to board came between us. I backed up and let them fill up the space that had been left by the two missionaries. I made my way back to the pole in the middle of the train. It wouldn't take Victor's suits long to figure out that these two girls were not who they were looking for, but it might just be long enough to help me get away.

The three tones chimed and the doors closed. Sister Allphin hadn't moved. She watched the train move away for a second before putting the book under her arm and following Sister Swanson toward the orange exit sign.

They'll be fine, I tried to tell myself. The suits wouldn't have any reason to harm them after they finished interrogating them about the patch inside their book.

"Prochain station Sherbrooke."

My hands shook slightly as I fished Mirlande's patch out of the Starbucks cup. The water was only lukewarm now. Placing the patch in the center of my palm, I pressed the crease of my thumb against it to keep it steady while I slipped the glove over my hand. The gloves were slightly too big, but it was the best I could do for now.

We came out of the tunnel at Sherbrooke station, leaving several passengers behind and exchanging them for new ones. The car was firmly packed, with very little room to breathe, when we finally reached Berri-

UQAM. The train crawled to a halt. All of my senses sharpened, watching the platform for men in suits with glasses.

Moving right behind a group of students in black coats, I stepped off the train. All I had to do was let the stream of passengers carry me up and out of the station, but I felt like I was drowning in a sea of unfamiliar faces, all speaking a language I didn't understand. I kept my arms folded and my eyes open for signs directing me to the buses. Skylights above the train tracks let in the full morning light. I was near the top of the station. *It shouldn't take me long to get to the bus terminal.*

The students followed the exit signs that would lead them to the University of Quebec at Montreal. I stayed close to them, only splitting off when I saw a sign for the bus terminal. The sound of shoes clicking against the tile dissipated as I traversed the long corridor that led to the terminal.

A row of ticket windows lined the right side of the station, but only one person stood in line. What if Victor's suits had already linked my chip to Mirlande's? What if her chip had already been flagged and the ticket agents were looking for her? Maybe it was too risky. Maybe I should just walk out of the station and find another way to get out of the country. I froze, trying to convince myself to proceed with my plan. My eyes swept the station a second time, and this time I noticed a semi-circular kiosk in the middle of the station with four computer screens facing toward the outside of the circle. The sign above the kiosk read *Billet.* A self-service kiosk? Somehow it seemed much less risky. I moved over to it, turning my face away from the ticket windows as I passed.

Taking the glove off my right hand, I touched the screen where it let me choose English instructions. A list of destinations appeared. I scanned over the list. Ottawa seemed like as good an option as any. The first bus was scheduled to leave at 8:30 a.m. It still had seats available. I touched the screen and barely skimmed the information that came up about baggage restrictions. I continued clicking next until the payment screen appeared.

Chip payment. I touched the option, then looked for the scanner under the kiosk and waved my gloved hand below it like the image on the screen demonstrated. The scanner beeped softly when the light passed over the chip. An hourglass came up on the screen while the transaction processed.

Electronic ticket or paper, the next screen asked. I clicked on paper and waited for the ticket to print. Part of me was vaguely aware that Victor's suits weren't the only ones who would be able to track my transactions. When Damien and the others were safe, they would know that I had made it to Berri-UQAM. Mirlande would tell them what my plan was. Would they try to stop me from going to DC when they knew?

There was no one in the area, but I still felt like someone was watching me. I looked over my shoulder around the station before returning my focus to the screen, purchasing three more tickets: one bound for New York City, another for Detroit, and finally Boston. All had departures within the next twenty minutes.

With the tickets in hand, I turned back toward the metro lines, scanning Mirlande's chip at the turnstiles to re-enter. There were even more people on the concourse than before. I weaved my way through the crowd, suspiciously eyeing anyone in a suit. I made it to the escalators without incident, but as I descended to the platforms an eerie feeling washed over me. Three train lines converged here. Where was the rush of trains entering and exiting?

When I reached the bottom of the escalator I glanced up briefly at the sign pointing to the platforms, but it didn't matter which platform I chose. I just needed to find a place to drop Mirlande's patch. It didn't even have to be on a person. I turned in the direction of Cote-Vertu.

While I walked, I tried to estimate how long it had been since I had given the book back to the missionaries at Laurier. The suits would have caught up with them by now for sure. It wouldn't be long before they were searching the station for me. I only hoped they would follow the live signal before searching Mirlande's transaction trail. By then, I would be aboard one of the buses on my way out of the city.

The station was still quiet. The only noise came from the footsteps and voices of waiting passengers. When I rounded the corner, I stopped dead in my tracks, then moved quickly over to the wall. The voices hadn't come from people waiting on the platform. The low murmur came from aboard the train that was stopped on the tracks with the doors open. All of the people waiting on the platform had already boarded and I hadn't been met on the escalator by a wave of departing passengers. This train had been sitting here for a while.

I turned around and quickly walked to the orange line platform headed in the opposite direction. Even before I saw the train, I heard the same soft hum of the engine and murmur of the people aboard. The trains were stopped. It didn't feel like a coincidence. Had the suits stopped them? I turned back toward the escalators. I had to get out of the metro station before they caught up with me. Sliding both gloves off of my hands, I waited until I reached the top of the escalator before tossing them inside a trash can.

Whether I was ready or not, I was completely off the grid now, with no money or identification, and the suits had the power to shut down public transit in the middle of rush hour. What else did they have power to do?

My heart beat even faster when I reached the top of the escalators and realized why the upper concourse was so crowded. I could feel the angry tension in the hum of conversations. There was no way that they could know that I had caused the delays, but I still felt like everyone was watching me.

"Someone said that Public Safety is investigating a bomb threat," a bald man in scrubs said as I passed by.

"Public Safety must be working with Omnibus agents. I saw them searching the trains," a woman in a trench coat replied. I hurried past, weaving my way through the stranded passengers.

"It's just the metros," a woman in a business suit said into her phone. "I have no idea when I'm going to make it in. I might try a bus, but I don't know how long that will take. There are lines for all of them. You'll probably have to start the meeting without me."

One third of the way down the concourse, I looked back over my shoulder at the escalators. A man in a black Omnibus suit rose up from the tracks below. He stopped, lifting the lid off the trash can I had dropped the patch in. He touched his glasses, then looked slowly around at the people in the vicinity. I ducked behind a newsstand. Had he seen me? I took a few deep breaths before looking around the side of the stand again. Three more suits came up the escalator.

"Are those Global Security guys?" a girl on the other side of the kiosk asked.

"Who?" someone else said.

"The guys in the suits over there."

The suit with the patch held it up, showing it to the newcomers. They began to spread out on the concourse, each scanning the crowd with his glasses. They were looking for people who didn't have chips. How many of the people in this crowd were still unverified? Could their OmniGlasses detect my heat signature or vital signs? I had no idea what they were capable of. I had to move before it was too late. A hush fell over the waiting passengers, who realized that they were being scanned.

I surveyed the station again, looking for another possible escape, but the only visible exit would take me into the line of sight of the suits. Their search was moving in my direction. Walls behind me. Door to my right. Escalators to my left. The one holding Mirlande's patch called out an order that I couldn't understand. He started to jog toward me. The others followed him. There was no way I would make it to the exit before they reached me. Hunching down, I covered my face with my hands.

Their heavy footsteps echoed like hammers down the corridor, stopping just before they reached me. I glanced up as the leader pointed at the sign for the buses. They didn't see me. Had they traced my transactions already? The bus tickets slid out of my hands onto the floor. The suits continued down the corridor without looking my way.

The noise of the crowd returned to full volume, but the electricity in the air was no longer angry. I scanned the concourse one more time before leaving the cover of the newsstand. I tried not to draw attention to myself, keeping my pace casual and my head down as I moved toward the door.

Light appeared through the glass doors ahead when I was halfway down the corridor. Freedom. It took everything I had to keep myself from sprinting toward them. I was only a few steps from the door when I heard a voice behind me.

"Yes, sir. The first and second buses have been swept already and passengers waiting for the third bus are being verified." His voice echoed down the corridor. "I'm securing the University exit. I've got four here. Only one is unverified."

I picked up my pace, my heart pounding.

"Excuse me, Miss!" he shouted, "I need to see your identification!"

I bolted for the door, throwing my shoulder against it, and burst out into the bright sunlight. The suit pushed through the doors a few seconds after me.

"I have her, heading south on St. Catherine Street."

A car coming through the intersection swerved and honked, and I almost plowed into a group of students waiting for a walk signal on the opposite side of the street. The suit's footsteps pounded the pavement only a few yards behind me.

A blur of brown brick buildings passed me on both sides. Through the intersection, I spotted a girl pulling a bike off a rental rack. I ran straight at her, pushing her and the bike to the ground. She screamed. I picked the bike up and continued running until the wheels began to wobble, then I threw my leg over the seat and jumped on. Glancing back, I saw the suit, already at the bike rack.

If he stopped to rent a bike, it would take him time to catch up to me. If he continued to pursue me on foot, he would fall farther and farther behind. I came to another intersection. Glancing up at the street signs, I decided to cut to the left. I had to get off of St. Catherine.

Sanguinet Street was a narrow one way, with traffic backed up almost to the next block. I weaved through the parked cars on the left hand side of the street and rode on the sidewalk until I came to a busier two-way street, then turned again. Aware that another left turn would make a square, sending me back in the direction of the metro station, I moved over to the right and prepared to turn.

As I was turning onto another one-way, St. Denis Street, I caught a glimpse of a black spot on two wheels just turning onto the road I was exiting. The suit was on a bike now and was gaining on me. My vision focused on the congested street ahead and I pushed my legs even faster toward a bus stopped in front of the line of cars. I moved over to the right, but quickly realized that the people exiting the bus would make it impossible to negotiate the sidewalk. I glanced behind me. The suit hadn't turned onto St. Denis yet.

Squeezing the brakes hard, I pulled the bike over to the edge of the sidewalk and jumped off. I angled my way through the passengers walking away from the bus. The doors hissed, closing just before I reached them.

"Wait!" I called, pounding on the glass.

The bus driver looked down at me and rolled his eyes before nodding and reopening the doors. His radio blared French announcers' voices, talking loudly over each other with accordion music playing in the background.

"Oui?" The driver's nasal voice urged me to make a decision. I stepped aboard. He closed the doors and took off through the intersection before the yellow light changed to red.

"Right here," he said, pointing to the scanner just to the right of his steering wheel.

Gripping the metal rail, I climbed the last step. My heart thumped twice as fast as the drum behind the frenzied accordion. With no chip, and no metro card, I was at the driver's mercy. Could I stall long enough to at least get to the next stop?

I strained to see through the passengers to the back window of the bus. The suit had just reached the intersection and was glancing back and forth between my abandoned bike and the bus. He touched his ear and moved his mouth mechanically. It looked like he was reading the number off the back of the bus. Turning away from the driver, toward the door, I waited, hoping he would ignore me. I had to get off at the next stop.

"Madame," the driver said, coughing. "You must scan your chip."

Just keep driving.

"Excuse me. Pardon," a gruff voice spoke.

I turned my attention away from the window in response to the commotion behind me. The crowd in the center aisle parted, letting through a salt-and-pepper-haired man in a red baseball cap. He was focused on me and only stopped pushing his way forward when he was standing directly across the aisle from me.

"This day is full of excitement. A bomb threat and a chase." He looked back at the intersection. The suit was only a small speck in the distance. The man's eyes turned back to me.

"What do they want with you?" he whispered.

I couldn't risk talking to this man. I shrugged my shoulders and took a step back toward the doors.

How long would it take the suits to access the chips of everyone aboard this bus? The driver stepped on the brakes and pulled over at the next stop. I was getting off.

A walkie-talkie mounted to the dashboard crackled through the driver's music and a voice started saying something urgently in French. The driver pulled a lever to open the doors.

"…jeune femme vetue de courir vetements noir," the voice on the radio said. I was halfway down the stairs when the driver pulled the lever back and shut the doors in front of me.

"Open the doors," the man in the baseball cap told the driver.

The driver shook his head, never taking his eyes off of me. He lifted the walkie-talkie away from its mount and touched the button to respond. I was trapped. I couldn't breathe.

"Elle est ici," he said, cutting off the voice that was still spouting information.

"I said open the door," the man in the cap demanded. Stepping toward the driver, he reached for the lever.

"Monsieur." The driver stood to fight the man for the lever, and dropped the walkie talkie in the process. It dangled from a spiral chord, swinging back and forth against the dashboard. The voice on the other end resumed talking, but now it was repeating a question over and over.

With both men's hands on the lever, the door opened a crack, letting out a small hiss. But the crack wasn't big enough to pass through.

"I said open it," the man insisted.

"You're crazy," the driver said. "She's a fugitive."

The man in the cap shrugged his shoulders and let go of the lever. I watched the crack in the door disappear along with my hope of escaping the suits.

"Sorry, friend," the man in the cap said. I looked over my shoulder just as he swung his fist at the driver's face. The force of the blow pushed the driver back into his seat. The man reached for the lever and opened the door, but the driver was already trying to regain his footing. The man pushed him back into his chair again, then turned to me.

"Go!" he shouted. I turned and stepped off the bus right into the line of people who were waiting to board.

"Excuse us!" the man shouted from behind me. The people at the front of the line stepped aside, and the man grabbed my arm, pulling me to the right. "Follow me!"

I didn't argue. The man led the way, running with long strides until we were well away from the pedestrians near the bus stop. We crossed the street and turned onto yet another narrow one-way called Bonsecours. I looked over my shoulder. No one had followed us off the bus. But I was certain that our location had already been given over the walkie-talkie.

"You shouldn't have done that. They'll be looking for you," I panted. "I can't stay with you."

The man ignored me, still holding my arm as he crossed the empty road toward a brick building with dark green wood trim and a gold-leafed sign. *Studio du Verre.*

He opened the door to the shop and waved me inside. "It's okay. I know the owner. We'll be safe."

"But they'll be tracking your chip," I said. "Probably listening too."

"You're not the only one still resisting." He held up his palm. Raising his heavy eyebrows, he beckoned me inside a second time.

I looked over my shoulder at the empty street before stepping inside.

The cramped shop was stacked with panes of stained glass against every wall. Light coming in through the windows refracted blinding rainbow patches. I squinted, trying to get my bearings.

The man strode past the empty sales counter toward a single door to the left of it. He knocked before pulling it open a crack. A rush of warm air and the hum of fans escaped.

"Rene?" he called. "Es-tu ici?"

One of the loud fans switched off. "Who is it?" a deep voice replied.

The man in the cap pushed his way through the door.

Rene was short with curly, copper hair, freckles and a beard. He held a heavy, metal rod in one hand and black safety glasses in the other.

"Jean-Baptiste?" Rene said.

Jean-Baptiste pulled me into the back room and shut the door.

Rene raised his eyebrows. "Who's this?"

"They've shut down the metro this morning because of her." The rate and pitch of Jean-Baptiste's voice escalated.

"Who shut it down?" Rene's voice flattened.

"They announced that Public Safety was shutting it down, but Omnibus Global Security was chasing her through the streets. She's not verified."

"And you brought her here?" Rene groaned.

"I thought I'd better get her off the street."

"You're sure she's unverified?"

"Yes."

Rene motioned for us to follow him to a couple of metal folding chairs. He set his rod down next to an open kiln.

"Sit down," he said. "You look like you need water."

Neither of us sat. Rene disappeared around a corner.

"I have to get out of here," I said in a low voice.

"First, tell me why they're after you."

Even if I wanted to explain myself to Jean-Baptiste, it would take more time than either of us had. My eyes shifted around the glass studio. Colorful blown vessels sat on a display shelf between where we stood and the kilns.

"They're looking for me because I'm not verified."

He furrowed his brows. "They don't shut down the metro and send Global Security after you because you're not verified. There must be something else." He crossed his arms over his chest.

I stepped back toward the wall. Global Security was on my heels. I didn't have time to explain myself to anyone.

Rene came back around the corner with two bottles of water.

"Please," I begged. "I have to find a way to get out of Montreal."

"Where are you trying to go?" Rene asked.

"I need to get to Washington DC."

"You're trying to get into the U.S. without a chip? It's impossible to cross the border without one now," Rene said.

Jean-Baptiste drummed his fingernails against the metal chair. "You won't be able to cross at a checkpoint," he said. "Even if they don't have Global Security posted at every border, they have a very good description of you."

"I'll walk if I have to."

The two men looked at each other. Jean-Baptiste scratched his chin. "It might be possible to cross over undetected in Ontario. If we can find an unmonitored inlet and make it far enough inland to avoid a border scan, you'd have a decent chance."

"How do I get to the border?"

"I think I can get you there, but you'll be on your own once you're on dry land."

"You have a boat?"

"I work for a jet boating company. I've been doing test runs down at the pier."

Rene shook his head. "You've had enough trouble with Global Security, do you really want to give them reason to open another investigation?"

Jean-Baptiste shrugged. "What do I have to lose?"

"They're not going to let you go with a slap on the wrist this time," Rene said.

"And what about this girl? What will happen to her if I don't help?"

"You're only one person, Jean. You don't have the power to stop them."

"Maybe you're right, but if I don't do something, I'm helping them."

Rene's eyes dropped to the floor and his breath hissed like a punctured tire. "What about your family, Jean?"

"I'm already lost to them."

A pained look passed between the two men. What had Jean-Baptiste done to draw the attention of Global Security and lose his family?

The faint sound of approaching sirens pulled all of our attention toward the door.

"Will you drive us to the pier?" Jean-Baptiste asked.

Rene hesitated. "What choice do I have?"

R ene started the engine, revved it, and tore away from the curb. "Stay low." The sound of the sirens pulled me down in my seat until I could barely see out of the side windows. Canadian sirens sounded like the car alarm that used to go off in the middle of the night at my apartment complex.

Rene turned onto a narrow one-way street. The small car jostled up and down as the tires clapped against uneven pavement. I pushed myself up enough to see the blue cobblestone lining the streets.

"You'll have to get out when we reach a traffic signal," Rene said. "I'm sure they're looking for my car by now. I can't drive you down the pier. I'll keep on toward one of the bridges. Maybe they'll think you're still with me."

"It will keep them busy long enough," Jean-Baptiste said. "How does the traffic look up ahead?" He pulled himself forward against the headrest.

"It's clear as far as I can see."

"Just a few more minutes," Jean-Baptiste said, touching my knee.

The spire of an old stone church passed on the right side of the car. The bumping continued until Rene took another turn, this time to the left.

"We're almost to the intersection," Rene said. "I'll slow down and take a right turn on Saint Gabriel. Get out when I'm around the corner." He glanced up at his rearview mirror.

"They will have tapped into all of the security cameras in the area by now," Jean-Baptiste said. "We'll all be better off if you let us off at Chez-Catherine near the umbrellas. They will camouflage us…at least for a moment."

Rene shook his head. "Whatever you say." He glanced up in the mirror again, his eyes squinting slightly, even though dark clouds had come in and were blocking out the sunlight. "Be careful, old man."

Jean-Baptiste reached his hand up and gripped Rene's shoulder. "You, too."

Rene stepped on the brake. "Now!" he said, keeping his eyes on the road ahead of him.

"Come out of my door," Jean-Baptiste said, reaching for my arm. He flung the car door open and stretched one of his long legs out. Ducking his head to avoid the door frame, he stood up in one swift motion. I scrambled to follow him out. When we were both standing on the street, Jean-Baptiste shut the tiny car door and Rene sped away.

My eyes scanned the crowd of people drinking coffee at the red checkered tables. "This way," Jean-Baptiste said. He took my hand in his and pulled me in the same direction Rene's car had gone, down the open street lined with old, grey stone buildings on our side and trees on the other. He kept his pace casual, except when we were under the colorful awnings, then his stride increased in both length and speed.

We reached an intersection just as a group of about twenty students that looked middle school aged reached the opposite curb—ready to cross from the other direction. I glanced up at the street sign. *Boulevard Saint Laurent.* We started into the intersection, but we were less than a quarter of the way across when Jean-Baptiste spun around, joining us with the crowd of pedestrians headed back in the opposite direction. After a moment of disorientation, I realized that he had strategically placed us in the center of the group, where we would be invisible to cameras on any side of us. Jean-Baptiste glanced to the right at a row of flags that led to a modern glass building, set back on the opposite side of the street. A glass top tour bus, painted and shaped like a long boat, approached the intersection and honked before turning onto the street with the flags.

Jean-Baptiste gripped my arm as the group moved forward into the crosswalk. Sirens in the distance rose above the conversations of the middle schoolers. They were coming from the direction of the glass shop. The tourists didn't appear to hear the sound of the approaching sirens as they mulled through the crosswalk. The group reached the other side of the intersection and began to spread out along the path heading toward the glass building. By the time the police cars sped through the intersection, we were several yards away. Neither of us looked back.

"They must have Rene's plate number by now." Jean-Baptiste ducked to the right of the crowd and picked up his pace to a run as soon as his path was clear. He glanced around several times to make sure I was still with him.

He turned onto a foot path that ran along the water's edge, and two seagulls cried out and swooped away.

"Almost there," Jean-Baptiste said, reaching again for my arm. The masts of several small boats became visible below us in the water. He led me down the cement staircase to the dock and stopped in front of a bright green tour boat.

"She's not much to look at, but she's very fast." I heard the sound of sirens again. Jean-Baptiste glanced up at the boardwalk. "Climb aboard," he said, jumping onto the deck of the ship and immediately beginning to untie the ropes that bound the ship to the dock.

I jumped across the small gap between the boat and the dock.

"Inside the cabin," he said, pointing up to the odd shaped tower at the back of the boat, "you'll find a life jacket and a poncho." He twisted the rope around his arm, then dropped it into a pile on the deck of the boat.

The boat rocked and swayed as it drifted away from the pier. Long rows of seating took up the entire midsection, with only narrow walkways on both sides. My legs felt like they might buckle, fighting the uneven motion, but I stepped carefully along the edge until I reached a rail at the back of the boat.

I'd just found a lifejacket when Jean-Baptiste pushed past me into the cabin. Bypassing the gear bin, he grabbed hold of the large, silver steering wheel. He pressed a button, and the low growl of the motor and swishing water masked the wailing of the sirens above us.

My eyes tried to stay level, scanning the dock for suits, but the boat was unsteady. I reached for a bar handle near the cabin door.

"Hold on." The boat lurched forward when we reached the end of the docks. Jean-Baptiste spun the wheel, turning toward the open water.

"We made it," I said.

"I wouldn't say that yet." Jean-Baptiste pushed the throttle forward, sending the craft speeding over the rolling waves. Leaning forward over the wheel, he peered up at the fast moving clouds. "Nobody at Saute Mouton will be looking for me. They were expecting me to test run the boat today. I work off the books for them. Global Security will have to question Rene to find out where we've gone. We have time."

With the skyline of the city fully visible from the water, I began to realize what Jean-Baptiste was sacrificing. I would be happy if I never saw Montreal again, but this was his home. What would this mean for a man who had already had trouble with the law?

The boat rocked, hitting a rolling wave. My stomach rose up with the boat but didn't come back down. I let go of the bar and wrapped my arms around myself, collapsing to my knees.

"Sorry," Jean-Baptiste said. "You should stay down there. It's going to get rough."

I couldn't speak. Barely able to keep myself from dry heaving, I tried to find something fixed to focus my eyes on, but the boat jerked unpredictably. Beads of sweat formed on my forehead as all of the heat tried to escape my body. A cloud, pushed aside by the wind, let through a flash of bright sunlight into the glass, reflecting back in my eyes just as the stabbing headache struck my temples.

* * *

I'm standing on a stone pedestal, surrounded by white curtains and mirrors. As much as I loved the dress she helped me pick out, wearing hers makes it feel like she's here, getting ready to walk down the aisle with me. Her wedding dress didn't have to be altered to fit me, and it's so well preserved it gleams. The eyelet lace is timeless, just like she was.

A soft knock at the door forces me to dry my eyes.

"Can I come in?" a familiar voice calls through a crack in the door.

Claire Trent is beautiful, wearing a merlot dress that brings out the same color in her cheeks and full lips.

"Oh, Jace. You're lovely." She comes toward me on the pedestal. I start to step down, but she motions for me to stay put.

She steps onto the pedestal with me, taking the veil out of my hands. "Let me help," she says, touching my shoulder until I turn back toward the mirror. After she pins the floral wreath into place, she rests her chin on my shoulder. I'm mesmerized by our infinite reflection in the mirrors.

My father is standing near the heavy wooden doors. He's avoiding eye contact. I put my hand in the crook of his elbow.

"You look like..." His voice trails off. I swallow hard. Squeezing his arm, I brush my cheek against his jacket. He pats my hand softly with his white gloves and clears his throat.

A hush falls over the crowd on the other side of the doors. The orchestra begins playing "I'll Be There for You" by Bon Jovi.

"Ready?" my father asks.

"I love you," I say, finally making eye contact just before the doors swing open. The guests are a blur of colors against the garden backdrop. My father's eyes fill with tears, but he doesn't look away. He loves me too. He pulls me gently onto the stone path.

I can't see anyone except Corey when my eyes shift away from my father. Waiting for me at the end of the white, flower and lace-trimmed aisle, he stands out in his black tuxedo. He insisted on wearing one, even though I wanted him to choose something more casual—more comfortable. Like him. I'm not sorry now. The tuxedo looks elegant on his broad shoulders and tall frame. His bright blue eyes are prominent with his dark hair smoothed back. Eyes that know what I'm thinking and feeling without words being spoken. Eyes that are always looking for ways to make me happy and comfortable.

The closer I come, the more anxious I am for my father to transfer my hand to Corey's arm, but he stops a few feet away. Finally, he squeezes my hand and gives it to Corey.

I sing in my head as the music plays. Warmth rushes through me. Despite the struggle it's been to get here, my father was right not to let me postpone the wedding. She wouldn't have wanted that.

My father takes his place, holding one corner of the Chuppah. Corey's parents were married under it. Minny and David Stein. *Their names are embroidered on the white cloth, edged with a thin, black border. I wish I could have known them.*

Claire and Victor stand in place of Corey's parents, each holding a corner of the Chuppah, and my mother's corner is planted firmly in the ground. Corey said that during the Chuppah ceremony, the couple's ancestors are believed to be present. Maybe it's my imagination, but I feel them in the warm breeze that ripples the fabric above us.

* * *

"Hey! Hey, are you alright?" His accent became more pronounced with his distress. Lifting my face away from the side of the cabin, I forced my eyes open, but I was too weak to lift myself from my knees. The memory of Claire standing with me on the pedestal on my wedding day was already familiar. I'd had a small flash of it before the Eruption on Mount Hood. I wanted to go back to that moment under the canopy on Corey's arm. I wanted to know more about a time when Corey and I had felt so right and comfortable together. But had there ever been a time when I hadn't felt comfortable with him? From the time I stepped into his apartment in St. Paul, I had felt at home. I'd never felt anxious or uncomfortable, even with his touch. And he still knew how to communicate wordlessly with me.

I turned my head slightly until I saw Jean-Baptiste's shoes. He was still at the wheel, and he hadn't slowed the boat.

"That's it." His voice registered relief. "It's much better if you can look out the windows. Can you stand up? If you can hold on to the wheel with me, it might help. You'll be able to anticipate the boat's movement. You need to focus on the horizon."

I took a deep breath and reached for the bar near the cabin entrance. Another wave tilted the boat hard to the right. It took everything I had to keep from falling to the floor again. As soon as the boat straightened, I shuffled toward Jean-Baptiste at the wheel. Then, reaching for the instrument panel, I let go of the bar behind me.

"Good," he said, letting go of the wheel with one hand. "Grab hold."

I obeyed, taking hold of the wheel and stepping in front of him. He closed his arm around me, gripping the wheel with his free hand. I tried to focus on the horizon to keep my motion sickness at bay, but I couldn't help watching the rolling current we were in. The waterway was wide and looked deceivingly calm from the banks. There was no way to see the danger of the swift current until you were already in it. I looked back over my shoulder. The city on the island became a blur as we moved away from it. Relief washed over me like a spray of seawater—taking away what was left of a bad dream.

"What happened with your family?" I asked. "You told Rene you were already lost to them. Did it have something to do with your trouble with Global Security?"

Jean-Baptiste looked down at me. "I spent six months in a low security correctional facility because of my protesting. I was asking too many questions. Stirring up too many people. My family didn't want anything to do with me after that."

"How many children do you have?" I asked. Jean-Baptiste seemed to be about my father's age.

"Just one daughter," he answered, adjusting his grip on the wheel on either side of me. "She was engaged to Rene. But she doesn't speak to either of us now."

"I'm sorry," I said.

He nodded slowly and glanced over his shoulder. "I don't see anyone behind us."

"How far is it?"

"It'll take a couple of hours."

Relaxing my shoulders and letting out a long, slow breath, the last of the nausea left me. I had already surpassed Mirlande's expectations—I was out of the city. Now I needed to think about how I would get from the border to DC without any identification or money.

"What's the name of the city with the unmonitored inlet?" I asked.

"Messena, New York," Jean-Baptiste answered. "It's only about an hour from Alexandria Bay. Interstate 81 is a straight shot to DC. I wish I had enough fuel to get you all the way to Alexandria."

"How far is it from there?"

"About five hundred miles. Maybe a little less."

Less than five hundred miles from my father. The boat caught air, jumping over a rolling wave.

"It won't be easy to travel without a chip," I said aloud. "I don't even have any cash."

"It wouldn't matter if you did. Very few places in the U.S. take it anymore."

The waterway narrowed as we passed to the south of a smaller island. The thick trees blocked out what was left of our view of Montreal.

Heavy raindrops began falling slowly. One or two at a time hit the windshield, the noise barely audible above the hum of the speeding engine. Soon the downpour wet every inch of the glass. As the wind and rain pushed against the boat, I was grateful for the protection of the cabin and Jean-Baptiste's steady arms on the wheel.

The small white boat looked like foam on the water at first, but its shape became more distinct as it sped toward us at an alarming pace.

I braced myself as Jean-Baptiste put the boat back into the middle of the fast moving current. Our boat skipped across the crest of the waves, jerking backward with each short landing.

"I had hoped we'd make it farther," Jean-Baptiste growled. "This will complicate things." He looked back again.

I gripped the rail tighter. "How far is it now?" I asked.

"Still another eighty kilometers to the inlets." He glanced at the left bank of the seaway. A few houses were visible among the trees. How far would the border be from here on foot? It wouldn't matter. They were close enough to see me. Jean-Baptiste couldn't just pull up to the bank and let me off.

I glanced back to see the progress of the boat behind us. It was gaining.

"I think I know what to do," Jean-Baptiste said. "But it will not be easy for you." His expression was somber. "Do you see the islands up ahead?"

Straining to see beyond the slight bend in the seaway, I made out a small island.

"Yes, I see it," I said.

"It's the first in a chain of islands that can give us some cover if we stay far enough ahead of them."

"Cover?"

"Yes," he said. "There are four or five of them that I can lead them through, just before we reach a small inlet that I think runs through the Wildlife Area." He looked up and down the shoreline again. "Yes. I'm almost sure. My daughter and I explored it once. It was years ago, but I'm sure it's there."

"And it's close to the border?"

"Not far," he answered, looking back over his shoulder again. "I won't be able to take you into the inlet, but I can come close enough that you can make it if you're a strong swimmer."

"Swim?" The rain had stopped, but the temperature couldn't have been over fifty degrees. Even out of the current, the water was turbulent. Wind pushed small waves into the rocks along the shoreline. I didn't consider myself a strong swimmer, but the life jacket would keep my head above the water.

Jean-Baptiste tossed me a blue ditty bag. "I wish I could offer more help." Sinking to the floor, I took off my shoes and socks and put them in the bag. Sealing the top, I held it against my chest.

My phone. It was still in my pocket. Unsealing the bag, I placed the phone carefully inside, hoping it was truly water tight. Corey's messages were the only link I had to finding him and my father.

I rose up to my feet again and reached for Jean-Baptiste's arm. "I wish I could repay you for what you've done for me."

"You can," he replied. "Keep fighting them."

Nodding solemnly, I looked behind at the white boat, which continued to gain. Turning, I refocused on the approaching islands. Jean-Baptiste pushed forward, navigating the boat into a narrow channel between the large island in the center of the seaway and a smaller island to its left. Soon, the smaller island blocked our view of the boat behind us.

"There's a narrow passage coming up ahead. I'll cut toward the inlet there and slow down enough to let you jump, then I'll circle back between the two islands just north of the inlet. Hopefully they'll be so distracted and intent on following me that they won't see you."

We came to the end of the island that stood between us and the shore. Jean-Baptiste looked over his shoulder at me. He meant for me to go now, to leave the shelter of the cabin, but my hand wouldn't let go of the bar. My body wanted to stay pressed against the control panel.

"Follow the river," he said. "It will take you all the way into Fort Covington."

Forcing my hand to let go, I stepped away from the window and the controls. The waterway widened again after we passed the end of the island and Jean-Baptiste moved the boat ever closer to the shoreline. Keeping my hand against the cabin wall, I pushed out into the wind and spray from the boat. It ripped my hair up and straight back. Blinded by watery eyes, I trudged along the side of the boat until I reached the end of the rail that was keeping me from flying off the edge.

The shoreline jutted out ahead. The inlet would be just around the corner. Jean-Baptiste steered close to the tip of the small peninsula, nodding to let me know that his signal to jump would be coming soon. I braced myself, barely breathing with the constant rush of air trying to fight its way into my mouth and nose.

Lowering my head, I took a few deep breaths, then looked back at Jean-Baptiste. He raised his arm up. *Not yet. Almost.* The boat came to the end of a long jetty and we rounded another curve. There was no sign of the boat behind us.

"Go!" Jean-Baptiste yelled, waving his hand up and down. The boat slowed abruptly and I stumbled forward. I hesitated, glancing back one final time before plunging feet first into the swirling brown river. My ears weren't even submerged when the engine roared again and the boat sped off.

Coming up to the surface, I gasped for air, the waves from Jean-Baptiste's wake filling my open mouth. Coughing and sputtering, I fought to keep myself pointed in the direction of the shore. The adrenaline coursing through me numbed me to the cold.

As the waves from the wake dissipated and the noise of Jean-Baptiste's engines faded, I glanced over my shoulder, looking for the white boat to appear around the corner of the island. Holding my breath in short gulps,

I listened for it. Soon, the waves lapping against the rocks on the shoreline completely drowned out the sound of Jean-Baptiste's boat.

After a few moments bobbing up and down, I began to pray that I would hear the other boat soon. My extremities felt like they were being pricked by hundreds of tiny needles. My teeth began to chatter.

Finally, I heard the higher pitched engine. The sound became louder and louder. Would they take Jean-Baptiste's bait, or had they already seen me?

The boat was coming up close to my position. If it didn't turn soon, I would know that they'd seen my pathetic shape moving on the waves instead of following Jean-Baptiste's bright green vessel.

Heart palpitations and shallow breathing started the flashes of black spots in my peripheral vision. Stabbing pain in my temples followed, then painful constricting of the nerves in my eyes. I knew what was coming—tunnel vision.

* * *

"Are you sure we'll be safe this close?" I ask in a low voice. The other researchers are several yards away, but I don't want to embarrass Corey.

"We wouldn't be doing this if it wasn't safe. You can stay with the helicopter if you're nervous." Corey picks up his backpack and slings it over his shoulder. "Mount Hood hasn't erupted in over 200 years, and we've got front row seats."

"Everything okay?" Victor Trent asks, buckling the chest strap on his pack.

I nod.

"I think we're ready," Corey says.

Victor pats Corey's shoulder. "You must be excited. You just joined a team that's going to make history and revolutionize the future of communication."

* * *

A wave washed over my face, jerking me back to the present. The hum from the boat motor was to my right now, and it was moving away from me. I blinked the rain water out of my eyes and turned to see the back of the boat on almost the exact path that Jean-Baptiste had carved in the waves. The wake sent me drifting toward the shore.

Slowly, I flipped myself over and began to stroke, creating as little splash as possible. Movement in the water intensified the cold. The gravity of my situation hit when the chattering of my teeth became uncontrolled muscle twitches throughout my entire body. The shore was within reach, but it didn't seem to be getting closer as I struggled to pull my arms and legs against the water.

The sound of the boat behind me was completely gone now. My breathing was intense and labored, warm puffs of steam leaving my mouth with each exhale. At least the rain was beginning to slow. Only small drops tapped against my head and shoulders now.

Finally, I caught a current that pulled me toward the inlet and my progress improved. Within minutes, I reached the bank, where my feet struck the sandy riverbed. But gaining a solid foothold was difficult with my numb legs and bare feet. The buoyancy of the life-vest was no help—it wanted to continue on with the current.

Somehow, I managed to push my way into shallower water with a combination of swimming and stumbling along. When I could touch the grass and rocks on the bank, I used my arms to pull myself out of the water. Each breath of air burned my throat and lungs as I lay, unable to move. The slight breeze felt like an arctic blast against my waterlogged clothes. I couldn't stay here. I had to dry off and raise my body temperature.

My fingers could barely grip the plastic closures on the life jacket, but I managed to release them, slipping it off of my shoulders. I tried to force my hands to stop shaking, but they trembled no matter how I stiffened my muscles. Finally, I was able to unseal the ditty bag, but pulling socks on over my damp skin almost took more strength than I had.

Follow the river. Jean-Baptiste's directions had sounded simple enough, but now I realized that hiding from view would be difficult. There were no trees or bushes to camouflage me, only tall grass. Bulrush and cattails. I stumbled through the grass near the bank of the river.

Behind me, I heard the faint noise of an engine. Could the suits have already realized I wasn't aboard Jean-Baptiste's boat?

No. The sound was coming from the sky, not the water. Helicopter blades.

I didn't look back to see the progress of the helicopter until I was crouched down in a patch of bulrush. It sped toward me for a few seconds, then turned toward the large island in the center of the seaway. Moving over the water to the end of the island, it stopped and hovered with its nose pointed down in the direction that Jean-Baptiste's boat should have been coming. *Jean-Baptiste's boat.* The helicopter dipped down until it was almost touching the water.

I waited, praying for the boat to come around the corner of the island, but the minutes ticked away and the helicopter didn't move. Had they caught up to him? How soon would it be before they realized I wasn't aboard?

My body wanted to stay frozen in the bulrush, but I knew I had to start moving. Running would put distance between me and the helicopter, and it would warm me up. My legs were stiff and unstable starting out. Uneven ground threatened to throw me off balance at every turn, but somehow I put one foot in front of the other, moving them faster and faster until I was jogging on the marshy ground.

Just before I reached the inlet river that would lead me to civilization, a massive *boom* rang out from the St. Lawrence behind me. I didn't need to look to know what had happened, but a glance confirmed my fears. A billowing cloud of smoke and flame rose above the water. *Jean-Baptiste.*

The helicopter hovered over the smoke, the blades dispersing it in every direction. The sound it made was muted by the distance and the dull ringing in my ears. As I stood mentally paralyzed on the bank I couldn't help remembering the other helicopter, and the smoke, and the helplessness I had felt watching Leo Belitrov disappear into the darkness of the eruption on Mount Hood.

Suddenly, the speedboat shot past the flames. The helicopter turned, and both came charging toward me.

Running through the bulrush near the river, I prepared to drop into the marsh if the helicopter came too close. The cold air circulating around me increased with my speed, but I pushed through the stinging. Somewhere up ahead I would find a small town. Getting there before nightfall was the only option.

Long after any trace of sound from the St. Lawrence disappeared, I still listened intently for the helicopter, but I couldn't hear it at all anymore. There must have been any number of places along the shore where Jean-Baptiste could have dropped me. I tried to picture the suits searching all of them. It kept my mind off of the numbness in my toes and fingers.

Eventually my clothes began to dry, becoming stiff instead of heavy. After what felt like about an hour, I came to a bend in the river. I hadn't heard a noise besides the movement of the river beside me, and the occasional cry of seagulls. Stopping for a moment to rest and catch my breath, I sat back against a large rock. Where was I now? Had I crossed over the border yet? The heavy clouds above were so low, they almost kissed the ground—making it impossible to determine the position of the sun. I could only estimate that it was moving into early afternoon now. Forcing myself up again, I continued on.

My progress slowed considerably over the next several miles, weaving through the bulrush. The landscape was still bleak from winter. The brown plants had only recently escaped the blanket of snow that had covered them, and the new grass was just beginning to push through in a few places.

Hours had passed and my throat was painfully dry, but whenever I slowed down enough to catch my breath, I could see Jean-Baptiste's flaming boat, like it had been burned into my retina. Trying to wipe away the image, I replayed all of the flashes of memory I had recovered. The Gates of Hell sculpture. Damien's funeral. My mom's accident. The wedding. And the white room where I was strapped to a gurney with Corey telling me he still loved me. I was missing the connecting link between the pieces of the puzzle.

Completely lost in the twists and turns of my own thoughts, I almost missed the sound of a car rolling along the gravel road on the other side of the river. The car was directly opposite me when I realized it was there. Ducking down in the tall grass, I watched it drive slowly by.

The next sign of civilization to appear was a powerline, spanning the river with a large pole on either side. Only a few steps farther, I passed by some mature trees and found myself standing in the backyard of a single family home. I wanted to collapse on the mowed grass and kiss it, but instead I spun around and looked across the river. Several more groomed yards and houses were visible on the opposite bank beyond the powerline. Following a narrow path along the edge of the yard and the bank of the river, I continued to move forward.

The houses were new construction, and some had vehicles sitting in the driveway. My stiff fingers moved up to my disheveled hair. Still slightly damp, the curls were oddly shaped and crunchy. Looking like this, I wouldn't be able to pass through the small town unnoticed. What would I say if someone questioned me? Everyone in the U.S. was verified. It was mandatory. I had to avoid talking to people at all. I couldn't risk letting Global Security know my position. They would be listening for suspicious conversations in border towns along the St. Lawrence.

My trail along the river disappeared just as the road in front of the houses curved and merged with a main road. Only a few feet past the intersection, a small building with a red and white striped gate sat in the middle of the street. Canadian and American flags blew above the building in the breeze. A border checkpoint. I stood behind a tree on the edge of one of the yards and watched the building for a few excruciating minutes. The road beyond the border checkpoint continued along the river, and would eventually reach the small town. I would have to show my identification if I crossed the border in a car, but there was no one to stop me from crossing on the side road that passed through the small neighborhood on foot. Trembling from a mixture of fear and cold, I continued walking until I was well beyond the checkpoint.

The neighborhood felt eerily abandoned, silent, except for the occasional chirp of a bird and the crunch of the gravel under my shoes. I had made it this far, in spite of the odds, but I still wasn't there yet. How was I going to get to DC? I needed to get my bearings and warm up.

Ducking into the yard of a small house on my right, I glanced in each of the windows as I looked for a back door. The lights were off, and the house was quiet.

Just before I rounded the corner into the backyard, I pressed my back against the brick wall. What was I doing? Real people lived in this house. People like Jean-Baptiste. He was dead now. Just like Leo and Megan. They all died trying to help me. Trying to help me defeat Victor. But was I any better than him if I was willing to leave behind so many casualties?

My teeth began chattering and I could barely keep my shaking hands under control. I didn't really have a choice. I had to keep moving forward. Stepping up onto the patio, I reached for the handle on the French door, but when I pressed down, it didn't budge. Locked.

My eyes fell to the doormat. It was weathered, with the words *Fishing Widow* printed in fading letters. Bending down, I lifted the corner of the mat. Nothing. Searching under each of the flower pots on the porch, I finally found what I was looking for: a shiny, brass key. It turned easily in the lock, and the door opened as I pressed the handle down.

The house was dark and still—full of odd knick-knacks, shelves covered with shot glasses, flags, buttons, and statues. Shivering, I moved farther into the house. The heat wasn't turned on. My feet squeaked against the wood floors as I passed through the kitchen and a hallway into a bedroom. I found a closet full of clothes that must have belonged to the Fishing Widow. She was only one size larger than me. I grabbed the first turtleneck that didn't have a pattern. After stripping off my running clothes, I pushed my head through the hole. Sifting through several thick, plaid jackets and knit cardigans, I finally found a grey hoodie sweatshirt, then I took a pair of jeans from the bottom drawer of an antique dresser and put them on.

I picked up my running clothes off of the ground. After retrieving my phone out of the ditty bag, I balled up the clothes and shoved them in. Holding the lifeless phone in my hand, I couldn't resist the urge to turn it on. It had stayed dry, but I wondered how much battery I had left. It only took a few seconds for the Apple symbol to appear, followed by the message that indicated that it was searching for a signal.

The dialog box popped up, giving me the option to connect to a Wi-Fi signal. The network name was a long series of letters and numbers. If it wasn't password protected, I could connect.

No. If I connected, they could trace the signal to my phone. They would find me.

I stared at my home screen, my mind racing. I had no way to get to DC. Even if I did make it there, how would I find my father and Corey? The Instagram messages from Corey hadn't given me any clues that would help me find him or contact him safely.

Except Sheila.

I opened the screenshot I had taken of Sheila's contact information.

If you need immediate assistance, contact my administrative assistant, Sheila Linehan 555-367-2956.

The Fishing Widow seemed old-fashioned. I hadn't seen any trace of Omnibus technology and she didn't even have a password on her Wi-Fi. Would she still have a landline that I could use to call Sheila?

I searched the kitchen counters, rifling through knick-knacks and loose papers. The Fishing Widow's house was overflowing with memories.

They must have been comforting to her, but they made me feel crowded in, stifled. Her fridge was covered in pictures of her children. Two smiling toddlers, a young woman in a graduation cap, a man sitting on the hood of an old car holding a cake with the words *Just Happy Birthday -TJ* written on it.

Finally, I found a black telephone next to the toaster. I dialed the number from the email and waited. *Pick up, Sheila!* I prayed, after it began ringing. Was this even really her number? It rang three more times with no response. My heart sank, and I was about to touch the red button to disconnect when I heard a click on the other end.

"Hallo?" a raspy voice answered.

"Sheila?"

"Who is this?"

"It's Jace," I said.

"What?" I could hear her shuffling around, "Who is this?" Her voice was a bit angry now.

I turned my back and took a few steps away from the counter. "I can't stay on the phone. I'm on my way to you now. I just need to know the address."

"I'm hanging up. This isn't funny."

She couldn't hang up on me. I had to think of something that would let her know that it was really me. "I never thanked you for packing for me when I left for New York," I said, forcing my voice to slow down, "I wish you could have been there when I found your little gift. It was so…unexpected." It had been three years, but I knew she would remember the lingerie she had packed when I went to New York with Damien.

"Jace?" Her voice cracked slightly.

"I can't talk long," I said.

"Where are you?" she asked.

"I can't tell you right now. Just give me the address and I'll tell you everything tonight."

Silence on the other end. "Are you okay? What happened to you?"

"I'll explain when I get there," I repeated.

"I'm in Arlington. 2100 N. Pierce Street. The Park Georgetown apartments. Will you be able to find me?"

"I'll be fine." Turning back toward the counter, I scrawled the address on a sticky note from the Fishing Widow's drawer.

"So glad you'll be fine. This'll be my first encounter with *The Walking Dead*, so I'm not sure if I can say the same." I heard a click and the line went dead.

The easiest way to get to DC would be by car. The lights and heat in the house were off. It seemed like the Fishing Widow had been gone for at least a few days. Was it far-fetched to hope that she had left a car?

There was wooden wall mount next to the door in the laundry room with four boys fishing carved into it. The metal hooks on the end of their fishing poles held four sets of keys. One of the larger brass keys had *Ford* printed on it.

I opened the door to the garage. Feeling for the light switch, I found it just to the left of the door. Harsh florescent tube lights illuminated a rust-colored Ford Galaxie. The paint was in mint condition and the chrome sparkled. The license plate said 1966. This was a car that would be missed. This was a car that couldn't easily be replaced. My heart began to pound and my head felt like it was being split in two.

The lights flickered and I reached for the wall to steady myself. Tunnel vision. Darkness.

* * *

"Ouch!" He gently unwraps her fingers from around his pinky. "Bridget means strong," he says, laughing.

"I'm still not sure," I reply.

"Or should we just tell them to put Mija on the birth certificate?" He smiles and brushes her smooth head with a kiss before transferring her back to my chest.

It's hard to believe she was growing inside me, but I've seen the shapes of her elbows and knees before in almost the same position, upside down and under my skin.

"Bridget Minny..." he says. "Minny Bridget."

"I love both names," I say, "but don't you think…" My voice trails off.

"We should name her after someone who didn't die a tragic death?" He raises his thick eyebrows, but his eyes soften when I don't protest.

"Maybe you're right," Corey says. "Have I ever told you that my mom was named after her grandmother?"

I look up. "No."

"She died during World War II. They found her remains near Dachau."

"A concentration camp?"

He nods. "She was part of Nazi low-temperature medical experiments." He strokes the soft fuzz on the baby's cheek and whispers, "Submerged in cold water until she froze to death."

The baby whimpers and I cover her with my hands.

"Minny is such an unusual name," I say softly. "What does it mean?"

"It's Teutonic. It means 'loving memory.'" His hand covers mine on the baby's back.

"Memory," I repeat. "Hmmm."

* * *

My eyes came into focus, looking at the tires of the car. The warmth of the baby against my chest was gone. Corey's hand no longer covered mine. I wanted to go back to that reality.

The baby's name was Memory.

A thin layer of dust covered everything in the room. Turning my head slightly, I watched the particles above me float toward the ground. My fall had disturbed the smooth blanket of dust.

My arms were weak when I tried to push myself up. I'd fallen on my right side and my shoulder had struck the concrete. Using my opposite arm to compensate, I finally managed to get back on my feet. When the stinging subsided slightly, I rotated my shoulder. It wasn't broken, but I had bruised it.

I pulled the car door open with my left hand and slid into the driver's seat. When I turned the key, the engine rumbled explosively and the fuel gauge jumped to full.

"Thank you." My eyes blurred with tears. I only had a rough idea of where I was, but I knew which direction I needed to go to find my father. Pressing the garage door opener, I flipped the car into reverse and backed out.

After only a short drive on the rural road, I came to a stop where it intersected with a highway. An oversized yellow atlas sat on top of the insurance papers and registration in the glove box. The road was empty behind me and only a few cars passed by on the old highway. When I found the map I was looking for, I traced the route to the east. Fort Covington, NY to Washington DC was roughly 550 miles. I searched the dash board for a clock, soon realizing that my arms were blocking the small square, smack in the center of the steering wheel. 3:38 p.m. Depending on how fast this car would go, I could be in Washington before midnight.

Dropping the atlas into the seat next to me, I spun the wheel to the right and pulled on to the highway toward Alexandria Bay. I couldn't help thinking about Jean-Baptiste again and what he'd sacrificed to get me to this point.

The radio dial beckoned, urging me to find music loud enough to overpower my thoughts. The first metal preset button was tuned to talk radio. I touched another button before I understood what the host was talking about. I didn't want to hear anything about the world or politics or Victor Trent.

The song on the second preset button had a heavy drum beat that sounded almost tribal. Combined with a dissonant, repetitive guitar and the garbled voice of the male lead singer, it reminded me of Nirvana, but I'd never heard it before. He was chanting more than singing about snakebite entering his veins and demons dreaming. The bass vibrated through me, in combination with the steady rumble of the car engine. The lyrics, though unfamiliar, described my situation with deadly accuracy. I'd been running away from the safety of Claire and her protocols since I'd woken up in the hospital. And now I was running toward the snake that had bitten me.

"And I don't remember why I came…" My foot pressed down like a boulder against the accelerator. Would I ever escape him? He had woven his way into my past, present, and future, entangling me in his suffocating grip, restricting my movements, depriving me of my ability to choose. What made me think I had the power to stop Victor?

The lyrics and music finally trailed off and I lifted my foot until the car slowed back to the speed limit.

"That's Voodoo, by Godsmack," the announcer said. "You're listening to 99.9, The Buzz." The station went to a commercial, reminding me that much of the world's population could still be concerned about getting the best price on an oil change. When was the last time I worried about that?

Pressing the rest of the preset buttons, I found everything but a classic rock station. Disregarding the presets, I turned the dial manually until I heard the familiar strains of AC/DC's *Highway to Hell*.

Wearing a red, flannel men's shirt and knee-high socks, Sheila looked as punky as ever. Her hair had been chopped into a pixie cut and dyed platinum blonde.

"You look terrible! Come inside." She grabbed me by the shoulders, pulling me past her before closing the door and double locking it. When she turned around, she looked me over again, then wrapped me up in a suffocating hug.

"You have no idea how good it is to see you," I said.

"I'm not sure whether I want to kiss you or punch you in the face," she replied, letting go of me and shoving me against the wall. "You're supposed to be dead!"

The sight of her small living room, furnished with everything from our townhouse in St. Paul formed a lump in my throat, and I couldn't answer her. I'd made it. I dropped my ditty bag on one of the end tables, next to the beaded lamps.

"How long have you been working for him?"

"Working for who?" Her eyes widened.

"My father."

"Why would you think that? I just agreed to store all of your things until he was ready to come for them. I never thought it would take three years, and I certainly didn't expect you to come yourself."

"You believed that I died in the eruption on Mount Hood."

"What else was I supposed to believe? I went to your funeral." She plopped herself down on the worn cushion right in the center of the sofa.

"So you don't work for my father, but you know how to contact him since you're storing my things for him."

She shook her head. "No. I gave him my number, but I didn't think I needed his."

She looked genuinely confused. Maybe Sheila really didn't know anything about this whole mess, but Corey and my father had led me to her. There had to be a reason why.

"I know this is going to seem strange, but I need your help. I need you to help me contact my father. I need to see him."

"Are you in some kind of trouble?"

How could I even begin to explain the trouble I was in? I glanced down at Sheila's palms. I couldn't take chances.

"I need a glass of water before we can talk."

"With ice?" She budged forward on the couch slightly. "Or I have tea. I put on a pot just before you got here."

"It's not for me," I said. "It's for your hand."

"My hand?" She narrowed her eyes. "What are you talking about?"

I moved closer and lowered my voice. "Omnibus chips don't transmit a signal in water. I need you to submerge your hand before we say any more."

Sheila shook her head. "Not necessary."

"You'll understand when I tell you everything, but I can't until you do it."

"You're the one who doesn't understand," Sheila said, holding her palms up in front of my face. "I don't have an Omnibus chip."

"You don't have a chip?" I searched her palms, but it didn't matter. A chip wouldn't be detectable if she had one. "I thought they were mandatory here."

She dropped her palms on her lap and pushed back on the couch again. "I'm not a citizen. I'm a resident alien, and my visa is about to expire. Most people in my situation volunteer in, but I don't want one. I'm going back to Sydney at the end of the month."

She tucked her legs up and pulled a crocheted afghan around her. I hesitated, glancing at her palm again, before sitting in the vintage armchair.

"Before you explain how you became *The Walking Dead*," she said, "how did you get my new number? How did you find me?"

"Your Instagram account. You followed me. The pictures you posted with the monuments—"

"You found pictures of me on Instagram? How many?" She threw the blanket off.

"You didn't open an account?"

"I don't have time for that crap!" She leaned across the coffee table and took hold of my arm. "And you remember how I just told you I thought you were dead? Yeah, why would I wait to follow you until after you died?"

I wasn't sure what to say. I stared blankly at her until her gaze softened.

"What happened to you, Jace?"

"I don't really know where to start," I said. "I guess it makes sense to start with the week I met Corey Stein. Do you remember him? You asked me about a text from him? You said I was two-timing Brad Pitt?"

Sheila grunted, feigning disinterest. "I vaguely remember that."

"The morning I met him, something really weird happened to me. Remember how I always used to have déjà vu?"

She was leaning forward now, and she looked annoyed when I paused, but she didn't ask me what happened.

"It was really bad when I went for my run that morning. Then something flashed in my eyes, and I had a strange memory of myself swinging on a swing."

"Swinging on a swing?" She motioned for me to continue.

"It was like I was actually reliving a moment from my childhood, from the time when my father was stationed in Italy. It was very short, only a few seconds, then I was back on the path. The bushes were whipping back and forth like an animal had just run into them, then I saw something sitting in the grass."

"What did you see?"

"An Omnibus tablet." I began to describe the images I had discovered in the maintenance closet at Omnibus and my "coincidental" meeting with Corey in the park.

"Wait. You didn't know Corey was working for Omnibus until you met him in the park?"

"No. I didn't really know him at all before then. He was my neighbor at Stanford, but he deliberately avoided me. My father was paying him to protect me." I stared out her window at the dark sky, remembering Corey's confession.

Sheila cleared her throat. "Protect you from what?"

Pulling myself back into the room, I began filling in the details of what had happened from the time I found the tablet until the eruption on Mount Hood. "That was when Corey told me my father was paying him."

My explanation about what happened after the eruption was abbreviated. I hadn't processed everything fully, and I didn't know what to say about leaving Damien and the baby behind.

"So you had amnesia, and while you had amnesia, you married Brad Pitt and got pregnant with his baby. And then you got over the amnesia right when the baby was being born?"

"Yes." I acknowledged Sheila's recap of my story.

"But now you have partial amnesia again and you don't remember anything about the three years between the eruption and the birth of the baby."

"Yeah. It's like a completely different person was living inside my body. I don't remember anything."

"That's terrible. If I was pregnant with Brad Pitt's baby, I'd definitely want to remember. I mean, I'd want to remember *everything*."

My eyes fell to the floor, my cheeks burning.

Sheila wrinkled her nose. "Okay, so based on everything you've told me, the machine only works on children...and you. Why is that, do you think?"

"I have no idea."

"Weird. You said you told your father everything before you had your memories erased?"

"They weren't erased; they were just locked away somewhere. But they've been coming back a piece at a time. Claire wanted to try a procedure that would speed up the process, but when I found Corey's message that told me to not trust anyone I decided I had to find my father, and the message on his out of office assistant gave me your phone number. He led me to you."

Sheila sat up from her reclined position. "Hmm."

"What is it?" I asked.

"I'm just thinking about how I decided to come to the U.S. A scrap of paper on the bulletin board at University...do you think your father knew my favorite color was purple?"

She was kidding, but I didn't laugh. She was the one person in Minnesota that hadn't felt familiar. She hadn't seemed forced or fake. Her unusual friendship had seemed genuine. Was it all just a coincidence, or had my father purposely placed her in my life like he had with Corey?

"Why did you come to DC?" My voice finally cut through the painful silence.

"Promotion," she answered. "The tips are much bigger at the Oval Room than they were at Denny's."

"The Oval Room?"

"It's an upscale restaurant near the White House," she said. "Your father came in once."

"He did?"

She thought about it for a moment before answering, "Yeah, I almost didn't recognize him. He was out of uniform."

That was unusual. "But still dressed up?" I asked, my heart beginning to thump.

"In a suit," She confirmed.

"Do you remember what day it was?" I asked. Before Sheila even responded I knew what she would say. My father had always been a creature of habit. Growing up, he'd gone to confession every Saturday. It was the only time he left the house out of uniform. He would meet us at a nearby restaurant for lunch afterward.

"Saturday," she said, confirming my hope.

My shoulders relaxed, a feeling of relief washing over me. "Do you know if there is a Catholic church near the Oval Room?"

Sheila shrugged. "I'm not religious. Why? Do you think he was coming from church?"

"Maybe," I said, trying to hide my excitement. I was willing to bet there was a Catholic church somewhere nearby, and I could almost guarantee that my father went there every Saturday before eating at the Oval Room. "Isn't tomorrow Saturday? I mean today," I said, looking at the clock.

Sheila looked from me to the clock, then nodded. "You think he'll be able to help you piece this all together?"

"I hope so."

"You said that you've been able to retrieve some of the memories yourself. Have they just been coming back on their own?"

"Yes. I thought I'd figured out what might be triggering them, but I tried it and it didn't work. It seems pretty random. Sometimes they come in clusters, and sometimes I'll just get a short flash."

"What did you think was triggering them?"

"Dr. Watts mentioned sensory and chemical stimulation along with hypnosis. I thought that flashing lights might be the key. It seems like the memories have always come after a flash of light, starting with the one I had before I found the tablet. But I tried to trigger one in the metro by purposely looking at the lights in the tunnel, and nothing happened."

"Because you were missing the hypnosis piece?" Her voice made it a question, but her eyes seemed certain of the statement. "Dr. What's-His-Name said sensory and chemical stimulation and hypnosis? If you were programed to forget using hypnotic suggestion, perhaps there would have been something specific in the programing that would allow you to remember. It's usually a key word that's spoken, or a visual or emotional cue."

"Visual or emotional cue?" I stared blankly at her. "How do you know that?"

"University," she replied, smiling wryly. "Before the purple paper of destiny. Before I decided I wanted to take a break and go on a walkabout."

I laughed, but it was from embarrassment. In the three months I'd lived with Sheila, I'd never asked her what she was studying before she left Sydney. I'd been too busy avoiding her unsolicited advice and her chaotic lifestyle.

"I was almost finished with my thesis. 'The Link Between Functional Amnesia and Posthypnotic Amnesia: How the Prefrontal Cortex Suppresses Memory.'"

The room fell silent.

"So you're an expert on memory suppression through hypnosis?"

She shrugged her shoulders. "Funny coincidence."

Electricity ran through me, leaving the hair on the back of my neck standing on end. I couldn't ignore the reality that my father had hand selected the people in my life. She'd never laid me down on a couch, but Sheila had always had a way of knowing what my psychological pressure points were and which episodes of Dr. Phil addressed them. Maybe this was the reason I was supposed to come to her.

"Do you think you'd be able to reverse hypnotic memory suppression?"

"I could certainly take a stab at it."

"What about the chemical and sensory stimulation?"

"If you've noticed a pattern with lights, I think you could be right about that for the sensory part. The chemical part is a bit trickier. Usually doctors use a verbal cue to trigger memories. In your case, it sounds like they wanted something a little more complex."

"Like what?"

"Think about the episodes you've had. Were you relaxed? Or feeling some kind of common emotion?" Sheila asked.

I hadn't considered it before. Was there a common emotion that had preceded the memories? On the path at Battlecreek. At the library with Corey after the break in. On the way to New York with Damien, then again when he'd kissed me on the plane to Mount Hood. Strong emotions had been present each time.

"Since they've been coming back on their own, I'm guessing that your body's chemical reaction to emotional stimuli could be triggering the memories."

On the train when the lights in the tunnel had triggered a flash, I'd felt anxious about Claire and the Alliance. The train had been packed. I'd felt like I was suffocating. Hope and excitement had filled me when I'd tried to trigger another flashback right after that. Maybe that was why it hadn't worked.

"Anxiety," I realized.

Sheila moved her head up and down slowly. "Anxiety dumps cortisol into your bloodstream. That could do it." She paused for a few seconds, lost in her own thoughts.

I looked at the clock. It was 1:14 a.m.

"How long would it take to try it?"

"You want to try now?" Sheila frowned.

"I need to remember. The tablet showed a completely different reality than I'm remembering. I need to know what's going to happen at the Point of Origin."

"It will all depend on how we're able to replicate the stimuli. I can handle the flashing lights, but what about the anxiety? What are some of your triggers? Do you know how to make yourself anxious?"

"I think so." So many things had made me anxious before the eruption that it would have been hard to choose, but now it was much easier to pinpoint the source of my fears. "Yes. I can make myself anxious. Do you have a pair of OmniGlasses?"

"My boyfriend gave me some for Christmas, but I haven't opened them."

"Perfect." The pieces were falling together. I was finally going to see the whole puzzle.

She stood. "Why don't you take a shower. I'll find the glasses and see if I can dig up a box of your clothes. Not to be rude, but you look like my grandmother and smell like a tuna fish."

"Could I get something to eat first?" I asked. "I'm starving."

* * *

With blinds drawn and curtains closed, the living room was almost pitch black. Sheila turned on one of the lamps before strapping my wrists to the arm of the dining chair with a belt as I instructed. Then she tied my ankles to the legs of the chair with cooking twine. Beads of sweat were already forming on my forehead.

"I never saw this technique in any Clinical Hypnosis manual," Sheila said, "but if you think it'll help—"

"It will."

She stood up and pulled another dining room chair around the corner until it was only a few feet away from me. The OmniGlasses felt heavy on my face.

"Are you ready?"

Lifting my arms until the belts cut into my wrists, I cleared my throat. "Yes, I think so."

"I'm not exactly sure how this is going to work. I would usually instruct you during the relaxation process to follow my voice commands, but that would be counterproductive."

"You won't be able to see what I'm seeing. How will you know what's happening?"

"Hopefully this will be a little bit different than the episodes you've had before. If we keep talking while you're transitioning into a memory, you should be able to tell me what you're seeing."

My pulse pushed against the belts on my wrists. "I'm ready."

She touched the side of the glasses until the green light appeared in my peripheral vision. "They're on," I said. The news feed began scrolling, but I consciously blurred my eyes so I wouldn't focus on any of the words.

"Okay." Sheila pulled the chain on the lamp, bringing us into the darkness again. The glasses responded by decreasing in brightness.

"Mount Hood Eruption," I said, focusing my eyes as the search results loaded. Four videos on the left lens were ordered according to length. The right side displayed news articles. I focused on the longest video until it began to play, filling up the entire room.

A narrator's voice introduced the video. "On September 1, 2015, Mount Hood became the deadliest eruption in U.S. history. 112 people died in the 15-mile radius affected by the blast and lava flow."

The footage cut to a helicopter view of the rising ash cloud. Seeing the ash cloud was enough to start my heart racing, but the noise of the helicopter blades magnified the feeling of being transported back to that day on the mountain.

"Good," Sheila said softly. "Think about the clock ticking down. You're trapped. It's coming and no one can help you." The strobe light began flashing, causing the video on the lenses to adjust repeatedly to the light changes. Stabbing pain. Throbbing temples. Restricted breathing. Racing heart.

* * *

"Where are you? Can you tell me what you see?" Her voice comes from a faraway place inside my head.

I'm in our apartment. There are dirty dishes in the sink. The phone is ringing. I'm upset.

"Why are you upset?"

I just put the baby down for a nap, and now she's screaming again.

"Hello," I shout over the cries.

"Jace?" It's Corey. His voice triggers a downpour of tears. "Hello? Is everything okay?"

"Shhh..." I bounce Memory slowly to try to calm her.

"I can call you back," Corey says as soon as her crying slows down.

"No! Just give her a few seconds. I miss you."

I continue to rock her, and it's only another moment before she closes her eyes and starts sucking on her fist.

"How did it go today?" I ask.

He's silent for a second. "Technically, it's now classified, but since you knew about it before I guess I can tell you that it was successful."

"It worked?"

"Yes. But there were some unexpected results."

I sink down into the rocking chair slowly, balancing the phone between my shoulder and ear. "What do you mean?"

"We had to recalibrate the machine several times because the eruption was much bigger than we'd anticipated," he says, lowering his voice. "We expected a small delay from the time we sent the message on the radio to the time it was delivered on the other end..."

"The delay was longer than you expected?"

"No." He pauses.

"What happened? I thought you said it was successful."

"We thought it wasn't received at all...until we reviewed the lab security tapes." He pauses again. "The messages came in before we sent them."

"What?"

"Victor had the radio we took with us tuned to the frequency we were planning to broadcast on. The messages were received on that radio 24 hours before we sent them.

* * *

My eyes began to come back into focus. The glasses had gone dark. The room was still, and the flashing had stopped. I struggled against the belts on my arms, searching the room for Sheila. She wasn't sitting in the chair in front of me anymore.

"What's happening, Jace? Where are you now?" Her voice circled around from behind me.

"I'm here."

"What happened? You were talking to Corey. He was telling you about a successful experiment. Do you think it had to do with the Point of Origin?"

"I don't know where he was." I cleared my parched throat. "They were trying to send a message on the shortwave radio back to a radio in their laboratory."

"But something happened?"

"Yes," I said. "They discovered that the message was received before it was sent. They discovered what the machine could do by accident."

"But there were no clues about where he was?"

I shook my head.

Sheila picked up the strobe light again. "Well, at least we know how to get you there. Let's try again. This time, concentrate on my voice. I'll try to guide you to what we're looking for."

My headache was completely gone now, focus was sharp, and my breathing was steady.

"Activate," I said. The glasses lit up. "Victor Trent."

Before I finished speaking his name, search results began to appear in my left peripheral vision. Top news stories had Victor suddenly leaving summit meetings in New York Friday night. Where had he gone? Had he followed me to DC, or was he already on his way to the Point of Origin?

I looked at the sidebar again and found a video of Victor Trent's speech at the UN. As I focused on it, the video began to play. His thick voice. His shiny head. The deep lines on his cheeks.

The strobe light started flashing slowly, but gradually picked up until it matched the tempo of my heart. It felt like my head was being squeezed in a vice. Why did it have to hurt so much?

* * *

"Good. Jace, listen closely. You're looking for the Point of Origin. Let your mind take you there."

I'm standing outside of the laboratory.

"Look at the details, Jace. You know where the lab is. Let yourself remember."

Corey's inside. I can see him through the window on the door. I'm holding Memory's hand.

"Can I enter the code, Momma?"

I smile and lift her up to reach the flat glass panel. She enters the numbers and the door slides open.

"Daddy!" she calls.

He pulls his eyes away from the microscope and she runs to his embrace.

"How's my girl?" he asks.

"Good. We brought you a sandwich." She snatches the sack from my hands.

"Thank you," Corey kisses me while Memory starts unpacking his meal on the desk.

"How's it going?" I ask.

"Huge steps forward today. We have a theory about why some of the subjects respond better to the chemical copying."

"Oh really?"

"Yeah, take a look here." He leads me toward the microscope. "We found a genetic anomaly after several of our successful test subjects had pre-seizure symptoms right after the copy was made. All of them had a mutated strand in their DNA. The mutation looks very similar but not identical to a sequence they often see in epilepsy studies."

I look into the microscope to humor him, but I have a hard time focusing when he tries to point it out. The truth is that I'm getting tired of him spending every waking hour working on this. I'm tired of tucking Memory in every night alone, then falling asleep on the couch waiting for him.

"Almost bedtime, Memory. Kiss Daddy goodnight," I say. "What time are you coming home?"

"I have a few more things to finish, but it won't be late. I promise."

* * *

Sheila's apartment came crashing back.

"What happened? Talk to me." She spoke immediately after my eyes opened.

Epilepsy. I'd read several articles describing the relationship between déjà vu and temporal lobe epilepsy after my mom died and my déjà vu had become a daily occurrence. I'd known something was wrong with me, I'd always known it, but somehow she had kept me grounded. With her gone, I hadn't been able to repress my feelings of self-doubt. My anxiety had skyrocketed. I had started to look for answers on my own—part of me guiltily thinking that I should talk to my father about it, to seek his help, while the other part of me irrationally feared his disappointment.

"They were testing the memory copying process," I said. "They found a genetic anomaly. A mutated strand of DNA that made the process work for some of the adult candidates while it failed for others."

"No mention of the Point of Origin? Do you have any idea where the lab was located?"

I shook my head.

She raised her eyebrows. "How are you holding up? Are you up for another try?"

"Yes. I'm ready," I said. Time was running out. I needed the pieces to fit together. Looking at the search field in the glasses until it enlarged, I didn't let myself think about it before speaking the words, "Bridget Vega Car Crash."

The news stories began to fill the screen. Pictures of her mangled car next to a picture of my parents from the Naval Academy ball from several years before the accident. The obituary.

When the strobe light began flashing, the pain was so excruciating that my arms pulled up to try to touch my temples, but the belt buckle on the left side was twisted and the sharp end pierced my wrist. Electrified by the pain, I was frozen with my eyes wide open. All light disappeared as my pupils constricted, and Sheila vanished into the ring of darkness.

* * *

I look over my shoulder. The rough road doesn't seem to bother Memory at all. Her glossy curls hide most of her face, but I can see that she's smiling.

"What are you drawing?" I ask.

She shows me with an elfish expression. Black pools, yellow earth, and smoke rising toward a blue sky. The illustration is labeled "fumaroles."

"Ha-ha," Corey laughs, looking at the picture through the rearview mirror. "She'll be giving her kindergarten teacher spelling tests."

The car slows as we approach the parking lot. "This is it. You can put away the map," Corey says. Coverage has been spotty, and I haven't been able to use data at all on the deserted road.

I open the glove box and tuck the map back into the black and orange packet they gave us at the rental office.

"Reykjavík Rent a Car." Memory's little voice reads the words on the sticker.

"You're sure it's safe for us to come along?" I ask after we're already outside.

"I wouldn't bring you if I wasn't," Corey says. "I'm glad you're going to see it now. It might look completely different in a few weeks."

"Inside a cave doesn't sound like the safest place to be. What does an eruption like that do to the glacier? You said it's predicted to be bigger than the one five years ago?"

"Don't worry. It's not going to happen today," he assures me, kissing the top of my head.

An unnerving tingle runs through my entire body.

"How far back are you trying to send the signal this time?"

"We're trying to send back more than a signal."

* * *

My mind spun back to Sheila's apartment. She was holding the strobe light right by my face.

"Your mind is taking you there, Jace. You're in Iceland. Was the Point of Origin there too?" Sheila's voice was urgent. She was hovering over me. I felt like I was suffocating. I pulled my arms against the belts strapping me to the chair.

"I can't!" I said, gulping for breath. "Let me out. I need a break."

"You can do it!" She squeezed my arm. "You're running out of time. You have to, Jace!"

My heart was beating so hard that it caused excruciating pain. I didn't want to go back. I felt overwhelming dread about what I was going to see next. My mind was already taking me there, but I didn't want to go.

Sheila adjusted something on the lamp. The flashing light became frenzied.

Shrill ringing filled my ears.

* * *

The sun comes out from behind a cloud, turning the ice walls the color of a brilliant sapphire. I'm taking pictures near the entrance of the cave when the black sand and lava rock rumbles beneath my feet. It's strong enough that I lose my footing.

"Memory!" I call, looking beyond the researchers and equipment. Finally, I spot her. Several yards deeper in the cave, she's tossing pebbles in the small stream that flows down the center.

Corey and Victor look like they didn't even feel the tremor, but I'm in fight or flight mode. The uneasiness I was feeling earlier in the day has turned to full blown foreboding. I want to get out of here, but the hike was long and tricky. Corey wouldn't want me to go back to the car with Memory alone. And I can't ask him to take us back. He has work to do, and I'm the one who wanted to come along.

"Memory!" I call louder.

She hears me this time, waving just as the ground begins to tremble again. It continues for several seconds, shaking more violently as time goes on.

Equipment topples.

"Memory!" I struggle to keep upright as I make my way toward her. She isn't moving, she stands frozen in terror.

The ground continues to shake. Corey calls out for her too.

Before either of us can reach her, the column of dripping icicles above her cracks like thunder, falling to the earth.

* * *

Lights still flashing. Blackness and pain sucked me back in.

* * *

I punch in Corey's security code, then walk through the laboratory door when it slides open.

Victor sets his tablet aside. "Jace, my dear. Lovely to see you. How is she? Any change today?" He doesn't wait for me to answer. "What brings you here this evening?"

"I just wanted to say goodnight to Corey. Do you know where he is?"

Victor shakes his head. Reaching for my arm, he rubs it softly before giving it a firm squeeze. "He left a few hours ago. He'd been sitting at his desk all day, recomputing all of the data." He steps toward Corey's workstation with his hand still firmly on my arm. The computer screen sits dark, covered in blue sticky notes. "I thought he was heading to the hospital."

"I must have missed him. I went home to shower," I say, my voice trailing off. Corey has been distant since the accident. He practically lives at the lab.

"I hope you're taking care of yourself better than Corey is," he says. "I've been trying to tell him that working himself to death isn't going to change what happened."

"He blames himself."

"It's really too bad we don't have clearance to test the machine on a human subject this time."

I look up from the floor. "What do you mean?" I ask. "Why do you say that?"

"I'm sure we've all been thinking we'd like to go back to before that day and prevent it from happening."

"Has Corey been talking about that?" I think about the countless hours he's been spending at work. "Is it possible? What would be the risks?"

Victor shakes his head. "I shouldn't have mentioned it. We don't even begin to understand the risks, and we have no idea what the ramifications might be."

Victor looks sympathetic, watching my deflation.

"He was prepared to try it in spite of all that," he says. "He wants to fix this as much as you do. If his DNA had shown the genetic anomaly, I believe he would try it, with or without Omnibus approval."

* * *

Dressed all in black, I'm staring blankly at my reflection in a mirror. Heavy makeup doesn't hide the dark circles, the redness, my swollen eyelids. Two months. No brain activity. With the doctors giving us no hope, we had little choice. It was the merciful thing to do. She was wasting away to nothing. I knew she wasn't there. She hadn't been since the accident. But that didn't stop me from begging God to bring her back from wherever she was.

But when the plug was pulled, the lines went flat. She didn't revive. My prayers were in vain.

They want to close the casket, but I'm not ready. What if I forget what she looks like? I try to memorize her face. The painted on glow of her cheeks makes her look more like herself than she did in the hospital. But the perfect, glossy curls look like they're on a porcelain doll, not on my baby.

"It's time. Are you ready?" My father's warm voice encircles me, full of empathy, full of emotion.

"Do you think Mom is with her?" My voice is barely a hoarse whisper. "I mean, they never knew each other, but do you think they are together now?"

"Of course," my father answers, guiding me away from the casket, toward the pew where Corey is sitting.

"If you could bring her back, would you?" I ask. I'm not sure he hears the question at first.

"Your mother?"

"If you could go back to that night, if you could do it again, would you come home from work? Would you stay at the party? If you could go back and do it all again, would you?"

He stops walking a few yards short of the pew. "Why are you asking me this? We can't blame ourselves for living life, mija. This is not your fault. What happened to your mother is not my fault."

"I'm not blaming you. I'm not blaming anyone. It's a simple question, and not a rhetorical one. What if we had the power to help them? If you could go back and change that one night, would you?"

"No. 'Suffering is an ineradicable part of life.'" His hand grips mine with surprising force. "We make hundreds of decisions every day, but we can't control the outcome of those decisions. We can only control our intentions, then trust in a higher power to bring order out of the chaos."

"I'm sorry. I didn't mean to upset you," I say. trying to pull my hand away, but he won't let me.

"You have to let this go, mija. Do what you can to help the living. The dead don't need us as much as you think they do."

How can he be so cold? Maybe mom doesn't need him, but does he think he doesn't need her anymore?

"He's wrong. He's wrong..."

* * *

"He's wrong."

"Who's wrong?" Sheila asked. "Jace, can you hear me?" Maybe she had been talking to me the whole time, but I hadn't been able to hear her. Tears were streaming down my face.

191

"She died, Sheila. After an accident in an ice cave, she was in a coma for two months with zero brain activity. When we finally pulled the plug, she died."

"I'm so sorry." She looked away. "Where were you? You kept repeating that someone was wrong?"

"My father. I was at her funeral. I told him something about going back to change the past. He said that the dead didn't need us. He wanted me to focus on the future and let go of the past."

She took a deep breath and lifted her head up. "I'm sorry I wasn't able to direct you more. As soon as you transitioned again, you were completely non-responsive. You went limp like a dummy. Could you even hear my voice?"

"Only in the first few seconds," I said. "But don't apologize. You helped me get there. We know how to do it now."

She put her hand on the belt that strapped my right arm down. "We're getting so close to finding it." She squeezed my arm. "You said you were at her funeral?"

I nodded slowly.

"Did you see or hear anything about the Point of Origin?"

My head wouldn't stop throbbing. Sheila's hand felt heavy.

"I'm exhausted," I said, the sound of my voice cutting through the ringing in my ears. "Can you unstrap me now?"

Sheila looked disappointed but nodded. "You've been through a lot. But how are you going to beat Victor to the Point of Origin if you still don't know where it is?"

"It seemed like Corey was saying that the Point of Origin was where they sent the signal back the first time."

Sheila nodded. "Maybe if we keep looking, we'll get a clearer picture," she said calmly. "Do you want to try one more time?"

Exhaustion. It was too much. *I can't think straight.* "Can we try again in the morning?" I said.

Sheila nodded. "You're right. You need sleep." She began unbuckling and untying my restraints.

Rubbing my wrists when they were free, I watched Sheila dig through a linen closet for sheets and a blanket. My eyes darted around the apartment. The furniture from St. Paul was arranged exactly as it had been, down to the placement of the antique clock on the end table. And the hint of the incense Sheila had been burning was familiar too. I blinked hard, trying to push away the fishbowl feeling. It almost felt like déjà vu, except my spine wasn't tingling, and I had no idea what was coming next.

Sheila dropped a pillow and sheets into my arms. "Need anything else?" she asked with a yawn.

I shook my head. "Thank you."

"Don't worry," she said, "when your mind is fresh, we'll find what we're looking for."

When she disappeared into her bedroom, I spread the sheets and collapsed between them.

I'm *in a never-ending hallway. Little legs in Mary Jane's tap against hardwood floors. I hear the beeping. I'm at the door at the end of the hall. I listen for a moment before reaching for the knob. He isn't home. He can't be in there, but fear still churns low in my stomach.*

Finally, I lift my hand toward the knob. They're not my little girl hands anymore. A French manicure and the exquisite emerald cut diamond. My hands tremble, but I know I have to do it. The beeping gets louder. My finger touches the metal.

A jolt of electricity throws my entire body into a door on the opposite side of the hallway. I crash through, landing on the hard floor. I'm next to a crib.

I've woken the baby. Her mop of blonde curls and bright blue eyes peek over the rails. She's so beautiful. She holds both arms in the air. She wants me to pick her up, but I'm frozen on the floor. It begins to tremble slightly.

"Momma?" She reaches for me, opening and closing her chubby fingers frantically. The house groans. The ground shakes. The wood flooring begins to break apart at the seams and glowing lava seeps in from below.

"Momma!"

* * *

Blinding sunlight flooded in through the window. I sat up. *Sheila's window.* What time was it? I sat still, listening for a moment. The apartment was quiet, except for Sheila's rhythmic breathing. How much battery life would be left on my phone? Lifting the ditty bag from the end table, I opened it and began feeling around inside.

It only took a moment for my phone to turn on. 8:38 a.m. Only nine percent battery left. I turned off the screen and sat back against the pillow, crushed by anxiety. My mind immediately began replaying everything that had happened the night before. Dr. Watt's theory that the Point of Origin was where my memories had been sent back was wrong. I knew that now. It was where they had first discovered that the radio could send the signal through time. Victor had been trying to get the radio back since Claire took it into the World Trade Center. I had to make sure that my father knew that Claire hadn't destroyed it.

Time was running out. I needed to remember. I got up and went to the box of clothes that Sheila had dropped in the hallway, choosing black dress pants and a plain white button down shirt. As soon as I was dressed, I would wake Sheila up, and we could try again before we went to find my father's church.

It should have been a relief that my father had placed Sheila in my life to help me, but I had a nagging feeling of dread about what was going to happen today. So many people had already died helping me. I couldn't stand the idea that Sheila's "purple paper of destiny" had lured her into danger. She didn't work for my father. She wasn't being paid to do this. She hadn't consciously chosen to be part of the plan. Before last night, she didn't even know about any of it.

I turned my phone on and clicked on Instagram, wondering whether it had been Corey or my father who had posted the pictures of her. I had only skimmed through them when they didn't seem to be part of the message. I looked at the ten images again. They had been posted several weeks before the string of pictures from the fake accounts. They didn't have geotags, and the captions were as quirky as Sheila herself. Like the fourth picture, a close up of a bottle of Little Creatures Pale Ale. The caption read "Putting my feet up while putting down a tallie." I recognized the Australian brand she had kept stocked in our refrigerator.

Sheila didn't know anything about this account, but whoever had posted the pictures knew her very well. I continued scrolling. The others were pictures of her and Josh at iconic DC locations. Except for the sunglasses selfie smack in the middle, taken in Sheila's living room. I almost scrolled past but stopped cold.

Thin framed, mirrored glasses. I gripped my phone to keep it from falling onto the floor.

"Perks from work," the caption read. *OmniGlasses.*

Trust only Father. The message had been clear, but they must have meant for me to trust Sheila. Both my Father and Corey seemed to be telling me to. The Instagram account. The email from my father's office.

Corey had warned me not to trust anyone except my father, but he had followed Sheila's fake account and made it clear that she was in DC. Why would he do that?

Unless that was a warning, too.

My stomach tightened. How could I have completely ignored these? *I have to get out of here now.*

The muffled sound of Sheila's snoring felt like a ticking time bomb. I had to get out before she woke up.

With my back still pressed against the bathroom door, I assessed my options. It would be crazy to think that I could hide from Victor's all-seeing eye in this city. Since I left Montreal, I thought I'd been hiding from him, but I had played right into his plan. Sheila had been trying to pry the location of the Point of Origin out of me. I had to find my father before it was too late.

The Fishing Widow's Ford Galaxie was still sitting in the apartment complex parking lot. My father would go to confession at a church near the Oval Room today, I could almost guarantee it. But I needed to know which church.

Looking down at the picture of Josh and Sheila, now dimmed on my phone, a thought struck. If I was going to get to my father, maybe I needed to use the Alliance's tactics. Hide in plain sight. Use Victor's technology against him.

With trembling hands, I dropped the phone back in my ditty bag. Sheila's OmniGlasses sat on the end table where I'd left them last night. I put them in the bag. With everything in my arms, I crept to the front door, but stopped myself. Sheila couldn't know that I suspected her. If she was working for Victor, they were waiting for her to get the location of the Point of Origin from me. Global Security would only be a step behind me.

My eyes darted around the room. I had to make it look like I was leaving to protect her. That might buy me extra time. Setting my things by the front door, I quickly folded the sheets and stacked them on top of the pillow. In one of her kitchen junk drawers, I found a sticky note.

I think I know where to find my father, but I've put you in enough danger already. Go to Josh's place for a few days. I'll contact you to let you know I'm safe.

She was still snoring when I closed the apartment door.

* * *

From the bridge, the dull, brown water of the Potomac was smooth like a sheet of glass. This was the view of the monuments from the Reclamation Day image on the tablet. Had the Omnibus banners and flags been a lie too? Why had my father given the tablet to Corey? Had it been part of the plan?

With the murky water behind me, I remembered my plunge in the ice cold St. Lawrence almost twenty-four hours ago. Experiencing the pull of the current without knowing what surrounded me in the water had been terrifying, but I'd managed to move myself through it. I'd been able to drag myself to the shore. That was what I needed to do now, just keep moving.

I had to assume that Sheila and Global security would be tracking me. I wanted them to. Taking the glasses out of my ditty bag, I put them on.

I touched the side of the glasses and waited for the green light to appear. Expecting the scrolling feed, I was surprised when a driving mode notification flashed in my peripheral vision.

"Navigation to the Oval Room," I said.

The word *verbal* appeared above the word *visual.* I looked at *visual* until a street view map appeared, overlaying the street I was driving on, labeling businesses and intersections as I passed. If Sheila was awake, this should let her know what I was thinking.

Less than ten minutes later, I pulled into an underground parking garage next to the Oval Room. I parked the car, but left the motor running.

"Catholic churches near me," I said.

A map of downtown DC filled my vision with churches, represented by red circular pins with small white steeples in the center, dotting the map.

The location of the restaurant became a small white circle with a fork and spoon in the center, situated just across the street from Lafayette Square and the White House. I focused in on the three churches that were nearest to the Oval Room. The Basilica of the National Shrine of the Immaculate Conception, St. Patrick's, and St. Peter's on Capitol Hill.

Looking at pictures of each of them, St. Patrick's captured my attention. It was smaller than the other two and not overly ostentatious. I focused in on one of the pictures of the interior of the church, and it grew larger until it filled my view. Simple white ceilings with classic arches and symmetrical stained glass windows framed the sanctuary. The crucifix was cut out of the same color stone as the alter. My neck began to tingle. I had been in the church before.

I looked back at the minimized map and it filled the lenses again. As I followed the route from the Oval Room to St. Patrick's with my eyes, business names began to fill in on the grey buildings surrounding the church. It was directly across from Madame Tussauds, and Martin Luther King Library was just north of it. We'd been to both places when I came with my parents after high school graduation. My father had stopped in at St. Patrick's to light a candle.

Business names continued to populate the map. When the word *Omnibus* appeared, among other businesses, on the building across the street from the church, I jumped. I pulled the glasses away from my face. After pausing to steady my heartbeat, I put them back on, looking at the word long enough for the business information to come up. *Temporary headquarters for Omnibus Global Security.*

I closed my eyes, waiting for the map to disappear. Would my father go to church directly across the street from Omnibus headquarters?

"National Shrine of the Immaculate Conception," I said, opening my eyes again. Focusing in on images of the ornate church, I recognized it too, but I'd never been there. The exterior was almost as iconic as the Washington Monument. Searching through the images of the interior of the church, I became more and more certain that my father wouldn't choose its opulent beauty over the understated simplicity of St. Patrick's.

I searched the third church, St. Peter's, but disregarded it right away. It was the farthest of the three from the Oval Room. He was a practical man. He would choose a restaurant closer to his church.

"Navigation to the National Shrine of the Immaculate Conception," I said. I wasn't absolutely certain that my father would be at St. Patrick's for confession, but I was confident that he wouldn't be at the National Shrine. When I reached the National Shrine, I wouldn't have access to the OmniGlasses anymore, and I didn't want to search a route from the Shrine to St. Patrick's, so I quickly planned my own. I just needed to take Rhode Island Avenue back to 10th Street.

Traffic was slow on Rhode Island Avenue. The OmniGlasses suggested an alternate route to avoid the congestion. Winding my way through the streets, I saw protestors with signs walking along the sidewalks. I held my breath as I passed several Global Security men controlling a crowd that had gathered in Franklin Square.

I made it through the commotion and parked the Galaxie near the Basilica almost twenty minutes later. Cars and tour busses filled the parking lot. I left the OmniGlasses on as I approached the church but turned them off just before entering.

If Omnibus was monitoring my actions, they would think I was looking for my father here. Now I needed to find a place to get rid of the glasses, somewhere that would keep anyone pursuing me busy while I made my way to St. Patrick's.

Only a few steps inside, I saw a large group of tourists congregating near an information desk. The sign said that a tour would be starting at 11:00 a.m. Less than five minutes. And tours lasted around an hour. I scanned the group for backpacks, purses and strollers. The OmniGlasses were small enough that I could drop them almost anywhere.

A green duffle bag on the ground next to the information desk caught my eye. The couple standing next to it had their backs turned to me. I moved toward the desk, picking up a brochure before bending down. The flap on the side of the bag was Velcroed shut, but I was able to slide the glasses through the gap in the fabric.

Striding away from the desk, I didn't look back until just before I exited the church. The bag was still sitting on the floor, completely unattended. I waited near a pillar until the tour guide gathered the group together. The couple standing near the desk were the last to join the group, but the man stopped to pick up the bag on his way to the large circle of tourists. He slung it over his shoulder without examining it.

I knew how to get to St. Patrick's. Without the OmniGlasses, I was off the grid again. I would leave the Galaxie in the parking lot for the suits to find. Walking wasn't the quickest option, but it was the safest.

I hesitated outside the heavy, wood doors, eyeing the circular window above the entrance of the gothic, blue-grey brick church. The sun was directly overhead, warming everything below it, but a gust of wind chilled me.

What if I didn't find my father inside the church? What if he didn't want to see me at all?

Taking in a deep breath, I pulled the door open. Inside, I waited for my eyes to adjust to the dim, yellow lights. Several patrons sat in the pews, and a few tourists milled around, taking pictures. I picked up a Mass and sacrament schedule from a display near the door. Confession didn't start until 4:30. It was just before noon now, but if my father's habits hadn't changed, he wouldn't come during the regular confession hours. He would schedule a standing appointment with the priest. In Corpus Christi, his appointment had been set at 12:30, but he had usually come to the church at 12:15 to pray and light a candle in preparation.

The confessional was to the left of the entryway, with the baptistery just beyond. Standing against the wall, I listened intently for a few moments for the murmur of voices, but heard nothing.

Moving farther into the church, I passed two stone angels kneeling on either side of the aisle. They seemed to be watching me, wondering why I hadn't stopped to dip my fingers in the holy water they were offering me—why I hadn't made the sign of the cross. I paused, just a few paces beyond them. Turning back, I reached my hand toward the basin, but stopped myself. Was I even allowed to participate in the ritual? I'd never been baptized. My mother hadn't been religious, and my father had never tried to force his beliefs on me. He had simply lived his religion while I looked on, wishing I was good enough to join him.

But he hadn't been the one making me feel unworthy. My doubts and insecurities came from deep inside my own mind. Maybe I had associated those feelings with him because he was the only one who knew my secret.

I bit my lip and brushed my fingers across the surface of the cold water.

More than ever before in my life, I wanted my father's wisdom and help. I needed to see him and feel that connection we had in his office in Sigonella so many years ago. I was willing to do whatever he asked to fix this.

A tear dropped from my eye the moment my cold finger touched my forehead. I brought it slowly below my breast bone and touched either side of my heart. *Please, let him come.*

I made my way up the aisle toward the sanctuary. None of the patrons looked remotely like my father. An elderly couple were in the pew to my left, the man kneeling in prayer, while his wife read from a prayer book. Near the front of the church, a young woman sat alone.

When I reached the end of the aisle, I turned to the right and walked past the Irish saints on the columns, each with its own shrine of candles. My temples began to throb. The flickering of the candles and the faint smell of incense started the strange fishbowl feeling. *I can't draw attention to myself.* The headache was getting worse. The light was getting dimmer. I staggered over to the nearest saint and knelt down in front of the candles, gripping the armrest for support.

* * *

I avoid looking at the massive shards of ice still piled on the ground where she had stood playing.

"Why do I need to be strapped down?" I ask.

Victor finishes latching the buckle before answering. "Good question. We used the straps for the chimpanzees because we needed them to be calm and still. Since you understand that this is going to be painless, I could probably trust you without them."

"It's fine. Let's get on with it."

Victor adjusts his equipment for a few minutes before returning to my side.

"Everything is ready. The machine will activate when the harmonic tremors reach the correct frequency."

"Thank you for doing this," I tell him. "Thank you for taking the risk."

The ground begins to tremble. Victor nods and touches my shoulder.

"Since we've never calibrated the machine for humans, I've given you a little leeway to make sure your memories arrive long before the accident." Victor taps on the controls, checking the coordinates a second time. "We already discussed the importance of making as few changes as possible, but I advise you not to come here that day. Stay away from the Point of Origin completely. I know you don't want to tell Corey anything, but if you can't convince him to stay home, come to me.

* * *

The candles were only inches away from my hair when the church came back into focus. My forehead lay on the armrest and my arms hung limp at my sides. Pushing myself away from the flames, I tried to get to my feet, but the pounding in my head hadn't stopped yet. I braced myself, gripping the armrest while my eyes rose up from the feet of the statue, past the crucifix against her heart, to the stone face of St. Brigid.

The candles flickered when the door opened. I tried to see who had come in, but my eyes began to constrict. I was swallowed again in the darkness.

* * *

"And I told you to avoid making other changes?" Victor says.

I nod. "But you must understand my dilemma. Something went wrong with the coordinates."

"You'll forgive me if all of this sounds a bit far-fetched." He stands up from his desk. "Can I get you a drink?"

"I don't blame you if you don't believe me," I tell him. "But I hope you'll listen to what I have to say. You sent me back so that I could save my daughter, but somehow I've traveled far enough to save your son."

"Damien?"

"Yes. He's a Navy SEAL," I say. "Is he in Afghanistan yet?"

Victor sits down, nodding slowly.

"He's going to be in a helicopter crash. March 3rd."

* * *

My head felt like it had been struck with a hammer. The sights and smells of the church returned, but the pounding only dampened slightly. With every ounce of energy I had, I turned my head, listening for footsteps. Had my father come in?

Silence surrounded me. Had I imagined the door opening? My heart began beating out of control. What did it mean? I couldn't breathe. *Help me understand, Father.* Throbbing, pounding, burning eyes. I turned toward the flickering candles.

* * *

White room. Sheer curtains. Stone pedestal. Mirrors. The same room.

My mom steps up on the pedestal with me. Our faces are reflected infinitely.

"You look lovely," she says, placing the wreath of baby's breath and white lilies on my curls.

I barely recognize myself. I couldn't wear her dress like I had the first time, and I didn't even try on the one we picked out together before she died. This moment should be joyful. She's here. I saved her. But the dull pain in my chest prevents me from feeling anything.

The dress I'm wearing has long sleeves and a high neck. I wish it was as easy to hide what I know from Corey as it is to hide myself. How would he feel if he knew what I did?

"Are you ready?" mom asks. "It's time."

I take a deep breath and nod.

It's almost impossible to focus on Corey with Damien in the audience and Victor holding a corner of the Chuppah. It's meant to symbolize the new life and home Corey and I will build together, with all four sides open like doors, inviting our family and friends to be part of our future together. The first time, I didn't know who we were inviting in.

* * *

St. Brigid and the soaring ceiling were spinning above me. I was lying next to the shrine. How long had I been like this? I tried to turn my head to look for my father, but the pain was still paralyzing.

My eyes opened to the bottom of the pews. I couldn't move.

The candles flickered. Darkness enveloped me.

* * *

"Do you really think it's a good idea to come?" Corey asks again. "She's so tiny. I hate the idea of taking her on an airplane."

I hold Memory a little closer to my chest. Taking her to Iceland is the last thing I want to do, but things are advancing so quickly that I can't be sure of what Victor will do at the Point of Origin. I didn't consider what telling him would mean. I explained what the machine was capable of, and things have changed drastically because of it. He's kept Corey completely in the dark.

"Please," I beg.

"Is this another one of those 'strange feelings?'" he asks.

I look at the floor, stabbed by guilt. I hate lying to him.

"I'll see if I can arrange to get you on the same flight," he says. "Or better yet, maybe I can talk the Trents into flying us on their plane."

I cringe inwardly, but I put on a smile. Each time I see Victor it becomes more difficult to keep his secret, even though I know that

205

telling anyone would mean revealing mine. He told me to stay away from the Point of Origin before he sent me back, but he's made it impossible.

"Do you think they'd let me tag along when you go to Mýrdalsjökull?"

He looks surprised. "I didn't realize you were listening. You want to see the ice cave?"

I nod. "It looks amazing in the pictures I've seen online. I could take my camera."

He hesitates. "We'll see if we can get you up there for some of the preliminary testing. But I don't want you anywhere near Katla when it erupts."

* * *

The glass doors opened and closed. The splitting pain in my temples eased until I was able to open my eyes. Black patent leather shoes, shined to perfection, tapped against the floor, stopping in front of the holy water. His shoes.

He didn't continue down the aisle as I expected, but immediately retreated to the vestibule. He was going directly to the confessional booths. I pushed myself up from the floor, careful to avoid looking at the candles.

The same patrons sat facing the front of the church. The woman at the very front's face was illuminated by the pale blue glow of her phone. None of them had been disturbed by the noise of my fall. I trudged toward the double glass doors, thinking about each painful step before taking it. *In through the nose on a three count, out through the mouth.*

The vestibule was colder than the nave had been. My shoes clicked against the tile until I was at the entrance of the confessional area. I stood, listening to the low murmur of voices inside one of the booths. What was my father confessing? Slipping off my shoes, I tip-toed over to the wooden booth and pressed my ear against it.

"God, the Father of mercies, through the death and resurrection of his Son has reconciled the world to himself and sent the Holy Spirit among us for the forgiveness of sins; through the ministry of the Church, may God give you pardon and peace, and I absolve you from your sins in the name of the Father, and of the Son, and the Holy Spirit."

"Amen," My father's voice was strong and firm.

Was it possible that he'd finished confessing already? I ducked around the side of the booth and pressed my ear against the wood again.

"The Lord has freed you from sin. May he bring you safely to his kingdom in heaven. Glory to him forever," the priest concluded.

"Amen," my father repeated.

"Go in peace, my son."

I held my breath, waiting for my father to exit the booth, but it was the priest who left after a few moments of silence. His footsteps echoed through the vestibule, stopping outside the glass doors before he opened them and disappeared into the church.

Standing only a few feet away from the man I had come hundreds of miles to find, I couldn't make my feet carry me to him. It wasn't just a wooden box that separated us. Years of secrets. Was I right to have come to him now? I'd been wrong about Sheila. What if he didn't want me to come at all? Should I have followed his protocols and waited for him to answer Claire?

But it was too late. Whether it was part of his plan or not, I was standing here. Walking slowly to the priest's side of the confessional, I opened the door and slipped inside. I needed to know the rest of the plan we had made in his office.

"Who's there?" My father's shadow leaned toward the wooden lattice that separated us.

"Is it safe to talk to you here?" I asked breathlessly.

"Jace?"

I put my hand against the wood and my fingers through the holes. "I'm sorry. I know I'm breaking protocols, but I had to talk to you."

"Mija?" His voice trembled. "How did you get here? How did you know where to find me?"

"I sent you an email." My voice was shaky. I took a deep breath. "Your out of office assistant said to contact Sheila. She told me about the Oval Room."

"I don't have access to my old email anymore. I haven't used it in over a year." He leaned forward, pressing his face against the lattice. "Does Sheila know you're here?"

"She knows I'm looking for you, but I think I was able to buy us a little time," I said.

"How long have you been back?" he whispered. "Why didn't Claire contact me?"

I shook my head, trying to dispel the ringing in my ears. "They wanted me to tell them where the Point of Origin is. Sheila was trying to get the location too."

"Did you tell her?" my father asked.

"Sheila knows it's in Iceland, but I realized she was working for Victor before I knew the exact location."

"You know now?"

I nodded vigorously, then opened my mouth to tell him.

The shadow of his face turned away from the lattice.

"No, mija," he said. "Not here. It isn't safe."

"I still can't remember everything," I said, leaning desperately toward the small holes. "I know we made a plan in your office in Sigonella, but I can't remember what I'm supposed to do next."

He turned toward me again, but didn't speak.

"I remember the pictures in the binder," I said. "I remember you told me you had a friend who could help Claire disappear. We took the radio from Victor, but it hasn't stopped anything. I need to know what's next."

"I don't know what's next, mija. You didn't tell me." He put his face close enough to the lattice for me to see his brown eyes through the holes. "Foreknowledge destroyed your future once...that's why you had to forget."

"What else did I tell you?"

My father cleared his throat. "When you came to me, you gave me a list of key points that happened in your first life, before the time travel. We hoped that if we kept the events the same, things would go back to normal. I was supposed to guide you toward those events, but you wanted to choose for yourself."

"But we were wrong. Nothing is the same. Why didn't it work?"

"Victor knew too much."

"The signal?"

"It did more damage than we thought it would," he said, nodding. "Victor became CEO of Omnibus. He knew what was going to happen to Damien, and he saved him." He paused. "Corey almost committed to Yale instead of Stanford. You never would have met at all if I hadn't...." His voice trailed off.

"You hired him to protect me."

"I didn't know what else to do," he whispered.

"I was supposed to marry him." My mysterious neighbor, the brilliant guy in my English class—the ally that showed up just when I needed him in St. Paul had never been a stranger to me. We knew each other intimately.

But if he knew that marrying Corey was a key point, why had my father given the tablet to him? The father of the little girl missing from the pictures. *Jace Trent* on my name card. It seemed obvious to me that part of the tablet's purpose had been to make me believe Damien was the father of my child. My father knew that was a lie.

"It doesn't make sense. If we went to so much trouble to erase my memories, why did you give the tablet to Corey?"

My father shook his head. "I didn't give it to him. I still don't understand where it came from."

Thump, thump, thump. My heart beat painfully slow. "You didn't give the tablet to Corey with instructions to give it to me?" Why would Corey have lied about that?

"No. I knew something wasn't right when I visited you in St. Paul, but Corey was being evasive. He didn't say anything about the tablet. I could see that you wanted to talk to me at dinner that night, but you waited to tell me until Damien brought you to me in New York. By then it was too late. Corey and Victor were already gone. Mount Hood was one of the key points, and the three of you needed to be there."

"I have to find Corey," I said.

"Yes, mija." My father lifted his hand to the lattice. "I'll take you to him."

My father left the confessional booth a few minutes before me, instructing me to wait near the exit inside the Carroll Square garage, across the street from Madam Tussauds.

Blinding sunlight overhead washed out the colors of the symbol on the Omnibus building. The sidewalk, which had been nearly empty earlier, now swarmed with people coming toward the church. Mass would begin soon.

I'd only been standing near the exit for a moment when my father's black sedan came down the ramp.

"Get in the back seat, and stay down," my father said through the open window. I climbed in and he drove away slowly. "Corey lives in the Senate Square apartments. The doorman is on my payroll. He said that Corey left about twenty minutes ago wearing running clothes."

"You've been keeping tabs on him?"

"He came to me when he first showed up in the city. He told me his theory about the Point of Origin. We agreed that he should go to Victor to try to find out how much he knew about it."

"Have you talked to him since?"

"No." My father glanced in his rearview mirror before turning a corner. "We agreed that we would completely avoid contact, except in the case of an emergency."

My father didn't look up from the road. After a moment, his phone beeped on the center console, and he glanced down at it.

"What time did you leave the safe house yesterday morning?" he asked.

"I left with Mirlande around 5:30 a.m. When we realized we were compromised, Mirlande went back to warn the others."

"If the safe house was compromised, I should have been notified immediately," my father said. Pressing on the brakes, he brought the car to a stop at a red light. "Look here." He lifted his phone to show me a green grid on the black screen. "The chips are all still active inside the safe house, broadcasting white noise activity. Including yours." He touched the screen on one of the red blips, bringing up my profile. "The history shows you leaving the safe house as you said, but then returning home just over an hour later."

I reached for the phone, watching the red blips on the screen. My mind raced. The suits must have recovered my chip from the girls on the train. What about Mirlande's chip? Touching the other red dots one by one, I pulled up the profiles of the other inmates of the safe house until I found hers. Her history showed her leaving the house at the same time I did but returning almost two hours later. The first wave of suits must have reached the safe house before they'd found Mirlande's patch in the trash can at Berri-UQAM.

"Don't worry, mija," he said. "My men will find out what happened."

We turned onto a divided road that rose above the new construction buildings surrounding us. I watched the colorful mosaics on the walls pass. The blocky artwork on the stark, white walls was meant to draw attention away from the train tracks below, but it had the opposite effect for me.

Slowing as he approached the red brick buildings, my father turned into the underground parking garage. The doorman stepped out of the shadows, ready to show us to Corey's apartment.

* * *

"Is he expecting you?" the doorman asked, passing his palm in front of a sensor next to apartment number 504.

"No," my father replied.

He wasn't expecting us, but I knew what I expected from Corey. Easy, wordless communications. His calm, rational explanation—some logical reason why he had left me in Montreal. And his warm, steady arms around me. We would face whatever the future held for us together.

The light on the sensor changed from red to green, and the doorman entered a code on the number pad. The locks clicked and he turned the handle. It was still early afternoon, but the apartment was black. My father stepped past the doorman into the darkness, and I followed him.

"I don't think he's ever had a visitor," the doorman said, touching a button that illuminated the kitchen, filled with dark, cherry wood cabinets and black appliances. A tan mug with the tea bag still hanging over the side and a plate covered with egg yolk sat next to the kitchen sink. A bowl half-full of dog food on the floor next to the island was the only other visible evidence of habitation. The counters and table top were completely bare.

"When do you think he'll be back? How long are his runs, typically?" I asked, moving farther into the apartment.

"Hard to say," the doorman answered. "He's usually gone for a few hours on Saturday, but he left much later than usual today." The door clicked closed behind him, and he backed up against it, folding his arms across his chest. "Last time I checked he was still at the dog park."

The doorman reached inside his inner suit pocket and brought out a phone identical to my father's.

"It looks like he's headed this direction now." He paused, touching the screen. "13 minutes at his current pace."

Walking even farther away from the door, my eyes scanned the sparsely furnished apartment. The black leather sofa and arm chair in the modest size living room faced a flat screen television in the corner. No rugs. No coffee table. Bare walls. It was a step up from his apartments at Stanford and in St. Paul, but I was willing to bet he had decorated himself. I opened the refrigerator. A carton of milk, a dozen eggs, and five white takeout containers. I smiled, wondering if he had eaten directly from the boxes.

"You know him pretty well?" the doorman asked.

After some hesitation, I said, "I used to."

"He's definitely not the most interesting surveillance subject."

Closing the fridge, I looked back over my shoulder at the doorman. "Why's that?"

"He works and sleeps. He doesn't have human friends, and he doesn't divulge much to his dog." The doorman smiled at this statement, but the thought of Corey being all alone in DC was painful to me. Circumstance had isolated both of us. We'd been in such close proximity since freshman year. We should have been together, but an invisible barrier separated us.

I peered down the dark hallway. Did Corey always leave his apartment completely blacked out and closed off?

Running my hand along the black granite countertop, I approached the closed door to the left of the kitchen. "Is this his bedroom?"

"Office," the doorman replied. "Bathroom is on the right and the bedroom is at the end of the hall." He turned to my father. "Is there anything else you need from me, sir?"

My father shook his head. "Just let me know when he's close."

The doorman nodded, turning to leave.

The cold metal knob twisted easily in my hand, and the office door fell open. With heavy shades drawn, the desk in the corner was barely visible, but the shapes of the binders became distinct, strewn across the work surface, even before I touched the light panel near the door. Hundreds of sticky notes on the wall spanned the length of the desk. Yellow, pink, and blue squares were grouped in straight lines according to color, making a paper mosaic rainbow.

I touched one of the binders, but didn't open it, my attention captured instead by the notes on the wall.

October 26, 2001 Patriot Act signed; March 19, 2003 U.S. invades Iraq; November 4, 2008 Obama elected. The yellow sticky notes appeared to be political events.

The pink notes all involved Omnibus. *April 12, 2003 Omnibus acquisition of World Com; January 13, 2012 Omnibus signs defense contract to rebuild communication in Iraq; August 29, 2015 OmniNetwork goes live;*

September 25, 2002 Ruang; January 27, 2005 Manam; April 14, 2010 Eyjafjallajökull. The blue notes were all volcanic eruptions.

My father looked down at his phone. "Corey just entered the building."

Suddenly standing next to me, my father reached for a chord by the window and pulled, letting in blinding organic light. Immediately hunching over to cover my eyes, the pounding started in my temples.

With eyes constricting, head throbbing, and heart beating out of control, I took my hands off my eyes and braced myself for where the future and the past would take me.

* * *

"Are you sure this is the only way?" Corey asks. I haven't told him definitively what's going to happen to me, but he knows it's not safe, based on the glance he had at Victor's research results.

"You saw the messages he was sending himself. Look at what he's been able to do with just the one piece of information I gave him." I pause, closing my eyes against the bright lights above the gurney. "Imagine what he'll do with stock tips and eruption dates."

Corey nods his head. He finally understands why I pushed him toward accepting the position with Omnibus. I've told him everything.

"I still think I should try to reason with him," he says.

But we both know that it won't do any good. When I confronted Victor about the messages, he tried to persuade me to join him. He's been trying to get me to tell him what I know since the helicopter crashed.

"If this is going to work, he can't know that I've told you," I remind him. "And if you don't send me back now, Victor's going to."

"And if this doesn't work?" Corey says. "If you can't find the radio?"

"I'll tell my father. I'll give him the key points, and then I'll find your friend that can repress my memories."

"And if that doesn't work..." he prompts me.

"I'll reset everything," I promised him.

"Say the numbers again," Corey says calmly. "43 15 13 02."

I repeat the numbers back to him slowly, then I begin the second set. "43 03 07 11."

He steps away from the panel. His shoes strike against the clean white tile until he is at my side. His bright blue eyes smile reassuringly at me, and he touches my cheek softly. The sleeve of his lab coat brushes against my neck.

"You don't have to do this," he says, looking away from me.

"I know."

"I still love you," he says, pulling my eyes to his. "That's never going to change."

I close my eyes. Hearing him say it warms me. He still loves me, even after everything I've put him through. I desperately want to tell him that I still love him too, but I can't. It will hurt too much.

"Are you ready, Jace?"

* * *

"Mija?" My father called, shaking my shoulders gently. "Where is he?"

My father touched a button on his phone. "He's in the elevator."

Footsteps in the hall. Metal clinking. A bark followed by scratching and pawing. The room was still spinning slightly, but I staggered out of the office, toward the front door. I didn't care that my father was watching, I wanted to be swallowed up in Corey's arms.

"What is it, Shane?" Corey's muffled voice cut through the wooden door.

The dog barked again in response.

"Wait," my father whispered, taking hold of my arm.

I watched the knob, waiting for it to move. Shane's barking became incessant.

"Who's there?" Corey called. Finally, the latch clicked and the door burst open. Shane stopped barking as soon as he saw me. Tugging against his leash, he pulled Corey into the room. The leather slipped out of Corey's hands when he saw me.

"Jace," he breathed.

My father let go, and I rushed forward, throwing my arms around Corey's neck with tidal force. Holding my breath, I waited to feel him exhale. His arms engulfed me and I closed my eyes. *Safe*.

The door clicked closed behind us, the only indication of my father's exit.

With my cheek against Corey's chest, I drank in his familiar scent. Finally at home in the arms that fit me so perfectly, I wanted to stay forever with my eyes closed, pretending that the outside world didn't exist. But after only a few short seconds, his arms loosened on my back.

"Why did you come here?" he whispered, his lips pressed against the top of my head.

"Your message…the pocket watch…" I stammered. "You were right about the tablet and my father."

"None of that matters now." Exactly what I hoped to hear, his words melted me.

"You knew I'd come," I whispered. Turning my face upward, I expected to find his lips. Instead, his blazing eyes met mine.

"So did Victor." His hands moved from my back to my hips and he stepped backward, forcing distance between us.

"I know," I said, shaking my head, "Sheila tried to get the location of the Point of Origin from me, but I didn't tell her."

"No, Jace," he said. "You don't get it. He played you…just like he played me." He let go of me completely. "We have to get out of here." Turning his back, he walked into the office.

"What do you mean?" I said, following him. Shane's paws clicked against the floor behind me.

Corey began digging through the drawers in his desk. "He only had to get us to believe one lie. The rest was easy."

"The tablet?"

He threw a set of keys onto the desk. "And the numbers on the control panel. He knew we'd try to change them, but we didn't change anything."

I shook my head. "That doesn't make sense. He was trying to send me back to Sigonella. Changing the numbers stopped it from happening."

"That's what I thought, too." He picked up the trash can and started ripping sticky notes from the wall. "But it didn't happen like that. It couldn't have."

"I don't understand."

"Victor never intended to send your memories back to kindergarten from Mount Hood. The date of the Mount Hood eruption was recorded in his notebooks from Sigonella. He knew the date, time, and V.E.I."

I nodded, remembering Dr. Watts's explanation. "The Explosivity Index?"

"Right. The eruption wasn't powerful enough. Mount Hood was only a four. He would have needed an eruption with a V.E.I. of six to get you there."

"What are you saying?"

"I'm saying that he intended to send you forward the whole time."

The color drained from my face. "Why?"

"To give him what he needed."

"The location of the Point of Origin?"

He shook his head. "He needs that now, but that's not why he sent you forward."

"What does he want?" I grasped the desk to keep from falling.

Corey ripped the blue note with the Eyjafjallajökull eruption date from the wall, crumpling it before throwing it in the garbage.

"Prince Charming came after you and left Claire to deliver your little gift to Victor." His eyes connected with mine. "I never thought you'd leave it behind for me." Setting the trash can on the desk, he opened the top drawer and took out a matchbook.

"The radio?" I asked. Head pounding.

Shane wound around my legs, rubbing his shiny black coat against me. Corey struck a match and dropped it into the can. Whimpering, Shane retreated to the kitchen.

"No," Corey said. "Your baby."

"Abby…"

Flames lapping higher. Smoke choking me.

"She's what he's been missing," Corey said.

Darkness swallowed me.

* * *

My father has my drawings spread across his desk, interspersed with timelines he has drawn himself and filled in with the information that I have given him. I smile to myself looking at his crisp handwriting and the precision of his lines. I didn't tell him everything, just the pivotal points that Corey and I identified.

"You're sure this is all?" he asks me softly. He's not looking at me, he's rereading his notes. Checking the dates.

"Yes." I look them over again to make sure. September 11, 2001, September 1, 2015, my eyes scan to the very last page: April 2018. The Point of Origin.

He nods, finally looking up at me. His eyes are somber.

* * *

"Jace." Corey put his arm under my shoulder, calling me back softly. Lying awkwardly under the desk, I tried to make sense of what Corey told me before the flash. Victor had Abby. *She's what he's been missing.*

"Why does he need her?"

"Because you're unique. You have a genetic anomaly that allows your memories to travel. Most adults don't. Victor tried to splice your genes with his own, but his cells rejected them."

"Does Abby have it too?"

Corey nodded. "He thought combining Damien's genes with yours organically would solve the problem."

"He's going to try to send himself back at the Point of Origin," I realized.

"Yes," Corey said. "He sent the tablet back to make you think Damien was the baby's father. To make all of us think that."

"We have to stop him."

"What if he wants us to try to stop him? We don't know how much of this is his plan."

He was right, but I couldn't wrap my head around the possible consequences of letting Victor send himself back. "What will it mean for us if he's successful?"

"If his memories are sent back, his body will die at the Point of Origin," he said. "But he'll create another splinter, where he has full first-hand knowledge of the future instead of just disjointed messages. We don't fully understand how the splinters affect each other—"

The front door burst opened loudly, interrupting Corey's train of thought.

"Global Security is outside the building," my father called. "We have to go now."

Wrapping his arm around my waist, Corey lifted me off the ground. As soon as I was firmly on my feet he took my hand and pulled me toward the apartment door.

Corey and I followed my father to a service staircase.

My father paused, touching his earpiece. "Copy," he said. "On our way up"

We bounded up three flights of stairs and burst out onto the roof of the building. A long, narrow swimming pool filled up most of the rooftop patio, but a black helicopter was already trying to land on the wooden deck between two tables. The helicopter blades caught the umbrella on top of one of the tables and threw it violently over the railing. My father opened the door, and we ran toward it.

"Hurry!" My father yelled, but it was barely audible.

Corey pushed me through the door first. He climbed in after me, followed by my father. Before the door was closed, bullets showered the side of the helicopter. Looking out the window, I saw two Global Security men running toward the helicopter from an open elevator at the far end of the pool, shooting as they approached. Corey pulled me away from the window, covering my upper body with his. The helicopter jerked into the air, and turned sharply. Fewer bullets connected with the metal door as we sped away.

Corey uncovered me, several seconds after the noise of the bullets stopped completely. My father was already strapping himself into the seat across from us. He smiled wearily at me while Corey and I caught our breath and found our seat belts.

After my father reached for a headset above him, I found mine hanging just to the right of my chair. Corey put his on too.

"My men swept the safe house," my father said. "There were signs of a struggle. They found the bodies of Dr. Watts and Mr. King."

Blood rushed to my head, and it began to spin. *Dr. Watts. Randall. Dead.*

Corey sat forward against the seat belt. "What about Leon?" he asked.

My father shook his head. "He hasn't checked in yet."

"Victor has Claire and the baby," Corey told my father. "But Global Security is still searching for the others. One of them has the radio."

"He knows that the Point of Origin is in Iceland, but he doesn't know which volcano," my father said.

"Not yet, but he's already on his way there." Corey reached into his pocket and turned on the Omnibus phone he brought out. He touched the screen several times before handing it to me. The deep red text seemed to jump off the screen.

Jace,
We each have something the other wants. Let's meet soon.
She has my eyes. Lovely.

The helicopter followed the path of the winding Potomac away from the center of the city.

My father leaned forward, looking at his phone. "The Alliance fleet has mobilized. They're moving toward Iceland," he said.

"Without orders from you?" Corey asked.

"The Alliance seems to be operating independent of my protocols."

"Who's calling the shots?" Corey asked.

My father continued reading something before answering. "With Claire missing and Randall dead, I'm not sure. It could be anyone. I've ordered a meeting." My father tucked his phone into his inner suit pocket. "It's time to dispel any doubt about who created the Alliance."

A peninsula jutted out in the distance where the Potomac and another smaller river converged into the Chesapeake Bay. As we approached, the shapes of the perpendicular landing strips stood out, forming a cement crucifix that nearly touched the water on all three sides. The helicopter descended, beyond the foliage of the thick trees, coming to rest in front of two enormous hangars. The words United States Naval Test Pilot School spanned the front of the two buildings in blue lettering.

My father reached up to take off his headset, but stopped when another message flashed on his phone. "Damien and Mirlande are here in the city," he said.

"They got to Sheila's apartment a few hours ago." Corey nodded. "She had orders to hold them there until Jace was located."

"I'm sending in a team to extract them." My father finished typing a message, then opened the door, beckoning us to follow.

Outside the helicopter, my father led us toward the open hangar until a detail of Navy men in flight suits approached us. He halted and pulled his shoulders back, saluting just before they reached us.

"The Poseidon is ready, sir," the dark haired officer said, nodding toward a stone grey plane that was taxiing away from the other hangar.

"Good," my father replied. "We'll have two more joining us."

"Yes, sir," the officer said. "Your uniform is onboard."

My father saluted again, then motioned for us to follow him toward the plane. It looked similar in design and size to a Boeing 737, but the Naval plane only had one window on each side, positioned halfway between the wing and the cockpit.

Following my father up the stairs, Corey and I reached for the rail at the same time, but he pulled his hand away awkwardly as soon as it touched mine.

"I'm sorry," he muttered.

My already heavy spirits sunk even lower.

"I'll join you shortly," my father said when we were aboard. "The lieutenant will show you to your seats." The lieutenant motioned for us to follow him. On the right side of the plane, the sailors who had climbed aboard behind us took their places at five computer consoles. Three rows of blue upholstered seats were situated on the opposite side of a narrow aisle.

"Make yourselves comfortable," the lieutenant said.

I glanced at Corey before sliding into the second row, leaving the seat on the aisle empty for him. He frowned, glancing at his phone before dropping into the aisle seat on the row just in front of me.

"Your husband is on his way here," he said as soon as the lieutenant was out of earshot.

"My husband is already here," I answered softly, trying to push away the sting of his words.

"How much does he know?"

"He knows I was regaining my memories," I said. "And he knows I'm not the girl he married."

"I doubt he's accepted that," Corey said, still facing forward. "He won't let you go without a fight."

And yet, Corey had. Fighting to control my emotions, I shook my head and rubbed my temples softly.

"How much do *you* know?" I asked. "What did you see in the messages from the signal?"

"I know we were trying to contain our mistake by sending you back," he said. "Corey from the other splinter was doing everything he could on his end to protect you from Victor. Somehow, he sent hundreds of messages on the signal. They were like grains of sand that needed to be sifted through."

"The entries about Memory?"

He finally turned around in his seat. "Was that her name?"

I nodded. "We wanted to name her after your grandmother. The translation was my idea."

"Yes," he said. "Those were the messages that gave me hope."

The lump in my throat was painful.

"Where do we go from here?" I finally said. "What do we do next?"

"You're the one with the answers inside you." Corey said. "You're the fruitful meadow."

I took a deep breath, "I had a flash of memory where I told you that if the other options failed, I would reset everything."

"What were the other options?"

I shrugged. "Plan A was to find the radio. If I couldn't stop Victor from getting the messages, I was supposed to tell my father about the key points, then have my memories repressed. And if that didn't work, I was supposed to reset everything. We talked about that right before you had me repeat the numbers I gave you on Mount Hood, then sent me back."

"The numbers?" Corey asked. "Do you remember them?"

I nodded. "I looked up the references."

"The first one was John 15:13, right?"

"Yes. Something about love, and laying down your life for a friend."

"What was the other set of numbers?" Corey asked, barely waiting for me to finish my thought.

"43 03 07 11," I said, searching his eyes to see if he recognized it.

He shook his head. "John 3:7? I've never used that one. What does it say?"

"I don't remember exactly, but the 11th word was 'born,'" I said. "Something to the effect of 'you must be born again.'"

Corey's eyes widened.

"You understand what it means?" I asked.

He was silent, his face unreadable.

"What is it?"

"I think I understand," He said. "But we'll never be able to convince anyone that it's a good idea."

"You know how to reset everything?" I asked.

"Theoretically," he said. "The beta-endorphin released during the birth process causes a memory reset for the baby."

"So the plan was to send me back to my birth?" I said in a low voice.

I heard my father coming back from the front of the plane. He was talking to the lieutenant near the observation windows, but I couldn't see him yet.

"The eruption at the Point of Origin would be powerful enough to send your memories that far," Corey said.

I shuddered.

"But it wouldn't do any good if Victor sends himself back first," he continued.

"Even if we do reset everything, wouldn't our lives just happen the same way they did the first time?" I said. "You would still go to the Point of Origin. We would still move to Iceland. Memory would still ..." I closed my eyes, remembering the ice falling. "Wouldn't it just start another cycle of the same mess?"

"Another loop," Corey muttered. "It's possible. We have no way of knowing."

My father and the lieutenant turned toward us.

"What do you think Damien will be willing to do to get his baby back?" Corey asked.

I shrugged. I didn't want to think about how Damien would react to the news that his father had used him as a human test tube. That Abby was nothing more than a pawn to Victor. My throat constricted.

"He'll give Victor whatever he wants to get Abby back," I said. "He doesn't think it's our responsibility to save the world from his Father."

"What if Victor wants you?"

I couldn't answer. My father came back through the curtain, dressed in his blue uniform.

"Any word from the Alliance?" Corey asked, adding "Sir," after a short pause.

"The fleet isn't responding to my order to hold their positions." my father said. "We'll get a secure connection as soon as we're airborne."

"The helicopter is on approach, Admiral," one of the sailors across the aisle said, turning away from his console.

"Good," my father replied. "Prepare for departure as soon as they're aboard."

My father glanced at me before walking back up the aisle and out of my view. Turning toward the wall, I imagined Damien and Mirlande approaching the plane. What *would* Damien be willing to sacrifice to get Abby back? It didn't matter how much Damien knew or didn't know about the other life I had lived. This was his reality. He and Abby belonged here. I was the one who was out of place. I had to get her back for him, no matter the cost. Too many people had already been lost because of my decision to send my memories back.

With headsets on, the sailors couldn't hear the clicking their fingers made against the keyboards, but the sound filled up the cabin like hundreds of tiny feet marching into battle.

"Admiral," I finally heard Mirlande's voice. "It's so good to finally meet you."

"Sir." Damien's voice.

"I'm happy you're both safe," my father said.

My eyes darted from the curtain that blocked our view of the doorway, to the back of Corey's head, to the blue monitors across the aisle. The two worlds I had been living in—one that had been chosen for me, and the one that I had chosen—were about to come face to face. They were going to collide and I couldn't stop it. I gripped the armrests with sweaty palms and braced myself for impact.

"Have the others checked in yet?" Damien asked. "We left before they did."

After a momentary silence my father's voice was somber. "We have a lot to discuss. Follow me."

Mirlande came through the curtain first, still wearing her running clothes from yesterday. Slightly swollen lips, cut on the right corner and a purple bruise in the arch of her eyebrow hinted at her struggles since I left her standing on the metro platform in Montreal. Her eyes narrowed when she saw us. Crossing her arms over her chest, she stopped and stepped to the right, making way for Damien.

He came through the curtain in one long stride, his weary eyes immediately connecting with mine. My heart pushed painfully against my ribs and my breathing became shallow.

"You're here?" Damien asked. He glanced at Corey, but quickly returned his focus to me, his eyes brimming with relief. "How did you…" he breathed. Bumping Mirlande's shoulder as he passed, he continued up the aisle until he was next to me.

I stood, with my elbows locked against my sides and my hands clasped in front of me. "You have no idea," he whispered, reaching for my arm and pulling me against the sweat stained collar of his grey t-shirt. "…imagining what could be happening to you. I never want to feel that again."

"I'm sorry," I said. Keenly aware of Corey's stiff form sitting right in front of us, I pushed against Damien's chest, but he didn't loosen his hold on my waist.

My father came through the curtains, his lips set in a stern frown. "If everyone could have a seat. We need to get in the air."

Damien let go of me with one arm, but kept his other on my lower back.

"Sheila sent a string of messages to my father about her conversation with Jace last night," Damien said. "They think the Point of Origin is in Iceland." He searched my eyes.

"But he doesn't know which volcano," I said.

"He wants Jace to give him the exact location," Corey said.

My father bowed his head. "And reassurance that he won't be disturbed when he arrives there."

Damien's grip on my waist tightened. "Why would we give him either of those things?"

My father looked up but didn't speak. He shouldn't have to. It was my mistake. I had to confess it.

Turning to Damien with my heart beating hard, I opened my mouth. "He has Abby and Claire."

His brows came together and the color drained from his face. "How? They should have only been a few minutes behind us."

"We don't have an exact timetable," my father said, "but Global Security must have gotten there just after you left. They took Claire and the baby and shot Randall and Dr. Watts."

"What about Leon?" Mirlande asked.

"He's still unaccounted for." My father shook his head. "I'd hoped you would know."

Mirlande took a step backward. "Claire sent him back for the radio," she said. "Maybe he was still in the basement when Global Security came in."

"It's possible," my father said. "The radio was gone. The safe was empty."

"Leon must have it," Corey said.

We all turned our focus to Corey.

"If Victor had the radio, he would have told me."

"Because he tells his Chief Information Officer everything," Damien said. "Am I the only one who doesn't understand why Corey is here?" His hand dropped from my waist.

"Calm down, Damien. Corey has been acting on my orders," my father said. "When he came to me, we agreed that it would be in everyone's best interest if he convinced your father that he could be trusted. We needed to find out how much he knew about the Point of Origin, and what he was planning to do there."

"I thought we all understood what he's planning to do there," Damien said, looking at me. "Isn't it supposed to be where they sent Jace back?"

"If you were paying attention to the tablet, you'd realize that doesn't happen for another five years," Corey said.

"If *you* were paying attention to the tablet, you might have noticed that you and my father seemed to be working very closely together. For all we know you could have been part of the reason we were burying her."

I shook my head. "They didn't kill me, Damien. The images on the tablet were from the splinter I created when I traveled back the first time." I paused. "I sent myself back the second time. I was trying to fix my mistake."

My words were charged with electricity and Damien stepped backward.

"The second time?" he said. "You went back twice?"

I nodded. "Omnibus. Your father's power. All of this is my fault."

"I don't understand," Damien said, rubbing his temples.

"Corey and your father were working together to develop new communication technology for Omnibus," I said. "They accidentally discovered that they could send the signal back in time at the Point of Origin."

"So naturally, they decided to see if it worked on humans? How did we get involved in this whole mess?"

"You weren't involved," I said.

We were both silent, but I could feel the impact of my words sinking in. As much as Damien had advocated for living in the present, he had built his life around the lies on the tablet. He had been ignoring the clues that should have warned him that his reality would eventually collapse.

"Where was I when all of this was going on?" he asked.

"Do you remember the flash of memory I had in the gym the night before I left Montreal?"

Damien nodded.

"I couldn't tell you about the memory then because I still didn't understand what it all meant." I took a deep breath. "It was your funeral."

Damien stepped backward into the aisle as if I had physically pushed him.

"I'm going to have to insist that we all take a seat," my father said, reaching for my hand. Placing it on the inside of his elbow, he guided me between Damien and Corey to the front row of seats.

Mirlande bowed her head and moved into the row behind us. Corey and Damien each seemed to be waiting for the other to make a move.

Finally, Corey went directly to the third row without looking at Damien. Damien's eyes still demanded answers, but for now, my father was in command. When Damien finally sat down next to Mirlande, I took a deep breath, allowing myself to feel a small moment of relief.

The plane had only been in the air for a few minutes and was still climbing in altitude when one of the men at the computer consoles turned to my father.

"Your connections are ready sir."

My father nodded toward the curtain. "Put it on the screen."

"Yes, sir," the soldier said.

A white screen dropped silently from the bulkhead.

"What are you going to tell them?" I asked.

"As little as possible, but enough to convince them that they need to stand down until we have Abby and Claire back safely," my father said. I was nervous to see the faces who had expected me to give them answers.

Answers I had been unable to deliver the last time. Now that I had the location, looking them in the eye would be even more difficult.

The lights in the cabin dimmed slightly and faces began to appear in a grid on the screen.

"Veritas Omnia Vincit." My father's deep voice spoke the same words Claire had used to greet the Alliance, but only half of them uttered the same words in response.

"You must be aware that the safe house was compromised." Omar Rahal was the first to speak. "With Claire and Randall gone, protocols directed that we should appoint a new leader and await your instruction. You'll forgive me that I didn't expect to hear from you so soon, if at all."

"Yes, Mr. Rahal. I understand that our communication restrictions have been difficult." My father took a deep breath and sat forward on his chair as the plane began to level out. "Due to current circumstances, our protocols are dissolved, and any future Alliance action will be initiated upon my command alone."

Omar cleared his throat. "Yes…of course."

Some of the faces on the screen looked agitated.

"Sir," an unfamiliar voice said, "you should be aware that our fleet deployed a few hours ago." He was a younger man with light brown hair. "It's en route to Reykjavík."

My father frowned. "What is their ETA?"

"The submarines are about three hours out."

"Our intel suggests that Victor is on his way there," Omar said. "We believe he knows where the Point of Origin is."

Omar's eyes turned to me. My father was silent.

"Has Jace recovered her memories?" Omar persisted. "Does she know the location?"

My father straightened his posture. "This Alliance was formed to protect my daughter from anyone who might try to recover her memories to use them for their own purposes."

"We were also promised that Victor would pay for his crimes," Omar said.

"And he will," my father replied. "After tomorrow is safely behind us, we will deliver the evidence we've gathered to the United Nations. Victor will be tried and punished by the world."

Omar cleared his throat. "Doesn't it seem a bit risky to wait until tomorrow? If he knows where the Point of Origin is, it may be too late. As soon as our subs are in range, we should take him out."

"Killing Victor was never part of the plan." My father's voice remained level. "You should have understood that before you signed on."

The plane tilted hard to the left and I gripped my armrests to keep myself from leaning with it.

"Claire seemed to understand the plan differently," Omar said. "Protecting Jace has been, and will continue to be, a top priority, but we're also sworn to bring Victor to justice. We've waited long enough. As soon as we have a clear shot, we're going to take it. He's not going to make it to the Point of Origin alive."

"There's more at stake here than just Victor's life." Damien finally broke his silence. "He's holding my mother and daughter. Are you planning to bring them to justice too?"

Everyone was silent.

"Claire made it clear that there may come a time when we would be called upon to sacrifice," Omar said. "If she were here, Claire wouldn't hesitate to order us to proceed."

"She's crazy," Damien said. "You're all crazy. Fine if you want to sacrifice yourselves, but how can you justify making that choice for an innocent child?"

"You forget that Victor may have already chosen their fate, regardless of what we do," Omar said.

My father lifted both of his hands, facing one palm toward the screen and the other toward Damien. "Gentlemen, we're wasting time. We need to step back for a moment and weigh our options. We're not going to do anything rash that would risk losing more lives needlessly."

Omar looked away from the camera.

"Command the fleet to hold their current positions," my father said.

Omar turned back toward us. His eyes narrowed, then he slowly nodded his head.

"Sir," Omar said, "with all due respect, your plan didn't work. The stakes are higher now than they have ever been and the advantage that Jace's foreknowledge could give us is about to expire. We need to know the exact location of the Point of Origin."

"I'm ordering you to hold your position and wait for my command," my father growled.

Every muscle in my body tensed, waiting for Omar to answer.

"We feel that the Alliance is more effectively run as a democracy," Omar said, staring at my father directly, without flinching. "The fleet will continue to move on their current headings. When Victor arrives in Iceland, we will be waiting for him."

Omar paused, anticipating my father's reaction.

"Then I will consider this notice that our Alliance is terminated. If you proceed, I will use whatever force is necessary to preserve the lives of Claire and my granddaughter."

"Consider carefully, Admiral. Remember why we were chosen to join you. Offer us another solution. It would be a tragedy to have to focus our firepower on each other."

Omar's feed was cut. His square flashed, filled with blank, white light. I pinched my eyes closed.

The Alliance had just fallen apart—like everything I had ever touched. My father squeezed my hand as I opened my eyes. He didn't speak, but sitting next to me in calm silence, he was the only thing holding me together. I wanted to shrink, to become the little girl in the Mary-Janes again. To sit secure in his lap, hidden from the world with my face against his uniform.

"What are we going to do?" I whispered.

"I don't know, mija. I've spent the past twenty years trying to give you the life you had before." He squeezed my arm gently. "And when I realized that Victor wouldn't allow you to have it, I did my best to protect you from him."

"I didn't mean for any of this to happen. I just wanted my baby back."

"I understand." His voice was almost inaudible.

He did understand. When my adult consciousness had been poured into his five-year-old daughter's mind, he had lost her too. Her simple innocence had been replaced by my years of accumulated insecurities, inhibitions, and compulsive habits.

"I was never the same, was I?" I said. "Even after the memories were repressed."

He shook his head. "You've always been you, mija."

Damien shifted in the seat behind me. I didn't look back to confirm, but I could feel him leaning forward, trying to hear our conversation through the crack between the seats. How could I blame him? He was suffering a similar loss. The other Jace had been like a child. He'd taken care of her and loved her until my shifting consciousness had overridden her memories. She was gone forever.

And now Victor and the Alliance threatened to take Abby from him permanently too. He didn't deserve any of this.

I leaned over and rested my head against my father's shoulder. I had to get them back. Damien, Claire, Mirlande, and Leon—anyone who had been serving the plan—deserved to be set free of it.

"Victor wants the location of the Point of Origin in exchange for Claire and Abby," I said.

My father shook his head. "Even if we were to give it to him, I don't believe he would release Claire and Abby without some guarantee that the Alliance isn't going to launch an attack."

My father was right. Victor wouldn't hesitate to take Claire and Abby with him to the Point of Origin. He would send himself back and leave them behind, just like he had left everyone at his laboratory on Mount Hood. I couldn't let them die like that. I had to do something.

"We can't let Victor kill them," I said, feeling completely hopeless. "I know where the Point of Origin is, but the plans we made didn't account for this."

"No." My father's voice was thick with emotion. "We'll land in Reykjavík in four hours. Maybe it's time we made a new plan, mija. Something the Alliance can stand behind."

I nodded, a chill running down my spine.

"Maybe it's time you told me where the Point of Origin is."

* * *

"The seismic readings are much stronger around Hekla. The Meteorological Office upgraded Hekla's status to red this morning," Corey said, looking at the computer screen. "You're sure it's Katla?"

I nodded, examining the map of the glacier. I recognized the parking lot where Corey and I had left the car when we went to the ice cave. "I'm sure."

"He's sending a car to meet the plane. They'll be there when we land," Corey said, looking at the message that had come in on his phone.

"To take us where?" Damien asked.

Corey glanced at his phone again. "Not us. He wants Jace to come alone."

My father and Damien both shook their heads.

"Absolutely not," my father said. "Jace has briefed me on the location. I can make the trade."

"Do you really think that's wise, sir?" Corey said. "You need to be here, making sure the Alliance doesn't lock their targets on Victor until we have everyone back safely."

"He's right," Damien said. "I should be the one to go."

"Let me see that," Mirlande said, snatching Corey's phone. "What makes any of you think he'll be willing to negotiate? He said he wants Jace. He knows that what he has is worth much more to us than what he's asking for. We're in no position to be making demands."

Silence. Everyone knew she was right.

"We have no choice," I said.

"Without a chip, we won't be able to monitor Jace," Damien said. "I don't trust that my father will keep his word."

"But you can trust that Jace will get Abby back for you," Mirlande said. "I think she's proven that she's capable of thinking on her feet."

We were all watching my father, waiting for him to give us the answer when a second message from Victor came through. Corey showed us his phone screen.

On second thought, Ms. Magloire should come along. I have someone here who is anxious to see her.

"He has Leon," Mirlande said, her tone flat.

"That means he has the radio too," Corey added.

"All of the Alliance's sources inside Omnibus have been cut off," my father said. "Victor's chip isn't broadcasting, and they still haven't been able to pinpoint his location."

"If we're going to keep the Alliance at bay long enough to get Claire and the baby back, we're going to have to promise them what they want," Corey said.

My father looked at me. "I can't be the one to make that decision," he said. "When you came to me, I promised you that I wouldn't use the information you gave me to play God. As many times as I've wanted to kill Victor because of what he has done, I've kept my promise."

"None of that matters anymore," I realized. "Killing him is the only way we're going to stop this."

Corey stood up from the table. "I know how we can do it," he said. He reached into his pocket and brought out the shiny silver pocket watch.

"Your father's watch?" I said.

"Victor's men will scan you for tracking devices before they take you to him, but this technology is so antiquated, they wouldn't be looking for it." He moved across the table to show me. "When you twist the face, the components come together to activate a homing signal. It transmits on a frequency that shouldn't be monitored by Global Security."

I nodded. "If I activate it and plant it on Victor after I tell him the location, the Alliance can wait until he's on his way and take him out before he even reaches the glacier."

TWO of Victor's suits were waiting on the runway in a red Jeep Renegade when we landed in the fog and snow. Mirlande and I descended the steps wearing oversized, blue camouflage parkas. The suits scanned us with their OmniGlasses, then patted both of us down. When the one searching me felt the watch in my pocket, I reached in without hesitating and handed it to him. He inspected it, touching the side of his OmniGlasses before handing it back and opening the doors.

I tried to relax, but driving through the streets of Reykjavík, with its colorful houses, felt intensely familiar. Corey and I had lived here with Memory before all of this started. Would I recognize the small, white row house with the blue roof if we passed it? I kept my hand tightly wrapped around the watch in my pocket.

Soon, the city disappeared behind us. Heading east on a mostly empty highway that followed the shoreline, we drove in silence through thick fog that covered the barren countryside. Mirlande kept her eyes focused ahead. The suits only spoke to each other occasionally, and their casual conversation wasn't in English.

Eventually, the terrain changed from black dirt on either side of the road to uneven lava beds. The volcanic rock was covered in patchy, dull, brown moss. As we rounded a corner, the mist cleared slightly and I could see smokestacks in the distance, adding their own steam to the humid air.

The suit who was driving slowed down as we passed a sign pointing us in the direction of the Blue Lagoon. The glass and brick resort materialized, almost like a mirage. The Jeep slowed, following the curve of the path leading up to the entrance through the nearly empty parking lot.

Mirlande and I exchanged a confused look. This wasn't where I would have expected to find Victor—with the eruption at the Point of Origin only hours away and the Alliance trying to hunt him down.

Mirlande and I followed the suits through the wood framed glass doors side by side. Dim natural light filled the interior of the spa. Stone floors and concrete walls amplified the sound of soft guitar music and trickling water. My eyes shifted left and right, looking at the empty conversation areas. I shivered.

I glanced over my shoulder as we walked away from the empty reception desk down a long corridor that ended at a fogged over glass door. The air was thick with steam and the smell of the sulfur rich mineral water.

"I don't like this," Mirlande whispered. "Where is everyone?"

When the suits reached the end of the hallway, one of them opened the glass door and waited for us to pass through.

Stepping outside, I was encircled by the biting cold. The glass door closed behind us. A series of paths and bridges framed the banks of the milky blue water. Empty chairs and tables on grey bricks near the water's edge hinted at the crowds that should have been bathing here.

Mirlande and I looked at each other.

"Where is he?" I whispered.

She shrugged.

We had been standing in the cold for almost a full minute before Victor Trent's shoulders and head appeared through the mist. He came toward us from the center of the lagoon. His face looked ghostly pale. It wasn't until he came closer that I realized it was covered with a thin layer of grey mud. Holding a bright green drink just above the water, he clinked the ice cubes against the glass and took a sip.

"Jace," he said, "I'm glad you made it. Have you been waiting long? I lost track of the time."

"Where are Claire and Abby?" I asked.

"We haven't seen each other in three years," Victor said. "Don't you think we should take a few minutes to catch up before we get down to business?"

"Why don't you stop pretending, Victor," Mirlande said. "We all know we're not here to chit-chat. Just give us Claire and the baby and Jace will give you the location."

"But aren't you even a little curious about why I brought you here? You can't tell me that this was a stop you were expecting to make on your tour of the Golden Circle today."

Mirlande looked at me. "Do you care why he brought us here?"

I shook my head. "I just want to get what we came for and leave."

Victor set his drink on the edge of the walkway. Reaching inside a wooden box behind him, he lifted out a ladle filled with mud. "Don't you find it interesting that nature's destructive forces leave behind everything needed to restore and rebuild?" he said. "People have understood the health benefits and anti-aging properties found in natural hot springs for centuries."

Mirlande glanced at me. "Is he joking?"

I shrugged.

He dipped his hands in the water and began washing away his mask. "Of course, this lagoon is man-made, fed by the runoff waters from the geothermal power plant, but the benefits are the same."

Nothing Victor was saying demanded a response, but my uneasiness built with each word he spoke.

"I often think about how the earth's powers have always been here, waiting to be harnessed, and I wonder where we would be now if they had been harnessed sooner."

Splashing his face with water one more time before wading to the edge, Victor stepped out.

"Can I offer either of you a drink?" Victor asked, pulling a thick white bathrobe over his shoulders.

"I don't want a drink," I said. "I want to see my baby."

He raised his eyebrows, seeming to sense that this was the first time I had called her that. I looked away.

"You're right. We should go in," Victor said. "It's much too cold out here for the baby."

I was silent, looking around at the volcanic rock, covered in soft grey silica. The lagoon was as unnatural as the glass and concrete resort built around it, and Victor belonged here, alone, covered in the mud that he believed would keep him young.

* * *

The suits were waiting just inside the door. They escorted us back to the lobby, while Victor disappeared into a dressing room to change.

"I have a bad feeling about this," Mirlande said. "He isn't in any hurry to get the location from you. Something is off."

"Try to relax," I said. "He's doing all of this to make us feel uncomfortable."

Mirlande shook her head. "I don't know, J. I still don't like it."

Victor rejoined us a few minutes later.

"Now that you've had your bath, are you finally ready to make the exchange?" Mirlande asked.

"I think we all realize that making the exchange poses a problem for me."

I stiffened. "We followed your instructions," I said. "We're here to give you what you asked for."

"Yes," Victor said, "But there is the small problem of your Alliance's fleet."

Mirlande's eyes widened.

"They don't know the location," I said. "And my father has ordered them to stand down."

"You'll forgive me if I don't trust that your father is in command of the Alliance." Victor said. "Claire made it clear that they have their own agenda."

"Where is Claire?" Mirlande asked through gritted teeth.

"I'm sure they're monitoring your movements. They *are* sworn to protect you, aren't they?" he said.

"You wanted them to track us here?" Mirlande said.

"I've always intended to take you with me, Jace," he said, approaching us slowly. "Even with as much as you've resisted, and tried to make it difficult, you are the reason I'm finally going to be able to travel."

"She's not going anywhere with you," Mirlande said.

Victor kept his cold blue eyes fixed on mine. He took a step closer and touched my upper arm. "I think she'll be persuaded."

I shuddered, instantly reminded of Victor's promise on Mount Hood that he would always be several steps ahead of my weak attempts to stop him. Raising his other arm slowly, he motioned for the suit who was standing near the entrance to open it. Mirlande and I both moved toward the doors. A black SUV with tinted windows was parked just outside. An armed Global Security officer pulled Leon out of the back seat.

Another armed suit waited while Claire stepped down, but his gun was pointed at the ground. She lifted the infant seat out and followed Leon up the path. The contrast between Claire and Leon's appearance was stark. Arms restrained behind his back, his clothes were torn and bloodstained. He wasn't even wearing a jacket. Claire was dressed in a fitted white ski parka with matching snow pants.

"Leon," Mirlande said, throwing her arms around his neck. The suit who was holding on to his arm didn't let go.

"Jace," Claire said, looking into my eyes for a moment before casting hers down to the stone floor. She took several steps toward me, then held Abby's seat out for me to take. Abby slept peacefully under soft white blankets. I wanted to take her out of the seat and hold her against me. I wanted to tell her how sorry I was, but I couldn't. Victor stood watching with a calculating smile, waiting for just the right moment to tell me what he had in store for all of us.

"I wish we had more time to spend together," Victor said, "but your Admiral will be waiting. I'm sure he's anxious to meet our granddaughter."

Her face blazing, Claire looked up from the floor. "She never should have been ours." Her eyes flashed. "Yet another thing you've stolen that eventually you'll have to pay for."

Victor waved off her comment. "I never intended to keep her, and I'm deeply grateful for what she's given me. It's unfortunate that she'll probably never understand the importance of who she is." He took a few steps toward me and pretended to admire Abby, reaching into the seat and almost touching her forehead. "As a show of good faith, I think we should send her to the Admiral now. What do you think Jace?"

I instinctively held the baby's seat closer. Mirlande made eye contact with me. We were both thinking about Corey's watch in my pocket. The plan was to activate the watch and send it with Victor so the Alliance could take him down before he reached the Point of Origin. If Victor took me with him, I couldn't activate the beacon unless I was willing to die with him.

"I'll tell you where the Point of Origin is," I said. "I'll go with you. But I won't do anything until I see a message from Corey confirming that everyone is safely back with my father."

"We think alike," Victor said, taking his hand away without ever making contact with the baby's head. "Let the pilots know we're coming."

Victor looked at one of the suits, who touched the side of his glasses and said something in Icelandic. The suit waved his arm, indicating that we should follow him through the doors. With his weapon held tight against his chest, he led us around the side of the building. The noise of the helicopters overwhelmed me long before I saw them, scattered across the otherwise empty parking lot. Seven of them. They were various models, different shapes and sizes, but all black.

"How confident are you in your father's ability to control the Alliance?" Victor yelled as we approached one of the choppers. "You should probably say your goodbyes, just in case."

I stopped several yards away from the helicopter, still holding Abby's seat over my forearm. Victor continued on, watching the suits push Leon aboard. Mirlande stopped next to me.

"I'm coming with you, J," she said, talking right next to my ear.

"You can't," I said. "I need you to make sure that Abby gets back to Damien safely."

She looked down at the sleeping baby. "What are you going to do, J? You can't activate the watch if you're still with Victor."

I nodded. "The Alliance is waiting for my signal. Tell them to go ahead with the plan. I'll activate the watch, then get as far away from him as possible."

Victor was several yards away, and the noise of the helicopters was deafening, but he smiled as if he'd heard every word I said.

"Are you sure you can do this?" Mirlande asked, her eyes glistening. Mine filled with tears too.

"Go!" I said. "I know how to run, and you taught me how to fight. I'll know what to do."

She threw her arms around me, squeezing me tight.

"Take care of her," I said, kissing Abby's forehead before handing the seat to Mirlande.

"I'll keep her safe until you get back."

"Damien, too," I shouted, but Mirlande had already turned to go. She climbed aboard the helicopter with Leon.

Claire stood several feet away from the helicopter, shouting something at Victor over the roar of the blades. Finally, she turned away from him, stepping toward the open helicopter door, but Victor took hold of her arm. The suit standing near the door nodded and closed it.

"What are you doing?" I yelled, coming at Victor. "I told you I'm not giving you the location until I know they're safe with my father. All of them."

"I'm afraid that isn't going to work with what I have planned." Victor said. "We'll need to have Claire with us to ensure that you suppress your need to self-sacrifice."

The helicopter lifted into the air, and Mirlande and Abby disappeared into the clouds. Claire watched them with tears streaming down her face. Victor didn't wait until they were out of sight to turn toward the largest of the six remaining helicopters.

"I'm sorry, Jace," Claire cried. "All of this is my fault."

I shook my head, the words my father had said to me at Memory's funeral coming to my mind. *We can't blame ourselves for living life*. I opened my mouth to tell her, but the suit standing behind us nudged me forward with the butt of his gun.

Victor was strapped into his seat with a headset on, looking at a computer console, when we boarded the wide helicopter. Six seats faced each other and Victor was nearest the opposite door. I took the seat farthest away from him. Claire sat directly across from me, tears still rolling down her cheeks, and two suits filled the seats in the middle.

One by one, we watched the helicopters take off, heading in different directions. Claire put on her headset and motioned for me to do the same. Her eyes looked wild and desperate. I put the headset on slowly, hesitant to hear what she was going to say. Clair didn't know about the new plan, and I couldn't tell her.

"You can't give him the location, Jace," she said, looking directly at me, but fully aware that Victor could hear her as clearly as I could.

I shook my head vigorously, hoping to silence her.

"He wasn't looking for the radio," she continued. "He doesn't need it anymore."

"I know," I said.

"We can't let him go back. He'll be undefeatable. His power will destroy all of us."

"My foreknowledge will *save* all of you," Victor said, his voice unreasonably calm.

"You'll use it for your personal gain," Claire said.

"Unlike your Admiral, who has had priceless information at his fingertips, but has squandered all of it."

"He's a man of restraint and integrity," Claire said. "He's spent his life serving and protecting those he loves."

"And yet, I find that very selfish," Victor said. "He's constantly willing to sacrifice the good of the masses to protect his favorites. The information he was given could have been used to save lives."

"Is that what you're pretending this is all about?" I asked. "That you want to send yourself back to save people?"

"There is no limit to the good I'll be able to do." Victor smiled. "And I'm not only talking about technological and medical advances. I'll bring down greedy world leaders. They won't be able to hide their lies. I'll put a stop to corruption and protect the people."

I shook my head slowly.

"I find that people really never change," Victor's cold voice continued. "They need to be watched over like young children. You've seen what my Global Security force and the OmniNetwork have been able to accomplish. People make much better decisions when they know they're being watched."

"They have no choice," Claire said, turning toward the window.

"The masses can't be trusted to choose wisely," Victor said, returning his focus to his computer.

He believed what he was saying, and his superior tone left no invitation for me to try to persuade him otherwise. Victor would continue to use his foreknowledge to force everyone to accept his ideas of perfection. Just as he had been trying to do with the world's conversion to the OmniNetwork. Just as he had done with the tablet. Just as he had tried to do with my life.

With only one helicopter left in the parking lot, Victor motioned to the pilot, and we lifted off into the air. Through the window, I watched the lagoon take shape below. I could see the water feeding into it from the Geothermal plant. Wastewater, reclaimed by bathers who believed it could still be used for something. They believed it could heal them and keep them young.

Clutching Corey's watch inside my coat pocket, I silently shook my head. This wasn't going to happen. I wasn't going to let Victor bind me down anymore. He may have left my life in ruins, using it for his own purposes, but I had the power to reclaim it.

"Mýrdalsjökull," I said. "It's the glacier covering Katla's caldera."

Corey's message and the pictures he sent of Mirlande and Abby safely aboard the Poseidon gave me courage. Mirlande would have given them my message. They would be waiting for my signal.

"Your researchers had equipment set up in a large ice cave," I said. "We drove there and hiked up to it. It took a few hours."

Victor nodded. "One of the vents," he said, his eyes glowing. He turned back to his computer screen. "It will be faster for us to access the caves from above."

Claire had been silent for most of the flight. Keeping her eyes downcast, she looked defeated. Victor knew where the Point of Origin was and she had no control over what the Alliance would do next.

As we moved east along the shoreline, I watched the sea, wondering where the Alliance fleet was positioned and how long it would take them to launch their attack after I activated the beacon. Would my father be the one to give the order, or Omar?

When the enormous glacier came into view, I shuddered. We followed the path of the road Corey and I had taken with Memory. Passing over the empty parking lot, the helicopter brought us to the face of the glacier within minutes, coming close enough for us to see the cracks and crevices. Snow and ice swirled around the helicopter as we touched down a short distance from the edge of the glacier. Victor had never spoken instructions about where to land; he must have been controlling everything through messages on his computer.

Claire and I waited expectantly while Victor continued typing. I turned the pocket watch over and over in my hand, thinking about where I would put it when it was activated. Time was running out. I had to find my opportunity.

"Notify me immediately if you're reading any aircraft in the vicinity," Victor finally spoke to the pilot. "Otherwise, maintain radio silence."

The helicopter pilot gave a thumbs up.

Victor waved us toward the doors.

"Leave Claire here," I said. "There's no reason for her to die."

Victor ignored me, climbing out of the helicopter. The suits pushed us toward the open door too.

The wind took my breath away. At the tail of the helicopter, the suits unloaded three small, white snowmobiles and a toboggan stacked with equipment under a blue tarp. The odd shaped object under the tarp didn't need to be uncovered for me to recognize it. It was a smaller version of the machine from the schematics on the tablet. The same machine Victor had hooked me up to on Mount Hood.

The suits pushed us toward the snowmobiles. I looked up at the sun breaking through the thick clouds directly overhead, then down at the snow covered glacier beneath my feet. I needed to activate the pocket watch soon and get Claire as far away from the glacier as possible. One of the suits was attaching the toboggan to a snowmobile, while the other secured Claire's wrists in front of her with a flexible plastic restraint, then she mounted the back of the snowmobile.

He came to me next, unlocking another set of restraints with his thumbprint before holding them out to me like he was offering me a birthday present.

"Do you speak English?" I asked.

The suit shrugged his shoulders.

"This volcano is going to erupt," I said, pointing at the ground, then attempting to illustrate an explosion with sign language. "We're not safe here."

The suit's expression didn't change and I couldn't see his eyes through the mirrored OmniGlasses. He reached for my wrists, but I pulled them away.

"Gefa mér þá núna!" the suit said. I stepped away from him, but he lifted his gun from a strap around his leg. These men had no idea what was going to happen to them. Victor hadn't told them that they weren't going to leave the glacier alive today. I glanced over my shoulder at Claire, then at the helicopter. The other suit had finished attaching the toboggan and was coming toward me now.

Victor shook his head and mounted a snowmobile. Without looking at me, he started the motor and pulled away from the helicopter, waving his hand in the air as he went. The helicopter immediately lifted into the air, leaving us behind in a swirling tornado of drifting snow.

The other suit reached my side. He jerked my hands and forced them together in front of me. I struggled against the restraints, but he was still able to locked them in place. There would be no hope of getting them apart without the suit's thumbprint to open them.

The ground trembled slightly beneath our feet. The suits looked at each other.

Victor stopped several yards away, adjusting the helmet he was wearing. He raised the mirrored visor and I could see his lips moving. His voice came through the suit's OmniGlasses, but I could just hear it faintly, and his words were translated into Icelandic. The suit forced me onto the back of the snowmobile, then climbed on the seat in front of me. He started the motor and lurched forward. I had to grab the back of the suit's jacket and squeeze my legs against the machine to keep from flying off.

Victor led the way across the rough ice and drifting snow. The helicopter had set us down somewhere near the center of the ice. Even if I was somehow able to set myself free, we would need one of the snowmobiles to have any chance of reaching safe ground before the volcano erupted.

After only a few minutes, a large opening in the ice appeared ahead. Victor stopped, turning on a head lamp attached to his helmet.

"We'll need to move quickly," he said. "Carry the toboggan in. You should find a surface flat enough to set it up about fifty yards down."

The suits nodded. Quickly detaching the toboggan, they pulled it toward the crevice. Following a trickling stream that gradually cut a path down into the cave, the suits carried the toboggan over the uneven ice. Victor watched until they were no longer visible, then turned toward us.

"I'm afraid this is as far as you can come. When the eruption starts, there's no telling what will happen to the glacier, but the ice caves won't be stable. I want you as far from here as possible." He came to Claire's side and touched her arm softly. "I can't have them tracking me into the cave."

Claire turned her face away from him. My stomach churned.

"I'm looking forward to being with you again at a time before all of this comes between us." He said. Claire refused to look back at him. His hand lingered on her arm for a moment before he finally let go and turned his attention toward me.

I swung my leg over the seat of the snowmobile and slid to the ground before he reached me.

"And you," he said. "I'll be seeing you again very soon too."

"It's not too late to give all of this up," I said, meeting his eyes. "The Alliance will back away. All you have to do is call your helicopter and leave this place."

The ground trembled beneath us. Before the motion stopped, thunderous noise sounded as the ice cracked in the distance.

"I think I can thank you for keeping the Alliance away long enough to get me here," he said. He kept coming at me until I backed up, pinned against the snowmobile. I tried to push him away with my bound hands, but he leaned in and kissed me slowly on the cheek.

The voices of the suits echoed, coming back toward us.

Victor turned, facing the entrance of the cave. He walked away, meeting the suits just as another tremor shook the ground. The instructions he gave them were brief, and I couldn't hear what he said over the thundering of the cracking ice.

The suits saluted him, then came running back to the snowmobiles. Victor stood watching me, his eyes never leaving my face. Before the suit reached me, I turned away from Victor, holding the watch tight against my chest. This was it. My only chance.

The cover opened easily when I pressed the button, but I fumbled slightly, trying to turn the face like Corey had shown me. The suit was shouting at me now. Probably telling me to get back on the snowmobile. I checked to make sure that the face had clicked into place before closing the cover again. Then, leaning backward slightly, I dropped my bound hands as low as they could reach and let the watch slide down my leg. It dropped onto the snow at my feet, and I immediately covered it with my boot without looking down.

The suit touched my back seconds later, shoving me toward the snowmobile. I climbed on, without looking at Victor, but I could still feel his eyes on me. The suit started the motor.

Claire and the other suit sped off in the direction we had come from. I held my breath, squeezing my legs against the sides of the snowmobile, waiting for it to jerk forward. But we didn't move. The suit lifted his hand to the side of his glasses and looked over his shoulder at Victor. Then he looked down at the ground beside the tread. The watch was partially pushed into the snow, but I knew he'd seen it even before the suit got down to retrieve it.

He said something to Victor, then shoved the watch in the chest pocket of his coat. My heart stopped. The suit climbed back on the snowmobile and sped forward.

Victor blew a kiss in my direction before turning toward the cave.

I could barely see Claire on the snowmobile in front of us, and the cave behind was becoming smaller and smaller. The wind dusted snow into the tracks we made, effectively sweeping them away within minutes.

The beacon had been activated, and we were moving farther and farther away from Victor. The Alliance would have already locked onto their target. It would only be a matter of time before they destroyed me.

The ice groaned again and cracked like whips on all sides of us. I squeezed my legs tighter against the seat as the suit twisted the throttle to full. I had to stop him. I had to go back.

Clutching the back of the suit's coat from the bottom, I realized that my body was the only weapon I had. Before I could think through what was about to happen rationally, I lay back against the seat and let go of the sides of the machine. The suit didn't realize what was happening until my legs were wrapped around his waist.

He let go of the throttle to try to push me off. We slowed down with a jerk. With only one hand on the bar, he couldn't hang on when I threw my body weight to the right. The snowmobile flew forward and the suit crashed to the ground on top of me, crushing me against the ice. My head struck the ground, making my eyes blur and the sky above me spin.

The fall knocked the suit's OmniGlasses off and the wind out of him. He moaned and scrambled up after only a few seconds. I staggered to my feet too, expecting the suit to try to subdue me, but the ground shook violently again, and the terror was obvious in his uncovered eyes. He shouted something I couldn't understand and turned around, running toward the idling snowmobile.

He can't get there before me, my mind screamed. I bolted after him, closing the distance quickly. Almost to the snowmobile, he slowed to looked over his shoulder at me, but I was already on his heels. I jumped at him, throwing my cuffed wrists over his head and my legs around his midsection. With all my strength, I pulled my restraints against his throat.

The suit brought his arms up, trying to tear mine away, but I held firm. He tried to shake me off as he gasped for air. I pulled back harder. The restraints tore into my wrists and tears poured down my face. Time seemed to stand still. Eventually, he sunk to his knees and fell face forward into the snow.

I waited a few seconds before untangling myself. The wind pushed even more violently against me as I flipped the suit over onto his back, retrieving the pocket watch from his coat. Then I took off his gloves and pressed his thumb against the plate in the center of my restraints, freeing myself.

The trail we had left in the snow was almost completely obliterated now. I did my best to navigate back to the opening in the ice using the snow covered hill on the horizon as a guide. Even at full throttle, the snowmobile seemed to crawl. Maybe it was because the watch in my pocket was counting down the minutes, or seconds to my death. I only prayed that I would be close enough to the cave when it happened that Victor would die with me. Until the eruption started, he could still be stopped.

Finally, I reached the mouth of the cave. The small stream that carved the path into the crevice was almost twice as wide as it had been a few minutes earlier. I followed it downward through the narrow passageway, ducking below a low ice ceiling and sheer frozen walls. But the cave gradually widened and expanded until I was able to stand upright. My eyes couldn't avoid the dazzling crystal walls of the cave, which had transitioned from transparent and white to an intense shade of aquamarine. I tried to keep my mind clear, but I couldn't stop thinking about the other cave somewhere on this glacier where the ice had fallen—taking Memory from me.

In the eerie emptiness, the rhythmic dripping from the walls and trickle of the stream flowing down the middle of the cave created music that felt familiar. It reminded me of my mother's music. The music from my wedding. Our song. "I'll be there for you" by Bon Jovi.

A tremor vibrated through the cave. My hair stood on end. Clutching Corey's watch with both hands, I kept moving, trying not to alert Victor of my presence with the crunch of the black sand and gravel under my feet. I couldn't be far from where the suits had set up the equipment. I was probably close enough now that I could drop the pocket watch and go back to the surface. I might still be able to save myself.

I shook my head. What if something went wrong? What if the Alliance didn't launch an attack? I couldn't rely on anyone else to stop him. I had to keep going.

A few steps farther, I spotted the machine, set up in the center of the cave. Victor had his back to me, standing at the control panel, which was attached to the machine with multiple colorful wires. A bag of IV fluids hung on a pole next to him, and a thin white device crowned his head, blinking red, green, and blue.

I stood frozen with my back against the cave, seething with anger. This man, who had exploited my weaknesses, the world's weaknesses, was finally going to pay for what he'd done.

A low rumble started in the distance. Victor looked up at the walls of the cave, then touched the control panel one final time before stepping away. The entire panel lit up, and the deep red numbers began counting backward.

The tremors increased in intensity and the roar of the cracking ice echoed through the cave. The pressure built until finally a massive explosion boomed in the distance, sending a shockwave through the cave that knocked me off my feet—into the ever widening stream of cold water running down the center.

Victor turned around when he heard the splash.

"My test subjects reported intense feelings of euphoria during the chemical copying, but I never imagined the heightened senses," he shouted over the continuous growl of the earth. "You should have told me."

Springing to my feet, I dropped the pocket watch and let out a guttural cry. His numbers weren't going to reach zero. He wouldn't be attached to the machine when it activated. I would stop him, or die trying. Victor's eyes widened as I charged toward him.

I slammed into him just as the ice over our heads shifted with an ear splitting crack. Victor barely budged against the full impact of my force. Lifting his arms, he circled his hands around my throat and squeezed, pushing me backward until my body was pressed against the frozen wall of the cave.

The lack of oxygen. The heat of his hands. The explosions above us. The light was becoming dim. Snuffed out. The numbers ticked closer to zero. Three minutes left.

Suddenly, I stopped flailing. He smiled at me like he'd just won, but I knew how to get out of this hold. The same move I used when Damien pinned me against the mirror. I lifted my left hand to Victor's outer elbow and my other palm to his chin.

Pulling inward on his elbow with all of the energy I had left, I twisted his jaw away. His hands were forced open when his head hit a jagged shard of ice on the wall, I gasped for air, staggering away. Through blurry eyes, I saw Victor lift his head and pull his shoulders back, preparing to come at me again, but I didn't let him. With explosive force, I ran at him, lifting my leg just before I reached him so that my heel struck his sternum, throwing him back into the ice. This time, the blow to his head knocked him to the ground.

"Jace!" Corey's voice echoed behind me like a trumpet above the cacophony of the eruption. "Step back!"

I immediately obeyed without looking to see if it was really him. I was only a few feet from Victor's limp body when a shot rang out. Victor's body jerked and his eyes opened wide. A small red circle in the center of his chest widened until reached the edges of his coat.

I didn't turn away until a wave of cold water enveloped my ankles. Corey was wading through it toward me, still holding the gun in his hands. The cave was illuminated now with a bright orange glow. I pushed my way toward him, but the water in the center of the cave was almost up to my knees, and flowing rapidly downhill.

Finally, we reached each other. I threw my arms around his neck and he pulled me against him, but the water was rising, trying to sweep us away.

"We have to get out of here!" I yelled.

Corey shook his head. "The lava flow," he said, looking over his shoulder. "It had almost reached the entrance. By the time we climb back out, the cave will be sealed off.

"Why did you come here?" I cried. "I activated the beacon. Why didn't the Alliance launch the attack?"

"Your father and I never would have let that happen," he said, pulling me even tighter against him. "We left as soon as Mirlande came back. We've been combing the surface of the glacier. But it was like looking for a needle in a haystack. I was praying you would activate it so I could find you."

The water was rising steadily, almost up to my hips now. Tears began streaming down my face. "There's no other way out?"

Corey nodded. "The third tier of our plan," he said. Looking over at Victor's body, which was almost completely submerged now, pinned up against a wall of the cave by the current. "You promised me you would reset everything if you couldn't stop him."

Before I could respond, Corey let go of me and let the rushing water carry him to Victor. Grabbing the blood stained white device from Victor's head, he waded back to the control panel and touched it until the numbers froze with only 30 seconds left.

I made my way to him.

"But we did stop him," I said. "And if we reset everything, you'll still die here."

"Sending you back will save me," Corey said, placing the device on my head and adjusting it until it was tight against my temples. "We have to follow through with the plan we made together, even if we don't understand all of it."

I clutched Corey's arm, shivering with cold. "I can't," I cried.

"We have to do this, Jace. The first set of numbers was for you. You have to be born again." Corey encircled me in his arms. "Maybe the second set was for me. I have to lay down my life for a friend."

"You really believe this is going to work," I said.

"Greater love hath no man…" he said, his lips close to my ear. "There's no one I'd rather die for."

I locked eyes with him, tears streaming down my face. "The 34th Canto," I said.

"Dante's *Inferno?*" Corey asked, looking at the ice surrounding us.

"In one of my memories, you told me I was your 34th Canto."

Corey's eyes filled with tears too. "That's never going to change."

He pulled me close.

"I love you," I whispered, completely immersed in his warm blue eyes. He pushed a damp curl away from my face with trembling fingers, and brought his lips slowly toward mine. His breath was like the breeze on a warm summer evening. I closed the distance between us.

Another wave pushed its way through the cave. The water rose above our shoulders. My feet would no longer stay planted in the sand. I gripped the control panel, wondering how much time we had left.

Corey struggled to make the final adjustments. I watched as he entered the numbers: 40 18 04 09, 38 13 09 13.

"It's ready," he said. "When I touch this, the machine will activate." It was a circular icon on the flat glass panel. He lifted two syringes, one filled with green liquid, the other with blue. "Take your coat off."

It wasn't easy to pull down the zipper one-handed while the flow of the water tried to pull me down to the bottom of the glacier, but I managed it. I barely felt the prick of the needles as Corey injected them one after the other into my upper arm.

"There will be a brief delay between the completion of the transfer and your loss of consciousness. Try to stay calm. As long as the headpiece stays in place, it will work," he said. "Just hang in there. Ready?"

"Are you?" I asked softly.

Corey pulled himself toward me, anchoring me to the ground again with his arm around my waist. "We should push it together," he said, grasping my hand. Fresh tears sprang into my eyes. We extended our intertwined hands to the control panel and touched the icon just as another explosion rocked the earth.

The machine activated, sending a beam of light into the ice just above our heads. We floated higher and higher in the cave, but the control panel couldn't rise any farther with us. The wires connected it to the submerged machine.

"Don't let go!" Corey yelled. My limbs stiffened. The same unearthly focus I had experienced on Mount Hood returned. Clarity. The smell of sulfur overwhelmed me and the sound of the lava crawling toward us threatened to deafen me.

Corey and I both filled our lungs with several shallow breaths of air before the water rushed over our heads. The temperature of the water grew warmer now. The walls of the cave wouldn't withstand the heat much longer. Would I still be conscious when it collapsed? Corey squeezed my hand under the water. I could see the lava flow coming, steaming and bubbling as it moved.

My lungs began screaming for air, but I was afraid to let go. Corey watched me, his eyes becoming more and more desperate by the second. Finally, he lifted his head above the surface. After a quick gulp of air, he submerged. I could see the questions in his eyes. Had it worked? When would I be gone?

He wove his fingers through mine and squeezed my hand. No light came from outside the cave. The sun had been completely choked out by the volcanic ash, but the glow of the approaching lava illuminated our faces.

I couldn't hold on anymore. The water had risen to the dome of the cave. The pain started in my temples but I didn't close my eyes. Corey squeezed my hand again, then let the water fill his lungs. I must have, too, because the burning stopped.

Corey held onto me as long as he could, but his violent jerking finally pulled him away. His eyes widened and his body went limp, his arms floating upward and out to his sides.

I tried to reach through the darkness for him, but my limbs were stiff. Not spread out, but folded across my chest. My heart beat painfully slow inside. My eyes close.

Flashes of red danced like fireworks inside my lids. The pain was gone.

* * *

My hair floats away from my face as I walk down the stone path on my father's arm. Rose petals beneath my feet and a crown of white lilies and baby's breath on my head in my mother's eyelet lace dress.

A camera flash blinds me.

* * *

Sitting in the classroom with the lights switched off, I want to put my head down on my desk and close my eyes. The news just keeps showing it over and over again. First one tower collapsing, then the other.

The teacher finally turns on the florescent lights.

* * *

Dizzy. I'm on a swing. Patent leather Mary Janes appear and disappear as I pump my legs in front of me. A mountain smolders in the distance.

"Jace! A woman's voice calls.

* * *

I'm still surrounded by water—arms folded across my chest, but I'm trapped in a small space with my knees shoved up next to my arms, being squeezed so tight I can't open my eyes. A loud, rhythmic booming vibrates through the liquid. The top of my head is pushed against something, maybe the top of the cave. My heart is beating again, but it's fast—too fast. Four beats for every boom.

I'm not breathing, but I don't need to. The crushing pressure suddenly releases. My head floats back away from the hard surface. My eyes open, but I can't see much. The water is thick and a soft pink surface is only centimeters from my eyes.

I can't see my body, but I can feel that it's different. I'm naked.

"Another one is starting," a muted voice says. "You're fully dilated. You can push with this one."

A cry that I can feel vibrates from below me. Above me. I'm upside down. It's her voice, crying out in pain. The pressure returns at the crown of my head, but the real pain shoots through my temples. The contraction squeezes me hard enough to stop my heart for a moment.

The top of my head breaks through. Soft cold air is a relief, even if it's only the very tip of me that can feel it.

"...I can't...Ahh!" That voice I know and love so well. The voice that sang Van Halen songs to lull me to sleep at night. I've never heard her in such pain.

Stabbing temples, crushing pressure. I want to cry out too, but I don't have a mouth. I don't have a voice.

"She's coming!"

My body slides inches forward, but my face is free of the water. Her cries stop. She's panting now. I hear it and feel it.

"One more good one. You're doing great!"

"...I don't...I can't..."

"You can," my father says, just barely loud enough to hear. "You're amazing, Bridget. Look what you've done. She's almost here."

"Uhhhhhhh..." The pressure builds all around me. Pinching at my shoulders. First the right is free, then the left. In one explosive movement, I slide into steady hands.

The room is cold. The beeping. I'm suffocating—drowning in a world of oxygen with my lungs full of liquid. A harsh plastic object is forced into my mouth, sucking it out. Two times in my mouth, then in each nostril. Finally, the air forces its way into my lungs.

I open my mouth to tell them to stop, but it comes out as a high pitched wail.

"She has a good set of lungs."

Mom's panting turns into a mixture of sobs and laughter.

My father laughs. "You did it!"
Nurses begin to congratulate them.
"She's beautiful."
"She's perfect."
I blink my eyes. Someone vigorously rubs a rough cloth against my bare skin. The room is still blurry, but I can see colors, silhouettes, shadowy figures. They're bundling me tight in a blanket. When a cap is stretched over my head, they move me toward the sound of my parents' voices.
"Good job, Mrs. Vega! You have a beautiful daughter. Seven pounds, six ounces."
When they finally set me in her arms she brings me close enough that I can see her features. Those beautiful lips brush across my forehead and linger there while she takes a deep sniff. Heaven. I can smell her too and it's intoxicating. So many memories associated with her arms and that smell.
I open my mouth to tell her everything that has happened, but suddenly my mind is foggy. I want to tell her about the world I just left behind. But I can't.
I want her to cry with me about Corey.
Garbled words. I don't understand what they're saying.
Father's voice. Soft. Strong. Steady.
Rough finger on my palm.
I squeeze.

October 15, 2023

I looked over my shoulder. The rough road didn't seem to bother Memory at all. Her glossy curls hid most of her face, but I saw that she was smiling.

"What are you drawing?" I asked.

She showed me with an elfish expression. Black pools, yellow earth, and smoke rising toward a blue sky. The illustration was labeled "fumaroles."

"Ha-ha," Corey laughed, looking at the picture through the rearview mirror. "She'll be giving her kindergarten teacher spelling tests."

The car slowed as we approach the parking lot. "This is it. You can put away the map," Corey said. Coverage was spotty, and I hadn't been able to use data at all on the deserted road.

I opened the glove box and tucked the map back into the black and orange packet they gave us at the rental office.

"Reykjavík Rent a Car." Memory's little voice read the words on the sticker.

"You're sure it's safe for us to come along?" I asked after we were already outside.

"I wouldn't bring you if I wasn't," Corey said. "I'm glad you're going to see it now. It might look completely different in a few weeks."

"Inside a cave doesn't seem like the safest place to be. What does an eruption like that do to the glacier? You said it's predicted to be bigger than the one five years ago?"

"Don't worry. It's not going to happen today," he assured me, kissing the top of my head.

An unnerving tingle ran through my entire body.

"How far back are you trying to send the signal this time?"

"We're trying to send back more than a signal."

The uncomfortable feeling intensified.

"This way, Daddy?" Memory had made her way past the other cars to a worn down path in the snow.

"You coming?" Corey asked. But I couldn't move. My vision had become distorted. The edges were unfocused, while Corey and Memory became crystal clear, centered in my line of sight. My heart began to pound and my head began to throb.

You shouldn't be here.

"Hurry, Momma!" Memory yelled back. She reached her hand toward me. A small stream of sunlight broke through the clouds above, flashing across my face, and the throbbing in my head became focused stabbing pain in my temples.

Unstable, I reached for the mirror on the side of the car to try to catch myself.

"Are you okay?" Corey asked through the ringing in my ears. He turned around and came back to me.

As Corey came closer, the headache faded just as quickly as it had struck.

"What's wrong?" Corey asked when he reached me.

"I don't know," I said, rubbing my temples. The headache was gone, but I couldn't shake the overwhelming feeling of fear the words in my head had left behind. *You shouldn't be here*.

"You're not feeling well. I can see it," Corey said. "Do you need to sit down?"

"I think I'm okay now," I said. I considered telling Corey about my premonition, but I dismissed the thought. I had been the one who asked to come along. We were hours away from home, and Corey had a full day of work ahead.

"What's wrong, Momma?" Memory asked.

"I'm fine. I just had a little headache."

Corey took my hand, checking my eyes to make sure they looked normal. I smiled.

"Did you get your camera?" he asked.

"Oh!" I said. "I almost forgot."

He unlocked the car for me and I opened the back of the SUV to grab my case. He waited for me to close it again, then took my hand to lead me toward the trail.

With each step, the unsettled feeling in the pit of my stomach increased until I felt like I was going to be sick.

You shouldn't be here. The voice in my head was almost shouting now.

I stopped just short of the snow-covered ice.

"Corey," I said, turning to him, "this is going to sound ridiculous, but I have a really bad feeling about this."

"You do?" he asked. "What is it you're afraid of?"

I shook my head. It wasn't that I was afraid. I'd been looking forward to this for weeks.

"You're serious," Corey said, searching my eyes. "This isn't like you."

"I know," I said. "You've got twenty researchers and a helicopter up there. I don't know what I'm worried about."

"Women's intuition?" he asked with a smirk.

I didn't laugh.

"You really are worried," he said, looking over his shoulder at the car. "Maybe we shouldn't ignore that."

A few minutes later, a very disappointed little girl was strapped back into her booster seat.

"Are you sure you'll be fine driving alone?" Corey asked through my rolled down window.

I nodded. My heart had calmed down completely, and I felt a deep sense of relief with Memory safely inside the car.

"I'll make sure Victor brings me home in time for dinner," Corey said, kissing me before tapping on the side of the car. He put his head in the window and looked at Memory. "Be good for your mom, and don't be so sad. I'll bring you something special tonight.

Memory's disappointment only lasted a few minutes, then she chattered happily all the way home. I felt almost euphoric all afternoon and into the evening as we prepared Corey's favorite meal for dinner.

I started to get a little worried about him after the sun went down, but he walked in the door just before I tried texting him. We barely had a chance to stand up from the couch before he had an arm around each of us, pulling us tight against his chest. He didn't say anything, and he didn't let go.

"Daddy!" Memory giggled. "You're squishing me."

He still didn't let go. I was pressed against his shoulder, and I couldn't see his face.

"Dinner's on the table," I said, pushing myself away. When he finally loosened his hold, I could see that his eyes were swimming in tears.

"I'm so glad—" he managed.

"What happened?" I whispered.

"There was an accident," he said. "An earthquake caused a partial cave in."

"Was anyone hurt?" I asked.

Corey cleared his throat. "Victor is in intensive care."

EPILOGUE

For weeks after the accident, I suffered from almost daily migraine headaches. I wanted to be there for Claire, but I couldn't even get out of bed for Victor's funeral.

Corey and the rest of the researchers were devastated when Omnibus cut funding for the project, but I was strangely relieved. Even with the debilitating headaches, I was able to pack up the contents of our small house in record time. I couldn't wait to be back home. I couldn't wait to see my father.

When the headaches didn't improve after almost a month, Corey insisted that I see a specialist, who immediately wanted to start me on an experimental new drug. I took my first dose of it yesterday morning, just after Memory left for school.

Within twenty minutes, it felt like it was starting to work. My head was exceptionally clear, and my senses seemed strangely heightened.

I was in the middle of vacuuming my living room floor when I stopped to open the curtains. The light streaming in from outside the window brought on a stabbing headache in my temples, just like the one that had stopped me from going to the ice cave that day.

It has taken me almost 48 hours to write down everything I remembered while lying there on the living room floor. Now, I'm going to lock the memories away. Put them in a safe. Bury them in the backyard.

With Victor gone and his research safely packed away in boxes at Omnibus, I could tell Corey everything. I know he would believe me. He would have so many questions for me.

But every time I open my mouth, I think of my mother, putting on her makeup at the vanity before a party, dancing and singing along to "Jump" by Van Halen.

Instead of telling him, I turn up the music and dance like she would have. Eventually, Corey and Memory stop laughing and dance with me.

ACKNOWLEDGEMENTS

When I started writing Reclamation, I thought the process would be easy. After everything I had learned while writing and editing Eruption, I wasn't a novice anymore. I had some experience.

But I soon learned that writing a sequel has its own special challenges. I struggled to keep the characters and plot consistent with the first book while creating a new, unique story. I had to start from scratch several times, and I continued to re-write sections again and again until I was satisfied with them.

Now that I've reached the end of this long road, I want to thank the people who helped me through and got me to the finish line.

To my friends, who understood when I became a complete recluse and were willing to listen when I needed to bounce new ideas or vent about frustrations. Thank you for continuing to invite me, even when I couldn't always come.

Thank you to my extended family (both the one I was born into, and the one I married into), who shared their excitement about Eruption with their friends and made it such a success. Brothers, sisters, aunts, uncles, and cousins on all sides of my family have offered so much love and support. I truly have the best family in the world.

To my writer's group and beta readers, for offering honest and timely feedback. Your help was invaluable.

My children—thank you for the unconditional love you give me. Thank you for making me want to be a better person. Thank you for everything you do to pick up the slack around the house so that I have time to work. Thank you for never complaining, and always encouraging me.

Thank you to my parents and Phil's parents, for being such a huge part of our lives. I'm so thankful we get to live close and spend so much time together. Your encouragement and support means the world to me. Thank you for always being there.

And Marnae—where do I even start? Your quiet wisdom. Your endless honesty. The hours and hours and hours you spent by my side, patiently and kindly helping me edit and polish. Your integrity, grace, and beauty shine in everything you do. You have an incredibly brilliant mind. Thank you for giving so freely.

Finally, I want to thank Phil for being the perfect friend. For always being in my corner. For listening and knowing when to offer advice and solutions, and when to just let me talk things through. Thank you for pushing me to be my very best. I love you.

ABOUT THE AUTHOR

Adrienne Quintana is the author of Eruption and Reclamation as well as several children's books, but as a teenager, she started out writing epic fantasy about fire-breathing dragons and bad Star Trek fanfiction.

When she isn't writing, Adrienne enjoys running, hiking, and matchmaking. (Are you single? She probably knows someone perfect for you.) She lives in Arizona with her husband and four children, who give her love, support, and plenty of good material for Instagram.

www.ingramcontent.com/pod-product-compliance
Lightning Source LLC
Chambersburg PA
CBHW072357110726
47909CB00003B/725